I0731102

A Spell of Rowans

BYRD NASH

ROOK AND CASTLE PRESS
SAINT CHARLES, ILLINOIS

License Notes

Copyright © 2021 Byrd Nash
www.byrdnash.com
Cover Art by Rook and Castle Press
Editing by Emma's Edit
Published by Rook and Castle Press

All Rights Reserved.

ISBN 978-1-954811-03-4

All rights reserved. This book or any portion thereof may not be reproduced or used in any manner whatsoever without the express written permission of the publisher except for the use of brief quotations in a book review

This book is a work of fiction. Names, characters, places, and events in this book are either products of the author's imagination or are used fictitiously. Any resemblance to actual events, places or persons, living or dead, are purely coincidental.

Byrd Nash

Publisher's Cataloging-in-Publication Data
provided by Five Rainbows Cataloging Services

Names: Nash, Byrd, author.
Title: A spell of Rowans / Byrd Nash.
Description: Tulsa, OK : Rook and Castle Press, 2021.
Identifiers: LCCN 2021913057 (print) | ISBN 978-1-954811-02-7 (paperback) | ISBN 978-1-954811-03-4 (paperback) | ISBN 978-1-954811-01-0 (ebook : Kindle) | ISBN 978-1-954811-00-3 (ebook : epub)
Subjects: LCSH: Family secrets--Fiction. | Women--Fiction. | Magic--Fiction. | Magic realist fiction. | Fantasy fiction. | BISAC: FICTION / Fantasy / Contemporary. | FICTION / Magical Realism. | FICTION / Women. | GSAFD: Fantasy fiction.
Classification: LCC PS3614.A724 S64 2021 (print) | LCC PS3614.A724 (ebook) | DDC 813/.6--dc23.

BOOKS BY BYRD NASH

Contemporary, Magical Realism
A Spell of Rowans
Breathings of the Moon

Madame Chalamet Ghost Mysteries
Ghost Talker #1
Delicious Death #2
Spirit Guide #3
Gray Lady #4
Haunted Grave #5
Ghastly Mistake #6

College Fae Series
Never Date a Siren #1
A Study in Spirits #2
Bane of Hounds #3
Knight of Cups

Romantic Fairytales
Dance of Hearts (Cinderella retelling)
Price of a Rose (Beauty and the Beast retelling)

Revisited Mystery Classics
Lady Molly of Scotland Yard
The Old Man in the Corner

Collections
The Wicked Wolves of Windsor and other Fairytales

If you cannot get rid of the family skeleton,
you may as well make it dance.
George Bernard Shaw

Dedications
To all who have known
the danger of families.

To my Reed.
Who saved me,
despite myself.

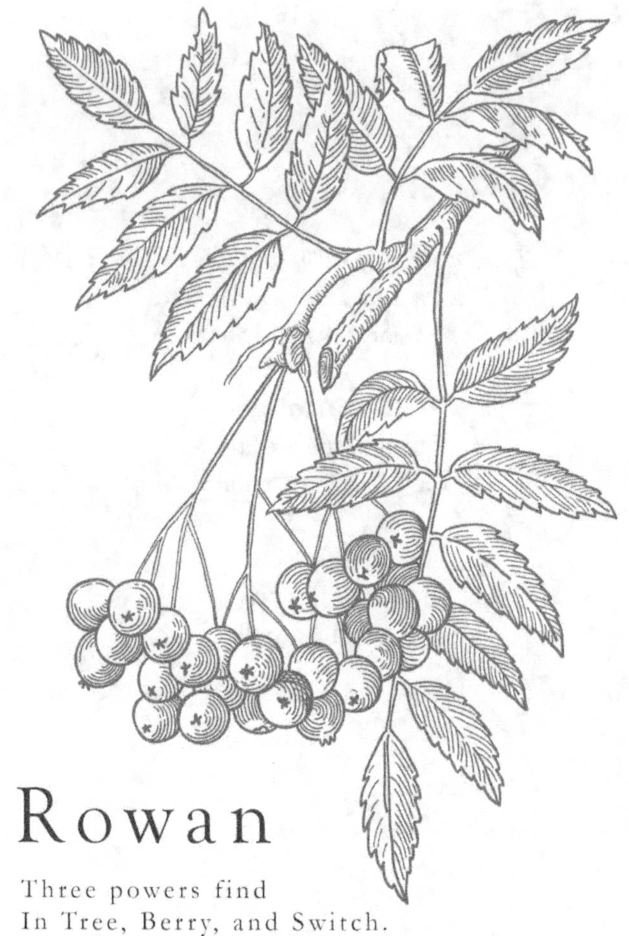

Rowan

Three powers find
In Tree, Berry, and Switch.
A remedy for a body's ills,
A vision true from the oracle,
But greatest of all is its ward,
'Gainst darksome haint and evil witch.

Chapter One

My brush was finishing the left nostril of the Madonna when the call came. From long practice, I ignored the ringing and smoothly completed the stroke on the board. Painted in the late 15th century, the portrait's age demanded respect, even from a modern device.

I stepped back from the painting and examined my restoration work with a critical eye. Nice. I turned off the lamp.

I was cleaning my brushes when the phone rang for the third time. Wiping my hands on a towel, I tapped the phone, putting my sister on the speakerphone to hear her announcement.

"She's dead."

The cutting of the bond between myself and my mother early this morning had woken me from a dead sleep. I thought I was past the need for confirmation but found myself asking anyway, "It was around 1:30, wasn't it?"

"Yes." There was a pause before Phillipa said, her voice breaking, "Ding dong."

I couldn't agree more. Indeed, the witch was dead. I asked Phillipa, "What's the plan?"

My older sister was a big planner. I imagined she would have a mental spreadsheet in her head of what she would do once our mother died. It wasn't like she hadn't had time to plan: our mother had broken her hip a few months back. Her long-desired death was not exactly an unexpected event.

"How soon can you get here? There are things we need to discuss as a family and not on the phone."

"I'll come this evening via train."

"You sure? What about the crowds? Wouldn't a rental car be better?"

"It's fine. A crowd is anonymous. I'll be okay. Besides, I let my driver's license expire."

Phillipa let big-sister exasperation leak into her voice. "Really, Vic? What if you needed ID?" When I didn't respond, she gave an aggrieved sigh. "Will you stay at the house?"

"Seems easiest."

"Liam refuses to go inside."

My brother had a talent for psychometry, a method of reading an object's past by touching them. I could only imagine how uncomfortable he would feel within the family home. However, a house empty of people presented no danger to my talent. I only needed to keep the right doors closed.

My mind was on death, both past and present, so Phillipa's next words jarred me out of my abstraction. "Will work give you any trouble?"

"During the summer? For the death of a family member? No trouble at all."

When I called to ask for time off, my boss at the university was all concern. That didn't surprise me. Tony was a soft jelly type of man who remembered his staff's birthdays and always let them have a half-day on the Friday before a holiday weekend.

Whenever I had to be in the same room with him, his emotions were like being stuck in marshmallow-goo. I tried to keep as much physical distance as I could between us; I didn't want to get attached to niceness. It was messy.

"Take as much time as you need. Losing a parent is hard."

Was it? Probably for normal people with average parents, it was. For now, I was still assessing my own psychic damage. I probed that lost emotional connection, like a tongue touching the place where a tooth was suddenly missing. Eventually, I would get used to the sensation of loss. Life continued. That I knew.

For now, though, I was feeling lightheaded, floaty, from the relief of Rachel Rowan's death. Tony's voice on the other side of the phone startled me.

"Where should we send flowers?"

"I'll let you know when I get the details."

Ha! Flowers? He should send a bouquet of vervain and dill. But for all of Tony's historical knowledge, I doubted he would get a reference to plants traditionally used to ward off witches.

"What about the Madonna? Do you want me to return her to the university?"

"Your studio is secure, and covered by insurance. It would be safer there, for now. I have my hands full here with an emergency fumigation. Some idiot brought in a cardboard box from outside, and now everyone is seeing bugs."

My studio, where I worked by myself, far from people, was indeed secure. Its security system was probably better than the university's.

"I'll keep you updated about my plans by email," I told him.

Taking the train was a calculated risk. I chose a time when it would be crowded with people all rushing to get home from work, their tired minds on getting dinner and not much else.

The larger the crowd, the more muddled the emotional output. My empath abilities registered it as white noise.

I watched the scenery flying by. The train was already out of the city, passing through the suburbs. It was all achingly familiar, and the dead link between me and my mother gave me an eerie feeling. Like I had forgotten something.

But I hadn't. That was the problem. I hadn't forgotten a damn thing.

At each stop, more passengers left to enjoy their ordinary lives. This line would eventually take me to Grimsby. It was the last stop before the train returned.

Tired from my interrupted sleep last night, I found my head starting to nod. My forehead pressed against the cool glass of the window, and to the rocking of the train, I fell asleep.

In the water, I was drowning. My hands flailed upward, trying to connect with something, anything. A hand pushed my head under the surface. I opened my mouth to scream. Stinking lake water entered my mouth, suffocating me.

I awoke with a start, choking, my heart pounding from fright. Still panicked, a voice made me jerk in surprise like a frightened deer.

"Pleasant dream, Vic?"

The carriage was now empty except for a man sitting opposite me, nearest to the aisle. A face I had known once as softer, more lively. Now his features held the neutral stillness of the experienced hunter. It assessed me with stony eyes.

My talent hit a blank emotional wall. I knew only one person that could do that: Reed Easton.

Like I didn't have enough ghosts from the past. Some of what I felt must have shown on my face, for he said with a voice deeper than I remembered, "Not pleased to see me, old friend?"

"Good evening, Reed."

He gave a gracious nod of his head, as if he were royalty, acknowledging a peasant. I wondered how long Reed had sat there watching me sleep. Was his interest creepy or romantic? Knowing how we had parted fifteen years ago, my guess veered towards unsettling. And dangerous.

As if he had read my thoughts, he asked, "Returning to Grimsby after all these years?"

I might not be able to read his emotions, but I was experienced in matching feelings to faces and words. He still held a grudge, while I had no regrets over burning that bridge. I was a talented bridge-burner, and had learned long ago: never look back to see the fire.

Suddenly, I became aware of how wrinkled my shirt was. Wearing the most paint-stained but comfortable jeans from my closet did not exactly scream: 'look at how successful I am without you in my life.'

I pulled the sympathy card. "My mother died."

"Ding dong, huh?"

Considering my mother's reputation in Grimsby, I had already figured the turnout for any memorial service wouldn't be numerous. But Reed's words made me wonder. Maybe a crowd of Grimsby residents, all holding pitchforks, would storm the house, wanting confirmation that the witch was dead. As well as her spawn.

"Your sister seems to be doing well."

"Yes, she is."

How much longer before we pulled into Grimsby station? Could I excuse myself and hide in the bathroom?

"And Liam?"

I tried not to wince. Liam was not faring well. He had his reasons, but I wasn't sharing them. I said politely, "He's fine."

Reed gave a small chuckle that I remembered all too well. "Still hiding the truth, Vic?"

I saw the silhouette of the town's water tower against the setting sun. Good, not much longer. I reminded myself to act like an ordinary human being. I was experienced with pretending.

Keeping my voice level, I asked pleasantly, "Your family?"

"Fine," he said, giving a smile that was sarcastic, acknowledging the game we played.

The adult version of his face had no softness, only angles. Reed, once a star athlete on the high-school swim team, was still lean and muscular. He wore crisp jeans, sharply pressed, a light blue jacket, and an Oxford shirt with the top button undone. It all fitted with immaculate tailoring. Well. Hm.

The train stopped. I practically jumped from my seat, grabbing my bag. Slinging the strap over my shoulder, and my eyes downcast, I muttered, "It was nice seeing you after all this time—"

With the speed of a cat, Reed was at the door, blocking my exit with his arm. He bent to me, his breath on my ear softly fluttering my hair. I shivered.

"Was it nice? Seeing me?" he asked softly.

I kept my eyes forward, looking straight through the glass to the platform beyond. Freedom was so close. When I didn't answer, he pulled back, his light jacket flaring open with the movement.

I shoved the door open as fast as possible. As I hurried away, I wondered why my old high-school boyfriend would be wearing a gun.

Chapter Two

I hid in the women's bathroom of the train station and texted for a driver. I didn't want to risk any more chummy meetings with old flames. Talking with Reed any further could become quicksand, that I would have a hard time escaping.

The driver was pleasant, and the car was clean. Unfortunately, his emotions were not as tidy. It took me a full five minutes to stop tasting the acid-weeping flavor of them.

From a lifetime of experience I knew what a combination of guilt-loss-sad-worry-despair meant. The driver had a loved one who had recently died, or was about to.

When we pulled up to my parent's old house, a sharp headache was slicing my head in half. This is why I had a private studio: to avoid people and the migraines their messy emotions give me.

Standing outside the car, I felt a reviving breeze. I pulled a twenty out of my pocketbook and handed it to the driver through his window. I was careful not to touch his fingers; touching people only made the emotional output stronger.

"You pay through the app," he started to explain.

"I already did. This is a gift to you."

He reluctantly took the money, still protesting. "Tips also go through the app."

"It's not a tip," I explained patiently. "It's a gift. Because I like you. Good luck."

Before he could argue further, I turned and walked up the drive to the house. Fifteen years. Well, the place was the same.

I stopped and took a deep breath while I surveyed it.

Our house was on the corner of a street in an area Grimsby residents knew as Claypit. The unappetizing name came from what had once made Grimsby great: the manufacturing of bricks.

My great-grandparents' house was gifted to my father upon his marriage. A Victorian Italianate candy box. A stolid square built with the local dusky-rose brick, with a flat roof and tall, narrow windows.

One of those homes that would make an ideal setting either for a romance movie or a horror show. Like many things Rowan, there was no in-between.

I remembered Mother being very proud of it. To visitors, she always pointed at the circular plaque on the porch that certified 'built in 1869' from the Historic Register. My mother had worn the mantle of my father's prestige so well that the town forgot it wasn't hers to begin with.

I passed the bronze sign with barely a glance.

The light at the porch was on. Did Phillipa do that for me? Or was it a forgotten relic from when Rachel Rowan toppled down the stairs (and off her throne) three months ago?

Mother had never liked the dark, and always insisted that the house be well lit. Perhaps she should have focused on illuminating the dark corners of her soul.

Weeks back, Phillipa had mailed me a copy of the house key and directions on how to turn off the burglar alarm system. I used the key and that information now. It wasn't sophisticated. I thought of three ways I could bypass it as I punched in the buttons.

Inside, I turned on more lights as I explored, letting Claypit know a Rowan had returned to the nest.

I wandered through the ground floor, finding that little had changed in fifteen years. Her dollhouse was still waiting for my mother's entrance. You could almost hear the click-click of her heels over the original heart-oak boards.

I shook myself. *You don't care about ghosts, remember?*

On the first floor was the entrance to my mother's sacred place: the formal living room. We kids had only been allowed there when cleaning it. Or when summoned for punishment.

I walked boldly into her space and as I sat down on the sofa, gave a brittle chuckle. No one could stop me. That moment was when I knew she was dead. Truly dead.

As my hand stroked the polished wood, I thought about my many connections in the fine art world. I knew several auction houses that dealt with furniture. I would speak to Phillipa about disposing of our mother's prize collection as soon as possible. The idea gave me sadistic glee.

With the Power of Attorney from our mother, Phillipa had kept the utilities turned on. Speaking from her realtor experience, Pip said nothing aged a house faster than it being deserted.

I imagined she had a good idea of the house's value. Yet, oddly enough, thinking of the "For Sale" sign Phillipa would quickly put on the front lawn bothered me a little. A feeling of nostalgia, a yearning for something that never really existed, came over me.

To slap away this sentimental nonsense, I deliberately thought of the rooms upstairs I had yet to see. Ha. Yeah, the house could be sold. The quicker, the better.

In the kitchen, I found a hand-written note tacked onto the fridge door: *'I'm sure you haven't eaten. Stuff in the fridge.'* It was signed with my sister's very decorative 'P' in the same script she used to decorate the cover of her high-school notebooks.

My stomach rumbled, and I realized that my big sister was right—I hadn't eaten since early that morning. I pulled out the containers, and flipping up lids, chose pasta. I automatically sat down in my usual place at the table, triggering a stream of memories, mostly bad, of sitting there with my family.

"Let it go," I commanded myself. I refused to see ghosts. The dead weren't my bailiwick.

Despite my self-talk, the Alfredo sauce had turned to glue in my mouth. I forced myself to continue chewing, making my body straighten from the cringing, head-down posture it had assumed.

When I was cleaning up in the kitchen, Phillipa called me again.

"All good?"

"It's fine." That word again. I needed to take a course on how to make pleasant chit-chat. Pick up a few more phrases I could use to perfect my camouflage.

"I thought we could meet at Vincent's for breakfast. Liam is willing. We can decide on our next move."

So many things to discuss, but more not to.

"Vincent's?"

"Dominic's old place. Dom retired after a heart attack, and his grandson has it now. I know you won't believe this but it's not a greasy spoon anymore—it's a hipster cafe!"

"There are hipsters in Grimsby?" The town was bricks, lumber, and railroad. Where was the proud blue-collar town I had left?

"You're out of touch, Vic. Grimsby is growing as a getaway spot. People are coming up here to shop at the quaint historic downtown, hike trails, and kayak on the lake."

"You don't have to give me the real-estate sell, Pip."

"I'm serious. There's a real revival happening here. Why do you think I'm so busy?"

I tried to wrap my mind around the idea. It seemed that not all things were going to be the same.

"Was the train ride okay?"

I was about to say it was fine, but stopped myself in time. I told her tentatively, "I saw Reed. Reed Easton. On the train."

Why had I said his last name? Pip knew who I meant.

"Oh? Well, his father still lives here, though he's not the police chief anymore. Retired. His mother died some time back from cancer. Maybe Reed's here for the weekend? I sometimes see him in town."

Today was Friday, so Pip could be right. Yet somehow, I couldn't shake the thought that his coming had something to do with my arrival. "Was Mother's obituary in today's paper?"

"Yes. I got it in right before the deadline. Why?"

"No reason. I was just wondering."

The beauty of electronic communication was, there was no emotional attachment to the words spoken. It was neutral. I leaned into that comfort. Tomorrow would not provide any.

Phillipa asked, "Do you want me to drive over to pick you up tomorrow?"

"No. I'd prefer to walk. It's just a few blocks."

I was so engrossed in reading technical journals that the rock flying through the glass window made me jerk from my chair. I flattened myself to the floor under the dining table and waited.

Lying on the carpet, panting, I got a fleeting taste of the vandal: an aggressive, masculine signature of smoky-hungry, burning-battery-acid that probably made him an absolute joy to be around. But even as I grasped his emotional energy print, it faded. He was out of my range.

Crawling out from under the table, I found the rock, bigger than my fist, in the middle of the carpet of my mother's pristine visiting room. I wondered if the vandal knew the irony of that. It had gone through a side window that looked out to the alley between our house and our neighbor's.

I picked it up and found curses and runes written on it with a black permanent marker. A fairly adequate beginner's curse. I took the rock to the kitchen sink and ran cold water over it, twisting it under the faucet to clean off its energy of ill intent. I dried it with a tea towel.

I found a black marker in the kitchen's junk drawer—still the same wonky drawer that refused to close properly. I doodled over the runes, transforming their shapes into fantastical dragons and trolls. As I worked, I hoped nasty guy felt the death of his magic.

Admiring the finished piece, I said with satisfaction, "And you said my art degree wouldn't be of any use."

But the person I spoke to was dead, lying on a slab somewhere, and if her ghost had made a caustic comment, I didn't hear it.

I convinced the alarm company not to call the police. I'd deal with the damage in the morning, and the police weren't going to be of any help. They seldom were.

I decided to sleep in the guest room. It held no memories for me and boasted a very comfortable mattress. I'd never understood why Mother kept the room, since we never had overnight visitors, but she loved the idea of it.

A room that would always be perfect.

I set my suitcase on a chair that had never enjoyed an occupant. The lace pillowcases and the extra bolster pillows I threw into the hallway. I removed the wall prints and tucked them behind the dresser so I couldn't see their false gaiety.

It helped make it habitable, but I couldn't open the window. Mother had nailed all the sashes shut long ago. It kept all the silent screaming neatly trapped inside the house.

Chapter Three

My morning shower, in the bathroom at the end of the hall, felt good. I dressed, and as I left the second floor, ignored the closed doors. I'd deal with them in good time, but that wasn't today.

I did lock the front door. Maybe no one would notice the big hole in the side window. I idly wondered if I would care if someone stole anything. I couldn't think of anything that would distress me if it was gone.

The corner lot ran parallel to a boulevard of other Claypit stately homes. Six blocks from these dowagers, and I was on the historic main street of Grimsby, where, naturally, everything was built from more brick.

Some things had changed: modern lamp posts with a vintage look; the cracked and uneven sidewalks were now as smooth as pancakes. That would disappoint the skateboarders. The pedestrian crosswalks were clearly marked and even had ramps. I passed decorative planters, trashcans, and benches. Most of the storefronts were now occupied, and the parking slots were getting full.

What town was I visiting?

There was no way to miss the new Vincent's. The diner was popping. I was waiting in line when I saw my sister wave. She was sitting at a table in the corner, near the back of the restaurant's long, narrow interior.

Beside her was my younger brother, Liam. I hadn't seen him in person for at least five years, and my oldest sister for about two. Most of our contact over the years had been by email, phone, and sometimes video chat.

In the flesh, I was always surprised we weren't kids anymore. Liam was bear-sized, much bigger than that boy my memory insisted on making him. Despite it still being summer, he wore gloves; a muffler was wrapped around his neck, and sunglasses masked his eyes.

There wasn't much to see of his face, which was deliberate. He hated the roundness of his features that made him look young and vulnerable. Hiding for Liam wasn't only vanity but a necessity for survival.

Phillipa was just as glamorous as I remembered, but maturity had put lines around her eyes, though they were barely noticeable under her pristine make-up. Saturday morning, and she was wearing a business outfit: a blouse of pale cream silk, a tailored navy jacket, and a matching skirt. Her shoulder-length blond hair was smoothly immaculate.

She was the type who could wear white and never get a mark on it.

"What do you think?" Phillipa waved her professionally manicured hand around, indicating the cafe.

"Distressed cement floors, check; rustic brick walls, check; and a wall displaying printed T-shirts for sale. Should appeal to the coffee-house crowd," I agreed.

The music wasn't too loud, but the metal chairs weren't very comfortable. No five-egg, ten-stack-pancake-with-a-slab-of-bacon breakfast, but they did have crepes, fresh fruit, and baked eggs that came in their own serving dish.

We were at a square table with four place settings. I sat opposite Phillipa, Liam between us, with his back to the brick wall. It was an old formation of protection that we Rowans knew well. All braced and ready for an attack from an outsider.

Thankfully, the morning crowd made an emotional white noise. Pip had chosen a good time and place to meet.

"Like the new beard," I said, picking up a menu. Liam's gloved hand stroked his chin.

"Not new, Vic. I've had it for at least four years."

I winced. I was just that good at avoiding people. Liam was even better at it.

"Wow! It's been that long since our last video chat?"

I almost reached out to connect with his emotions, but I shied from that. I had invaded his privacy too many times—perhaps with the best intentions, but I couldn't ignore the damage it had done.

I made sure to keep a blocking wall between myself and both of my siblings. It took a lot of focus and energy and wasn't something I could continue for a long period, but I'd rather be tired than hurt either of them again.

As usual, Phillipa wanted to be in charge. When the waitress came up to take our order, she suggested what I should order. I felt a whisper of resentment, that reluctance not to do what my older sister wanted. Contrary, I chose something different.

Liam gave his own request. He hadn't touched a menu, so I assumed he was familiar with the place, living in Grimsby.

Several people entered the restaurant. Most gave Phillipa a verbal greeting and wave. My sister's talent was to be loved, even by people who would like nothing better than to see us all drowned in a sack like unwanted kittens.

Like a car trying to start on a cold January morning, it took a moment before our conversation warmed. The three of us finally found common ground, and the talk grew familiar and easy. One of my comments startled Liam into a gruff chuckle; the sound of it tickled my shriveled heart.

Still, despite the camaraderie, each of us sat alone in our skin.

Liam pulled out a set of folding silverware from his pocket. I was about to put a forkful of egg soufflé in my mouth when Phillipa said brightly, "What do you want to do with her body?"

Before I could digest the comment or my egg, Liam suggested a tried-and-true option for quieting the restless dead.

"Cut the head off, pack it with salt, and bury her at a crossroads."

Phillipa countered, "I was thinking of something simpler— cremation. It's much cheaper. Then we could scatter her."

Liam continued, pedantically. "Ashes should go in a lead container, packed with salt. Then we bury it at a crossroads, under a stone to weigh her down."

"Will you stop with the salt and crossroads idea," Phillipa said crossly.

I took a few more bites, letting the friction between oldest and youngest settle before saying, "I don't want her buried next to Victor. The family plot is off-limits."

"That's a given," said Phillipa quickly.

Thinking of our dead parents, I added, "Why wasn't Victor cremated?"

Phillipa considered my question. "I guess Mother didn't want to do that. But we could have Victor cremated on the pretense we were going to spread their ashes together."

"Oh, like that wouldn't arouse anyone's suspicions at all," said Liam, giving a succinct and brutal analysis of the situation.

I asked, "You mean because of how he died fifteen years ago? Surely no one cares about that anymore?"

Phillipa gave me an unreadable look. "Your old boyfriend's dad may be retired from the police force, but Greg Easton goes out of his way to remind me that Victor's murder remains an open case."

In case I didn't understand, Liam clarified, "Chief Easton likes to threaten us. He thinks to keep us in line."

Victor's death was not forgotten, then.

"Seriously, cremation is fast, easy, and affordable," said Phillipa.

"The funeral home has her corpse in a private room," said Liam. "You could go spit on Mother before we torch her."

"You two didn't do that, did you?"

They both gave me round, owl-eye stares.

My sister finally said, "You don't have to go."

I hadn't seen Mother since the day our father had died. Thinking out loud, I said slowly, "I would like to see her. Unfinished business."

Phillipa went back to planning everyone's lives.

"Okay, when we get done here, I'll drive you over."

I spread jam on my toast. The jar label said it was homemade by a local farm. Very farm-to-table.

"I had a bit of excitement at the house last night."

I told them about the rock and the window. About the huge hole in it. Phillipa, the organizer, pulled out her cell phone and started calling to find a repair person. Liam asked me, "Do you want me to touch the rock? Find out who did it?"

Stupid me. I hadn't thought of that.

"I cleaned it. Sorry."

"How are you feeling about staying there?" His question surprised me.

"I'm fine."

I wondered how many times I would use that word before my visit to Grimsby was over.

The funeral director explained that this was a private showing for the family before they carried out the cremation. My mother would be in a natural state. After this appropriately solemn exchange, I entered the small room alone.

The walls were covered in somber blue drapery, so dark it was almost black. The only illumination was from a tiny lamp on a table next to a box of tissues and a Bible. Two chairs allowed families to collapse comfortably in their grief.

The first thing to strike me upon seeing my mother's body was how small she was. On the table, she appeared child-like. It wasn't fair. Evil should be larger than that. It gave me an odd feeling that none of this was true.

Her skin was pale and heavy like clay. Her dyed chestnut hair showed three months of snow-white roots. I was suddenly aware of how long fifteen years was.

I could say what I wanted in this twilight room, smothered in the thick folds of serious drapes. My lips trembled as they formed words.

"You've sent demands to me, through Liam and Pip, that I should come home. Here I am." My voice grew in volume. "No sneer? No nastiness? Well, being dead makes you finally powerless, doesn't it?"

I shifted closer, staring down at the slack face of the woman I hated. I tried to stop the words, gain control of myself, but I couldn't. I felt emotion clog my throat, tears of frustrated rage in my eyes. She didn't answer. I almost reached out to shake her. Force her to hear the words I should have said when she lived.

"What you did to Liam I will never forgive."

I took a deep, ragged breath and let it out in an explosive exhalation as the tension left my body.

"Ding dong, Mother, the witch is dead. You're gone, and I'll make damn sure—forgotten."

Phillipa was standing in front of her car in the funeral home parking lot. Next to her, I recognized the tall form of Reed Easton. I was in a mood to punch someone's face. He'd do.

But when I came closer, I saw that Pip's face had a dazed, pale expression.

"The police have Liam," she said.

Chapter Four

The Grimsbys' police building was the same, but even more tired than I remembered. Still grim and somewhat useful. It reminded me of an old vacuum cleaner that you were reluctant to replace, even though it left too many bits on the floor.

During the drive, Phillipa explained Reed had seen her when driving by and stopped to give her the news about Liam. I looked in the rearview mirror and saw Reed was following us to the station. Parked, I said nothing as I got out of the car.

Someone quickly buzzed Reed through the door that separated the public from the private areas. It left us womenfolk waiting.

Phillipa smiled nicely at the officer watching us from his duty desk, ready to work her charm on him. She could discover they were questioning Liam, but that was all.

I leaned my back against the cinderblock wall and slipped into a meditative state. Concentrating, I could feel the presence of about half a dozen people here. Overall, there was a level of thrilling excitement, like a kicked anthill. Something momentous had happened, but the emotional radiation was too strongly mixed. I couldn't pick out individuals, even one I knew as well as my brother.

I blinked, slowly becoming aware of my surroundings again. Leaning over to Phillipa, I murmured, "I didn't reach Liam."

Phillipa whispered back, "While you were under, I heard them discussing a murder. We need to get Liam a lawyer."

Murder? Liam? I couldn't wrap my mind around what Pip was saying. It made little sense, but one thing I knew.

"We aren't hiring anyone from this one-horse town," I told my sister.

I opened my phone and dialed Hunter Garrick. Would he pick up? Was my number still on his phone, or had he blocked it? I hadn't seen him in four years, after all. When he answered, he didn't give a greeting.

"The situation must be bad for you to call me."

In an expulsion of breath that hurt, I babbled. "The police are questioning my brother, Liam. About a murder in the town of Grimsby. Can you send someone? Or recommend someone?"

There was a pause, but it wasn't a long one. Hunter always made quick decisions in a crisis. "Grimsby is about an hour north of here by car. Tell them you have counsel. I'll get there as soon as I can."

"Thank you, Hunter."

"Tell them your brother has counsel," he insisted again, in a firm, slightly louder voice as if I were hard of hearing. Hard-headed, I grant you, but my hearing was fine.

"I will."

When I hung up, Phillipa was staring at me like I had grown a second head. "Who was that?"

"Hunter Garrick, the best criminal defense attorney in the city."

Phillipa recognized his name. Who wouldn't? He was on television enough. She gasped. "The Hammerby murder trial lawyer?"

"He says to tell them that Liam has counsel."

I used Hunter Garrick's name to bludgeon my way to Liam's side. When I entered the interrogation room, Liam didn't acknowledge my entrance. He was silent, staring at the opposite wall.

My brother sat at the desk, stripped of his protective shields. His hat, gloves, and muffler lay on the metal table. Without his sunglasses, Liam's baby blue eyes and pale round face had no defenses.

He looked much younger than his twenty-nine years.

Seated across from him was a guy I faintly remembered, though I had to look at his nametag to nudge my memory: Deacon Hayes. Greg Easton's second-in-command fifteen years ago, an older version than I remembered.

It seemed he was now police chief. Deacon Hayes had moved up from ticketing kids who loitered at the strip mall past curfew.

In a town that had made many a big man, Deacon was a toad-shape of fat. His gut overhung his belt buckle, and his neck was a column of jowls and chin. His eyes were cold, mean, and far too watchful.

In the corner of the square pea-green room stood Reed, arms crossed, his hip against the wall. I thought I was starting to under-stand the reason for the gun on the train.

Bad cop and murky cop.

"Liam, you have counsel," I told him. "Your lawyer advises you to stay quiet until he arrives." As I took a chair next to my sibling, I asked Deacon, "What is this all about?"

I couldn't feel anything from Reed. No surprise. Still a blank wall. Mr. Inscrutable.

From Deacon, I gained a mix of satisfaction-smugness, with just a shadow of uncertainty. He said, "A man of your brother's description—"

"Don't give me that bullshit," I said, my voice dripping with cold scorn. "That's a lame excuse. Tell me why you have my brother here."

The empath-pathway worked both ways. Yes, I could feel another's emotions, and could also make them feel mine. I touched Deacon's uncertainty and leaned. It was a skill I had stopped using a decade ago, seeing how it damaged Liam. Emotions made dangerous tidepools.

But Deacon had a hard core of self-belief, he refused to doubt himself. "Back in town, twenty-four hours and cocky as ever, Victoria Rowan. Shouldn't you be home, overcome with grief?"

"When evil dies, do you mourn its loss?"

I felt a flash of surprise from him, quickly smothered.

"We do have a description, and your brother is very distinctive. Hard to forget. A man who walks around mumbling to himself? Who wears gloves, a muffler, and a hat in the middle of summer?"

"Liam isn't saying anything without his attorney, Mr. Hunter Garrick."

Deacon gave a low whistle. "Already got the rich lawyer lined up, huh?"

"What about you?" Reed's voice caused me to break my staring contest with Deacon. I felt a quick, sharp prick of irritation from Deacon. The police chief wasn't keen about Reed being here. Interesting.

Reed pushed himself away from his corner and came closer to where we sat. Was he trying to intimidate me?

"Can *you* talk?" he drawled.

I shrugged, playing at being nonchalant. There was nothing I could say, as I knew nothing. Reed continued.

"What do you know about your father's death?"

Oh, that same old song and dance.

"No, Reed, I don't know who murdered my father. Maybe you should open an investigation into it, since your father didn't do such a great job in solving it."

I smiled pleasantly and batted my eyelashes at him.

"You left Grimsby shortly after your father's death."

"Yes, to attend university. Scholarships don't wait on grief."

"Why leave in the middle of the night telling no one?"

I raised an eyebrow. "Were you hiding in the bushes, watching me say my tearful goodbyes? Why do you think it was in the middle of the night? Maybe it was after breakfast? Before supper?"

Deacon interrupted our duel of words.

"Look, Easton, I let you in on this interview as a courtesy to your dad. The FBI has no jurisdiction in this matter, so stand down and let me do my job."

Deacon's remark must have caught Reed on the raw, for, without warning, he suddenly tossed something toward my brother. Liam instinctively reached up to catch it, but my brother was barehanded. He screamed as his skin touched it and fell from his chair to writhe on the concrete floor.

Scrambling after him, I pried open his hands. He was holding a set of keys with a dangling double-R fob. I threw my mother's keyring as far from us as possible.

Liam curled tighter into a ball. I put myself over him, holding him tight against me as I broke my promise and opened a forbidden door. The connection sprang back into place in one breath. I felt Liam's terror, its pungent stink burning my nostrils.

I should never have left him. I should have stolen him away with me all those years ago, when I had fled. Guilt made me open the floodgates with no care for myself. Once again, I was my brother's keeper.

I grew lightheaded as I brought it deeper into myself, past the boundary that separated our sense of self. Connections continued to be made, but it became too much. Flooded, it sucked me down in a tidepool too strong for me to fight.

From a long distance away, I could hear Phillipa outside the steel door. She was shouting and pounding on it. How uncharacteristic of her. How impolite. Mother would be angry with her.

"Vic! Victoria!" That was Reed.

"Get a paramedic!" another voice shouted. That jerk Deacon Hayes. It would serve him right if I died here under his watch. I rolled off Liam, who was now quiet.

Eyes closed, lying flat on the floor, I could smell concrete, pee, and cigarettes. Underneath the stench was a faint whiff of bleach.

"What did you do to my sister?!"

Oh, your sister did it to herself, Pip. Like she always does.

Chapter Five

I woke up in the hospital, hooked up to a heart monitor. There was also an IV.

It wasn't a private room; whoever was on the other side of the curtain was snoring. Strangely, I felt little emotion from my roommate. It could be because the occupant was asleep, but I didn't think that was why my empathy was on the blink. There was a strange quiet in my head.

Oh. Now I remember. I probably temporarily burned myself out. I've done that a few times as a kid, but never as an adult. *Well, better find out what happened.* I checked to see if someone had left my phone on the side table. No.

My movement must have alerted a nurse, as I heard footsteps. He came around the curtain, a stethoscope around his neck. Behind him stood Reed. I choked back a snarl.

If I took in too much emotional output from others, I needed time to void it safely. Right now, Liam's fear was a ball of murderous rage inside me that wanted to strangle Reed.

"How are you feeling?" asked the nurse. He came to the side of my hospital bed and started checking all the devices attached to me.

"Fine." To be fair, I felt fine. I wasn't sure why I was here.

The nurse explained that I had collapsed at the police station. "Do you or your family have a history of fainting? Has anything like this happened to you before?"

"No."

"The doctor wants to keep you for observation over the next few days."

I thought of all the things I needed to get done before I could leave Grimsby.

"I do want to speak to the doctor."

"She'll be doing her round in the late evening."

"Uh, okay." The nurse left. I asked Reed, "Do you know where my phone is?"

He opened the drawer of my nightstand and pulled it out. I didn't thank him for it: he was the reason I was here. I texted Phillipa.

awake where is bro?

lawyer w liam. yummy

Okay, so Pip had met Hunter. The guy was bonafide honey-smooth Hollywood Glamour, updated for the modern palate. I hoped my sister hadn't devoured him yet; those two would be two suns colliding. They might produce a black hole.

where?

my condo

Good. Liam wasn't sitting in a jail cell.

when can u get here?

in hospital, lobby now.

I leaned back on my pillow, laying the phone on my stomach, satisfied.

Reed cleared his throat. "How are you feeling?"

At least he had the decency to look shamefaced. That didn't mean I wouldn't kill him later. I gave him an icy glare. "The next time you arrest my brother—"

"It was Hayes who brought him in for questioning. I found out about it over my dad's police scanner."

I mulled over his explanation as he stared out the window, avoiding my gaze. Greg Easton was exactly the type who would have a police scanner at his house. Still living the job.

"You haven't asked why we were questioning your brother."

"Whatever it was, Liam didn't do it, so why should I care?"

"It's murder." Did he think that would shock me? Murder and I were nodding acquaintances. Bedmates. Soulmates, even.

He told me who. "Patty Maxwell."

I shrugged. "Don't know her."

"Your mother knew her. Patty was Rachel's assistant at her antique shop."

"I haven't seen my mother in over a decade. Why would I know some employee of hers?"

We were both saved from further arguing by the entrance of my sister. Pip was wearing slacks, heels, and a v-neck pullover that showed off her swan-like throat.

"How are you feeling, Vic?" Ignoring Reed, she gently rolled the IV stand back so she could come to the side of the bed. Phillipa didn't touch me, which I appreciated. Even though my empath ability was on a low battery, I felt shaky. Raw.

"Fine. How is Liam doing?"

She looked at Reed and said, "Family matters."

When he didn't move, I told him, "You're dismissed, copper."

Under our twin glares, he left. I suspected that he was still lingering in the corridor with his ear to the door. My sister must have felt the same, for she bent over and said in a low voice, "Liam's doing a lot better since you almost killed yourself to drain off his energy. That was a stupid thing to do."

I neatly pleated the hospital blanket and sheet over my stomach. It allowed me to look down and avoid her eyes. "Update me on what's going on. Reed said they brought Liam in about a murder? Some woman named Patty Maxwell?"

"Patty was killed, strangled, in the alley behind Mother's shop."

"Reed told me she was Mother's assistant. What has that to do with Liam?"

"Liam entered the shop about an hour before the murder happened behind the store. They have him on a security camera."

"Has he told you why he was there?"

I could tell from her hesitation that Phillipa was reluctant to explain. "He worked for Mother sometimes."

"She wasn't making him use his talent for some scheme, was she?" Despite myself, my voice rose in volume, outraged. Pip's shameful grimace confirmed my guess. If our mother hadn't died, I'd have killed her.

"I don't know all the details of what he did. He didn't want me involved and refused to discuss it."

Mentally, I cursed my mother. I hadn't known about this; when I talked with my siblings, we avoided discussing her. I hadn't asked questions because I wanted to keep my head buried in the sand. I should have asked questions.

Phillipa said, "Everyone in Grimsby knew Liam didn't like Patty. They had several public arguments. Especially after Mother's fall."

I gestured to Phillipa to pour me some water from the pitcher at my bedside. My mouth was dry and gummy. She handed me the foam cup, and I tried not to splash water on myself as I sipped it.

"The weird thing is, Patty died the same night Mother did."

"Phillipa, that's a mighty big coincidence, don't you think?"

"Well, it has to be a coincidence. Mother died in her bed of natural causes."

"Did she?"

"She had emphysema, Vic. After breaking her hip, she went downhill fast. When she died, it surprised no one. Not myself or her doctor."

I had left the burden of looking after the old witch to Phillipa.

It was part of the oldest sibling's burden as the responsible one. The Mother's Helper.

Because of her Charming talent, Mother had always treated Pip best, and that made her feel guilty about the attention she received. To tell her of things that happened when she wasn't around would have been cruel. To speak those things aloud would have made the monster real.

I could have felt guilty about leaving, but I didn't. Not much. In the end, I had left Grimsby because if I had stayed, I would have died.

I handed her back the cup. I was proud to see my hand wasn't shaking.

"What does Hunter say?"

Phillipa's face lit up as I mentioned the attorney. "Where did you meet him? He's gorgeous."

"Don't gobble him down in one bite, Pip."

She gave a suggestive lick of her lips before becoming serious. "Hunter thinks Liam is on the spectrum. It might help his case if we get him tested."

"How would that help?"

"The police went well beyond what they should have in that interview. Hunter wants to use it to set up a defense or counter with a civil action against the Grimsby police department."

"But is Liam truly disabled? I know he has his issues, but—I mean, isn't it like a chicken-and-the-egg kind of thing?"

Phillipa understood immediately. "Like, did his talent cause him to be this way, or do people perceive he's different because of his talent?"

If it came down to it, a psychiatrist could have a field day with the entire Rowan clan. Phillipa may have fooled people into thinking she was normal, but we both knew what a lie that was. She was a Queen Bee whom all the other drones couldn't help but come to.

I doubted normal would get me commissions from around the world for art restoration.

"Look, I'm staying here overnight to talk with the doctor, but I'm checking out in the morning."

"I don't know if that's a good thing, Vic. It was scary seeing you collapse. For a moment, you weren't breathing."

I didn't want to think about that. "I'm fine. The emotional overload overwhelmed me, but that won't happen again. Don't worry about it."

At my words, Liam's dragon stirred inside me again like a powerful hurricane swirling. It was gaining momentum. I was in the eye for now, but I would need to shed this maelstrom soon. I couldn't maintain the boundary between Liam's fearful rage and my own emotions for much longer.

I didn't want to think about that either, so I changed the subject. "Where's Hunter staying?"

"He's at the house, using the guest room." At my look, she said defensively, "The other bedrooms are locked."

"Not a good idea, Pip," I warned her.

"I know! But after I told him about the busted window, he insisted." She raised her hands in a helpless gesture. I sighed. Why was this growing so complicated?

"I wanted to talk with you about some things without Liam around. Are you up for it?"

What now?

"Go ahead. I'll tell you if it's too much." I gestured with my thumb at the curtain, reminding her we had neighbors. She picked up the television control and set it to a game show, then went to the other side of my bed and pulled up the one guest chair close to my bed. She put her elbows on the mattress and leaned close.

"It's about Mother's estate. She has a lot of money. A–lot–of–money."

Hm. Knowing Mother's nature and seeing Phillipa's expression, I knew I would not like this. Heaving a sigh, I said, "That antique shop. It isn't legit, is it?"

"I don't see how it can be. When she woke up in the hospital after her fall, she was frantic. Insisted that I go to the shop and get the accounting book. She also gave me an account number. I don't think she wanted Patty to have them."

Mother might have treated us all like garbage, but we were still family. Keep the family close with the secrets. That way you can stab the dagger in deeper.

"How much money are we talking about?"

Instead of answering me, Phillipa typed a number on her phone and showed it to me. It took me a moment to figure out how many commas I was seeing. No way was this honest money. I had a terrible feeling about this... and Patty's murder wasn't exactly comforting.

Phillipa's phone rang, and she answered. I could see from her expression that it wasn't good. Matters were going to hell in a handbasket by the minute.

"Thanks for telling me. I'm with Vic right now. I'll be over as soon as I can. Don't worry, Liam. This won't change things." She hung up and said, "The police have stopped Mother's cremation. They've ordered an autopsy."

Chapter Six

I escaped from the hospital two days later. Phillipa brought me to her car in a wheelchair. At my grumbling about the humiliation, Phillipa explained, "It's a precaution in case you faint again."

It was an embarrassing way to meet Hunter Garrick, especially when I remembered my abrupt last text four years ago about not needing him. I would have preferred to be standing on my own two feet with sass in my step. Instead, my sister reached across to pull my safety belt over me as if I was a child. I swatted her hand away to do it myself.

After a hello and "Hope you're feeling better," Hunter turned his attention back to my sister. Sitting behind him, I had a perfect view of the back of his head. Tightly cropped black curls showed off a perfectly shaped skull. His cool black skin was a dazzling contrast against the white collar of his shirt.

Why did he have to glow? *Tone it down, show-off.*

He and my sister already appeared to be on good terms. Their playful banter darkened my mood. I sulked in the back seat.

Sure, Hunter and I had parted over four years ago and my

sister wasn't poaching a turf that I hadn't already abandoned, but wouldn't it be nice if someone acknowledged that I had almost died a few days ago?

Pip pointed out the few interesting landmarks in Grimsby as she drove. They already had a jest going about her trying to sell him a condo by the lake. Coyly, he got her hopes up by saying how nice it would be to have her as a neighbor.

Before he could sign anything, I interrupted.

"Where's Liam?" My demand sounded shrill and petulant.

Phillipa used the rearview mirror to meet my eyes. I promptly stuck my tongue out at her—a gesture seen by Hunter, who had turned in his seat to address me. Could this day get any more embarrassing?

"Your brother is at Phillipa's condo. He's quite comfortable and has strict instructions not to let anyone in. If the police show up with a warrant, he's calling me immediately."

"Good." I stared out the window while Hunter continued to watch me.

"That's a cute look, with your hair sticking up in the back. It makes you look younger, more vulnerable."

"Bedhead isn't cute." I snapped back.

"Don't fret, Vic, we all know you're still tough as nails."

He grinned, flashing his bright white teeth in his movie-star face. He gave a sideways look at Phillipa's profile and said, "Imagine my surprise to learn you have a family. And a beautiful sister. Something you've never mentioned to me."

I could feel the bonding, like warm, sticky honey, forming between them. My injured talent was healing. And it confirmed Hunter's interest in Phillipa. While I definitely didn't want to renew an intimate relationship with Hunter, it still stung my pride.

I said crossly, "If you're done giving the nickel-tour, Phillipa, can we get to the house?"

After my shower, I came downstairs to find Phillipa and my ex at the formal dining table going over documents.

"Mother's?" I guessed.

Phillipa nodded. "We've been going over the books. On the surface everything looks correct, but—"

Hunter explained. "Rosemary Thyme seems to be an ordinary antique business dealing with high-end pieces. But antiques, like real estate, are often a preferred method to launder money, since their values fluctuate. The real value is exaggerated, and the difference becomes the rake-off."

Phillipa said, "The big problem? The customer's addresses don't exist. Or at least not in the MLS."

"MLS?" I asked. The two of them were like watching a friendly tennis match.

"Multiple Listing Service," explained Phillipa. "Realtors use it to list a house, but all legal addresses can be found in the database even if they aren't for sale."

With plenty of time in my hospital bed to think over what we knew, I gave my conclusions. "Why was Patty in the alley behind the shop? Was she meeting someone? And why there, and not somewhere else? More importantly, why was Liam there about the same time as Patty?"

"He won't talk to us. But he might to you, Vic. You two were always close as kids."

I was doubtful about that. I had walked away from my brother's plight more than a decade ago, so it wouldn't surprise me if he blamed me for the way his life was. I would. Would he chit-chat to me about what he and Mother had been doing? I thought not.

"What do you think of the case against Liam?" I asked Hunter.

"Officially, there is no case, as he was only brought in as a person of interest. However, he was in the area, and his dislike of Patty Maxwell is common knowledge. They had a heated exchange earlier in the day, observed by several people. He was possibly on the premises when the murder happened. However, as far as I know, there is no direct evidence he murdered Patty, but the police don't always show all they know."

"How are my mother's keys involved in this?"

Phillipa gave me her full attention. "What do you mean?"

"It's what got Liam upset. Reed tossed her keychain at us, and Liam caught it barehanded."

Phillipa understood immediately. "What a bastard." To Hunter, she added, "My brother has a phobia about being touched. It's called haphephobia."

That was the cover story we all used. Nowadays, though, how much of a story was it, really? Coming home was making me rethink all of my assumptions, and Phillipa's chicken-and-egg comparison had me wondering.

"That only gives us more ammunition in getting anything that happened in the interrogation dismissed. Evidence gained by coercion won't go down well with a judge."

"I'd prefer to avoid a Grimsby judge. We should solve this one ourselves." Neither of them seemed surprised by my statement.

"We agree," said Phillipa. "We stayed up last night discussing it. I don't think we can rely upon Deacon Hayes for justice."

"Your sister told me that your mother was universally disliked."

I almost laughed out loud, but coughed instead. "That's putting it mildly."

"Which gives plenty of choices for who might have killed Patty. Or who might want Rachel dead," Hunter said.

"I can't believe Mother was murdered," Phillipa said, shaking her head. "She was over seventy and in poor health. Why not let nature take its course?"

"At this time, Rachel's death hasn't been proven to be anything but natural," said our new lawyer.

I ignored Hunter and addressed myself to Phillipa. "If the murderer couldn't wait, that speaks of a time constraint. Whoever the culprit was, he or she couldn't wait a few months or a year. They needed her gone."

Phillipa opened her laptop and started to type.

1.) Patty Maxwell, murdered behind the shop. Died the same day as Mother.

2.) Mother. Natural or not?

"I wonder what time Patty was killed. Was it before or after Mother died?" I asked, and Phillipa added that question to the list.

Perhaps tired of being ignored, Hunter said, "Unlike murder shows on television, an autopsy will only reveal a possible window of time of when she died."

I trusted his knowledge. "Do you think you could get a copy of the autopsy report?"

"Perhaps."

"Vic, ask Reed Easton to get us a copy," Phillipa suggested.

"Are you crazy?"

"He's called several times to find out how you were doing. You could work on his old affection to get what we need."

Hunter's emotions became amused, tickling my nose like a fizzy soda. Smiling, he asked, "Did you dump him by text, too?"

Phillipa, who could be as manipulative as our mother sometimes, persisted. "Reed was truly upset about what happened. We could use that to our advantage."

Hunter's fizzy-interest was growing. Time to change the subject. I muttered, "If an opportunity presents itself, I'll ask him, but I'm not going out of my way."

Of course, at that moment, the doorbell rang. Looking over, I could see across the room that Reed Easton was at the door. It seemed my tally of embarrassments wasn't going to stop until I left Grimsby.

Phillipa jumped up and quick-stepped to open the door.

"Why Reed, we were just talking about you."

"Anything good?"

"*Nothing* good," I called out spitefully from where I was still sitting at the dining table.

My sister played the good hostess. "Would you like some coffee? I have some pastries from Nelly's bakery."

"Sounds good."

Did the man have no shame? Did he think he could just prance in here after what he'd done to Liam? I would have followed Phillipa to the kitchen, but I'd be damned if I gave any ground to Reed.

"Mr. Easton." Hunter shook hands with Reed. All congeniality on the surface. But he was wary of the newcomer, and that pleased me. Reed Easton was nothing. I was over thirty-years old and had a life far away from Grimsby that didn't include him. A grown-up life.

"Is this a social call, or do you have a warrant to destroy innocent lives?"

Reed ignored my testy question. "I want to know why Liam reacted so strongly when I gave him this." He dangled the key chain, the double R – Rolls-Royce's signature medallion—swinging.

Phillipa returned with a tray of coffee and pastry, and Reed's gaze traveled from me to my sister.

"What did Liam discover when he touched these? The identity of Patty's killer?"

Hunter Garrick pounced like a hawk.

"Say no more, Ms. Rowan. This smells like entrapment." Hunter's hostility increased, though his face didn't betray it. He controlled himself well; it was one reason I liked him.

"I only wanted to know why this might be in Patty Maxwell's purse," said Reed, his green eyes never wavering from mine.

Before Phillipa could get us into more trouble, I told him, "I would guess Patty had them for managing the shop while my mother was in a care home. She was my mother's assistant, after all."

"Wouldn't Liam be the natural choice to have them?"

Phillipa understood now what was at stake. She set down her tray, handing a mug and saucer to Hunter and then to me. "Liam wasn't as involved in my mother's business as you believe, Reed. She only gave him minor jobs to do to keep him occupied. It was a way of earning money, since people in this town refused to hire him."

Reed stepped closer to me, invading my space in a way he had to remember I disliked. I stood up so he couldn't loom over me.

He asked me, "You didn't answer me, Vic. What did Liam find out when he touched these keys? What made him scream and curl into a ball?"

"What do you mean?"

Reed's slight smile was sad. "Don't do this. Don't play these games with me."

"I don't know what you're talking about," I insisted, even as my mind frantically went back to when we had been teenagers. What had I told him about me? About Liam or Phillipa?

As if he was reading my thoughts, Reed said, "I can see you wondering what I know. I'll make it easy for you; you didn't tell me your secrets back then, Vic. But I wasn't blind or deaf. There were plenty of strange rumors about you and your brother going around the school. One day I saw him talking to a car, and I asked him why he did that. He told me."

As Reed talked, the snarling storm inside me awoke. The pain wanted someone to devour. I had two options: absorb it or release it.

I growled, "How dare you use my brother for your own end? You don't know anything about him!"

"Maybe if you'd let me in, I would understand!"

We were shouting, our faces only a few inches apart from each other, while Hunter and Phillipa stayed as quiet as mice.

"Do you really want to know what Liam felt? Want to know

about my family and me?" My hand, still bruised from the IV, reached out and gripped Reed's wrist tightly.

"Don't!" cried Phillipa, but I ignored her.

"Take it." My cool hand circled his warm skin, and I gave him the storm.

But as I slammed the spiky ball of howling pain at Reed, my strike hit nothing.

When I had met Reed Easton in high school, he'd been one grade above my own and a year older. He was the only person I couldn't read, whose emotional output couldn't swamp me. Now, I discovered he had no limitations in absorbing my own.

The pile of self-hate, disgust, frustration, and loathing was a rock I threw, but instead of shattering something, it sank. Reed was at the center of a downdraft, a vortex, and there was no bottom. Still attached to the transfer, it pulled me along into an infinity of nothing.

I kept falling. Falling...

As it all left me, I felt an inner peace I'd never experienced before. Reed took my fears and the trauma, feeling none of it.

The release gave me a blissful moment of not feeling anything, too. I could give him everything and never feel again.

"Victoria!" It was Phillipa who snapped me out of it, slamming me back into the chair I had vacated. Her hands on my shoulders pressed down, grounding me. My bare feet were flat on the rug covering the old wood floor. I felt dizzy and lightheaded.

"Haven't you done enough damage already?" Phillipa yelled over me at Reed. It wasn't often one heard my sister angry.

"Are you all right, Vic?" I heard Reed's voice floating like a cloud above me. Hunter must have moved, for his voice was closer than it should have been. "What happened? Is she having another episode?"

"I want to lie down, please," I mumbled.

Reed responded quickly, picking me up. Maybe he was

showing off to Hunter. I didn't care about his reasoning. I nestled into his outdoor-fresh-breeze smell and closed my eyes.

"This way," Phillipa directed. They lay me on my mother's sacred couch in her sacred sitting room, tucking a soft pillow under my head.

"Blanket?" I mumbled. It took a few more moments before it arrived. As my eyes closed, I fell down a dark hole full of painful memories.

Chapter Seven

My mother loved catching us kids out with our lies. And as we got older, there were more things we didn't want her to know.

But my mother's talent was sniffing out deceit. So we became mice to her cat as she sharpened her skills, using us as sport and to feed her self-importance.

On Sunday, she attended church with Victor. We did our assigned chores: dusting, vacuuming, and cleaning toilets. She said it built character. We must have built a lot of character in those days.

After church, my parents would dine at a restaurant with other notables in Grimsby. When they praised Rachel Rowan as a model for every woman in the community, she arrived home in a good mood. If not, things happened to us.

My siblings relied upon me feeling her emotions, and if we had enough warning, we would scatter out the back door to find some place else to be. On the days we weren't quick enough, once inside she would set her hat and gloves from church on the table near the door.

Victor always went upstairs. I still remember the heavy sound of footsteps, the latch of his door shutting.

Downstairs in her parlor, we lined up, waiting to be punished. For Mother needed to relieve her frustrations upon our heads. And there was always something wrong about us for her to find.

She would ask questions about how our lessons were going and who our friends were. Did teachers like us? Did we do well on tests?

Her voice, in that artificial breathy tone she thought sounded well-bred, would always begin with the same phrase: "Did you uphold the Rowan family honor?"

In this memory-dream, Phillipa was babbling, stretching out a story to make it last as long as possible. It was her technique to keep Mother's focus upon her alone. Phillipa's talent for charisma made her the favorite with Mother, which was in equal turns a blessing and a curse. She used it to shield us. But Phillipa was young, and there were limits to Mother's patience.

"And what about you, Victoria? What teacher loves you best?"

Her eyes turned to me, and I trembled. Beside me, Liam played with a feather duster, stroking it.

To avoid her stare, I looked at her pink purse sitting on the small round table next to the sofa, her keys on top with their distinctive keychain. The RR luxury car medallion she used to mimic her initials.

"None of them really," I piped up, my voice so young.

"None?" Mother repeated. She had a way of raising her chin and looking down out of half-closed eyes. Her mouth would give a faint smile, as friendly as a cobra's.

Strange how you can remember a voice, an attitude, so clearly when you can't remember where you parked your car after a concert.

"My dear Victoria, Rowans are always special. The Rowans are a founding family and the Grimsby community looks to us to be an example."

She gave me a backhanded slap that tossed me back against the wall. The house wasn't so big that my father upstairs wouldn't have heard it.

How many times had we hoped he'd come downstairs? Rescue us? But those wishes never came true. He moved like a ghost in the house, watching but never part of us. We stopped calling him father, preferring the name our mother used, complete with a sneer.

Next up for interrogation was Liam. While I might not be willing to play the game, at least I knew the rules. Liam was clueless. My brother never knew how to appease Rachel.

Beside me, he hummed to himself, twirling the handle of the feather duster in his hand. He was enjoying the memory of the birds in the silky feathers, unaware of the monster about to attack.

My mother snatched the feather duster from his hand. He looked up at her, frowning at the interruption to his game.

"Do you love me, Lee?" Oh, that voice! How I wish I could forget it.

In all honesty, because Liam didn't understand how to hide, my brother told her, "No."

And his beating began.

I woke up from my dream with acid on my tongue and a cold, sweaty neck. I fretfully kicked the blanket off, and a man sitting in the armchair across from me said, "How are you feeling?"

I sat up and told Reed Easton, "Irritated seeing you." It annoyed me seeing Reed emotionally healthy after I had tried to dump all of Liam's crap on him. "Why don't you go home? Have dinner with your dad and talk about how dangerous the Rowans are?"

"I told your sister I wouldn't go until you woke up. Phillipa and Hunter are upstairs. Together."

Did he think that would bother me? Yeah, well, my pride might bristle a bit, but Hunter and I were old news. It would never have worked out. That was why I'd dumped him.

"So you're a cop now, filling Daddy's shoes—?" I began, but Reed contradicted me sharply.

"No. That's what I wanted to talk with you about, if you're up for it. You don't look up for it. To put it bluntly, you look like death warmed over."

"It's because I'm hungry. I always look like the Grim Reaper when I need food."

I got up, and ignoring Reed's outstretched hand, made my way to the kitchen. He followed, soft-footed as a cat. From the microwave oven clock, it looked to be early morning, about an hour before dawn. I flipped open cabinets, looking for food.

It was strange to see the old plates, the glasses, and even a bag of coffee that my mother had enjoyed sitting on shelves as if nothing had happened. It gave me a weird feeling. Like she wasn't dead.

What an unpleasant thought.

She'd better be dead.

I filled a kettle from the sink and turned on the gas stove. I'd make some tea. Reed started speaking. "I'm a cop, but I don't work for the Grimsby PD. I'm with the FBI now."

"Yeah, I heard Deacon Hayes say that." Okay, so Reed was a top cop. Still, an overachiever, driven to do more than anyone else. "Let me guess. It was just a coincidence that you were in town when I arrived?"

I kept my back to him, finding things to keep myself busy with as I listened. Phillipa had left me another meal in the fridge. I didn't ask Reed if he had eaten; he could scrounge for his own food.

He didn't answer my question.

"Someone strangled Patty Maxwell to death in the alley behind Rosemary Thyme around 1 a.m. A security camera recorded Liam entering your mother's antique store around midnight."

He paused, as if waiting for a reaction. I didn't give him one.

"When my dad heard Patty's murder could involve Liam, he wanted to go down and be in on the questioning. I convinced him to let me go instead. But I'm not officially on the investigations about the deaths of Patty Maxwell or Rachel Rowan. Hayes let me sit in as a professional courtesy to the badge."

Not for the first time, I wished I could scan Reed's emotions, feel the inner truth of what he said, instead of having to rely upon my ears and eyes.

"Deacon ordered my mother's autopsy?"

"No, that came from the state coroner's office. Normally they wouldn't do one, since a physician attended her, and her death wasn't exactly unexpected. But with Patty's murder and your family wanting to cremate her, I think they felt they needed to step in."

I took out a tea bag and poured hot water over it. The tea was too hot. I always overdid things. "Liam had nothing to do with any murder, Reed."

"People around your family die, Vic. It makes people wonder."

"Wonder if we're murderers? That's what your dad's been thinking for fifteen years. Or so I hear from Phillipa."

"What information did Liam get from the keys, Vic? Does he know who murdered Patty?"

Without Liam's hurt on my shoulders and with a good night's sleep, I was feeling very calm. If Reed wanted an exchange of information, I'd do that. Besides, what could he do with the information I was giving him? Nothing. And I could do a lot with what he was telling me.

"No. His talent doesn't work like that. When I was at the hospital, Liam told me it was an emotional residue from our mother owning them. It shocked him. It's complicated, but he learns things-stuff, not people-stuff."

"And you know people-stuff, don't you, Vic?" I said nothing and Reed abruptly changed tactics. "Why did you leave without telling me?"

I knew we'd get there. Best drive through it, knocking aside all the flashing red-light barriers, and push the pedal to the floorboard to drive off the cliff.

"We'd fought. Or don't you remember?" I did. Vividly. We had agreed to leave Grimsby and attend the same university. We'd go together. While Reed was a year older, we were still in the same graduating class because of his birthday being late in the year.

That was the plan—until Reed decided we both should wait another year before escaping. His decision had precipitated a series of horrible events, but I wasn't ready to confide in him.

As he had long ago, he said, "I know I agreed to leave, but the time was off. I couldn't go, not then. You should know why by now."

"Still don't know," I said, pressing my lips into a thin line, the mug uncomfortably hot in my hands.

"The day before you asked me to leave, we were told my mother had cancer."

I felt I had punched someone, but they had dodged the blow, making me look an idiot. Phillipa had told me that Mrs. Easton had passed away, but had given no details.

"Sorry. I didn't know." Sure, it was lame to admit that, but I needed to offer some sort of apology. His mom had been a nice lady, unlike mine.

I took my food and beat a retreat to the dining table. Again, he followed. Taking a chair to my left, he watched my face in that intense, focused way of his that hadn't changed since our teen years. No, it had changed. Now it made me feel distinctly uncomfortable.

"How do you know Hunter Garrick?"

I waggled my eyebrows at him and gave him a knowing look.

He didn't appear happy with the confirmation of something he had probably already suspected. Too bad.

"Why don't you tell me about Patty Maxwell. Off the record. You aren't here officially, right?"

"And if I do? What do I get?"

The teen Reed would have done anything for me, but this was a man who could stand firm against a girl's eyes. Not as malleable. Someone had rubbed away that teen naiveté and shown him that women could count the cost and give no change.

I wondered what girl had hurt him.

Oh, right, that was me.

"Maybe I'll answer a few questions. Nothing incriminating, though."

"Maxwell's body was found in the early hours of the morning on Saturday, August 12th, by a delivery driver. He'd pulled into the alley to make his regular stop at the bakery next door to your mother's shop. Maxwell was on her back, a bill clutched in her hand. Scattered around the alley were the contents of her purse. Including the keys."

"Sounds like a robbery gone bad to me."

He continued as if I hadn't interrupted. "The preliminary autopsy shows she died by strangulation. It broke her hyoid bone."

He waited for a response. I shrugged. "The only physiology I studied at college was the naked human form in life drawing classes, so you'll have to explain what that means, Sherlock."

"It takes a great deal of force to break the hyoid in the neck. It's a type of breakage you see in car accidents or hangings. From the marks on Patty, it's as if someone grabbed her by the throat and throttled her face-to-face. To put it bluntly, he wrung her neck like a chicken's."

My brother was over six feet and built like a linebacker. I saw where Reed was going with this, but Liam wasn't the only big guy in town. Men in Grimsby were shaped by hard work. It was why the football stadium had artificial turf; the team did well against teams of scrawny city boys.

I shook my head. "Still doesn't implicate Liam."

"Earlier in the afternoon, Patty and Liam argued in front of Nelly's bakery. It drew quite a crowd, and witnesses described it as acrimonious. Some heard your brother threaten Patty, saying he'd see her dead before he accepted her as his boss."

While my brother may have said those words, I couldn't imagine Liam yelling. I didn't answer, keeping my interest in my food. Dang, this ravioli was good. I wondered where it came from so I could get more. I loved Italian.

"When they renovated the main street area, they installed cameras at the traffic lights. One caught your brother going into Rosemary Thyme around 11 p.m. and leaving around midnight. From the coroner's report, Patty died between midnight and three in the morning."

Why did I have the strange feeling that Patty had died at 1:30 a.m., at the same time as my mother? An icy shiver went down my neck, and the hair on my arms prickled. To cover my sudden fear, I snorted in disbelief.

"So what if Liam was inside the store when she was dying out back? That's thin. Any DNA, fingernail scrapings, or hair of my brother's clutched in the victim's hands?"

"It sounds like you know your way around a crime scene, Vic," said Reed.

I shrugged. "I watch a lot of crime shows."

Chapter Eight

The others stumbled downstairs, and we all decided to pick up Liam for breakfast. We pointedly did not invite Reed, so after giving me one last pointed stare, he left.

Perhaps the server would have refused to seat a bunch of Rowans, but the charm of Phillipa and the star presence of Hunter Garrick won the day. Hunter's face was recognizable to anyone who watched the news stations. And as soon as we entered Vincent's, he attracted attention.

Holding his arm, Phillipa introduced him to Grimsby notables while Liam and I squeezed past to find an empty table near the bathroom. My brother was back to his sunglasses, hat, and gloves. I said little while sharing the back seat of Phillipa's car, though a lot needed to be said.

Hunter and Phillipa joined us in a warm glow of bouncy energy. She was another person I needed to talk to privately. I put it on my to-do list to determine her intentions towards Hunter. It wouldn't do to anger our attorney before he got Liam off for double homicide.

A council of war began over crepes and French toast, while we sipped gourmet coffee blends.

Hunter told us, "As a family, I'll see if you can request a copy of your mother's autopsy once it's completed."

"Is that possible with one of us being a suspect?" Phillipa asked doubtfully.

"Until Liam is arrested or charged, we may get some information. Still, they may try to drag out supplying it because Rachel's death is being investigated. I'll see what I can do."

This is why I had called Hunter. He would make calls. Things would happen. Strings pulled.

As plates arrived, Phillipa said, "I have a couple of house showings this morning. When should we meet up again?"

Hunter spoke first. "I need to head back to my office tomorrow morning. But today I'll be at your house making my phone calls and doing online meetings. I don't want to leave Grimsby just yet."

He smiled at Phillipa. I put my coffee cup down and told them, "I want to go by Rosemary Thyme. And I want Liam with me."

"Is that a good idea?"

Liam stirred.

"I'm not a child, Phillipa. Stop treating me like one. If Vic wants me there, I'll go."

His words silenced us all. Finally, Pip said lamely, "I thought maybe going there would upset you, since you didn't want to come to the house."

"The house is different. It's a poisonous place. We should get it sold quickly to someone we dislike, as a curse. Or burn it to the ground."

Now that was an idea.

"I see the gears turning in your head, Vic Rowan," Hunter warned me. "Arson would be a terrible idea."

"Bad. Bad idea," Phillipa repeated, shaking her finger at me and using a deep warning voice that made us all laugh.

"When did Mother start the shop?" I needed more information to solve this whole puzzle.

Liam answered, "Three years, two months, and five days after you left."

"Hm. Why? I never imagined her as a business owner. Was it a vanity project?"

"After Victor died, she lost a lot of prestige in the town," said my sister. "I don't think she ever realized how much Victor's presence was part of why Grimsby society welcomed her. The committee work dried up. No more invites to lunch. No more plaques and ribbon cuttings. I think she was bored and wanted something to do."

"Not bored," corrected Liam, who was never keen on inaccuracy. "She was seething over being snubbed. Mother wanted revenge."

That sounded like Mother. Funny that Liam, the one who liked objects over people, would be the one to hit the bullseye for explaining her motivations.

Hunter asked, "They spurned Rachel, and she retaliated with an antique shop? How does that work?"

While I wanted Hunter to be on our side, how much truth about our family did he need to know?

Before we had left the house, while Hunter was showering, Phillipa had confided that he didn't believe Reed's comments last night about Liam's talent. Further, while Phillipa had shared the Rosemary Thyme accounting information with him, she had not told Hunter about the off-shore bank account.

"That's what we need to find out," I said. "Looking around Rosemary Thyme is a good start to answering that question."

Phillipa cleared her throat. "After Mother fell down the stairs, Patty called for an ambulance. She was at the house that evening, you see. When Mother came out of surgery, she was confused and worried. She wanted me to get the books. I thought it would make her rest easier just to do what she wanted, so I went over to Rose-mary Thyme."

Phillipa daintily patted her mouth with a napkin.

"I found Patty at the store. I didn't think much about it at the time because she was Mother's employee, but she looked strange. Pale and sweating. And she wouldn't meet my eyes. The whole situation gave off a weird vibe that made me very uncomfortable, so I grabbed the accounting books and left."

Liam was staring down at his pancake stack. He had cut it into a grid of perfect squares. "That wasn't the book Mother wanted you to get, Phillipa."

My sister looked confused. I asked gently, "What books did she want?"

Liam dropped the bomb.

"Mother was blackmailing people in town. She discovered their secrets and made them pay. A special book lists all the transac-tions, and that was the one she wanted."

I knew it was going to be something manipulative and nasty. Mother's signature style.

Hunter said in the stunned silence that followed my brother's statement, "Thank you, Liam. That explains things—why the people I've spoken to would either heap outrageous praise upon her or refuse to discuss Rachel at all."

"When did you have time to talk with anyone?" I asked, surprised. Hunter had only been in town for a little over three days.

Phillipa spoke up. "I put him in touch with some people mentioned in Mother's paperwork. People who bought things from her."

"The Persian rug that wasn't."

"What was that, Hunter?" I asked, confused.

"One item mentioned several times in your mother's paper-work is a Persian rug. About eight feet by eleven, over one hundred years old. A field of red, with blue and gold highlights. She sold that identically described rug a dozen times last year. While you were in the hospital, your sister and I interviewed three of the local buyers we could find an actual address for."

Hunter and Phillipa's eyes met. Sharing something. I was thinking things had progressed faster than I had supposed. Maybe pillow talk had already happened? Hunter seemed to take the revelation of our family's dirty linen well.

"Not one of them had a rug they could show us," Phillipa said. "We were told it was being cleaned or already given away. One person slammed the door on us. On *me*!"

If my sister's honeyed charm wasn't working, matters were indeed serious. I had some experience with fraud, because of painting sales in the art world. I gave them my thoughts.

"So Mother discovered people's dirty little secrets. If they paid up, she kept quiet. Like Hunter guessed last night, she used antiques to conceal dirty money. People bought a phantom rug to explain Mother's bank balance. The shop was a front—a piece of fakery."

"Seeing the store every day as they drove through town must have tormented her victims," said Phillipa, horrified. I nodded. Sounded sadistic. Sounded like Mother.

"As her assistant, Patty probably knew what Rachel was doing. How long did she work for her?" asked Hunter.

"I remember her at the party Mother held for the opening," said Phillipa.

Finished with his pancakes, Liam dropped another bombshell.

"Patty was Mother's go-between. Sometimes she collected the payments for her. Patty kept doing it even when she was in the hospital."

"How do you know this?" I demanded, fearing the answer.

"I was helping them do it. Do the blackmail."

I felt Hunter struggle to control his impatience when Liam refused to answer any further questions. However, Phillipa and I were familiar with Liam's ways; when our brother finished talking, he was done. We discussed practical matters instead as we finished our breakfast.

I insisted we stick to the original plan: Hunter would work from our house, and we would meet for dinner before he left back to the city. Phillipa would do her house showings, while Liam and I checked out Rosemary Thyme.

It was the first time I had seen the place. It had hunter-green awnings over large plate windows, but lined drapes concealed the interior. Only the sign on the door hinted of what the place might be about: *Rosemary Thyme, Secret Treasures.*

Oh yes, how Mother liked her games.

Liam used his key to open the door. Inside, he entered the burglar alarm code while I got my first look at my mother's business.

In my line of work, I'd visited many museums. I had been behind the scenes at some of the finest institutions the world offered. I'd seen private collections hidden away. So, while textiles and furniture were not my areas of expertise, I recognized quality.

Rosemary Thyme was quite the showpiece. It didn't hold a few treasures; it was bursting at the seams. To assemble all this in one place would have taken quite an investment—far more than my father's wealth or a life insurance policy could have managed.

Strangely enough, there were no paintings. After I left Grimsby, I cut contact with my mother. From Phillipa, Mother had known what I did, my degrees and job. The lack of paintings? I could guess why. The snub almost made me laugh.

Liam was walking through the collection, touching items as he named them.

"Side table, George II, walnut, highly carved. 1745. Cabinet, William and Mary, walnut, with marquetry. 1786. Chairs, two. Empire style, gilt over bronze. Mahogany. Right arm, hairline crack. Twentieth century. Porcelain, Chinese, blue and white with silver-gilt mounts. Flemish. 1748..."

My brother always preferred old objects, which he said had a rich, layered intensity. New stuff, still in use, projected a flat, one-note dimension.

The store was laid out in vignettes. There was a marble fire-place mantle, bracketed with chairs and side tables. Silver candelabra held candlesticks. A full plate service with cut crystal was on a dining room table, awaiting guests.

Rosemary Thyme was a playhouse. Here, Mother arranged her dolls on a stage and gave them their stories.

Liam continued to name things while I explored the private area of the store. A doorway led to an expensively decorated powder room with a heavy smell of gardenias. A short hall opened to a very tidy office. Here I found a partner's desk with two chairs; it allowed two people to face each other as they worked.

I sat down in a chair and started opening drawers. None of them contained the usual office paraphernalia, like paper clips or staplers. Only a few pens rolled around inside them.

There was no computer either. Would Mother have used one? Surely Phillipa would have mentioned it? But maybe Patty had taken it?

I thought again about what Phillipa had said about retrieving the accounting books and finding Patty here. What had the woman taken? Had she taken the blackmail book? Liam said she continued taking payments. Maybe that led to her death.

There was a gasp at the door. I looked up to see Liam staring at me from a white, shocked face.

"Sorry, I didn't mean to startle you. Is this where Mother and Patty worked?" He nodded. "They're dead, Liam. Dead is dead."

He took a hesitant step into the office.

"Whatever part you played in this sordid mess, we're going to get you out of it. It wasn't your fault."

He took the chair across from me. It must have been Patty's, because it was lower than my mother's and sagged in the seat. She would have chosen the best for herself.

"Did you kill her?" I asked.

He said nothing.

I knew things had been awkward between us since my return. There was a gap, a chasm, between our close childhood relationship and today. It was my responsibility to bridge that, not his. I was the one who had abandoned him so long ago.

The mass of emotional energy that I had removed from him at the police station and tried to re-gift to Reed had not just been from a keychain. It was trauma from years of abuse.

I reached my hands out across the oak desk, palms up.

"I'll take more if you have it."

His raised eyebrows over his glasses made a skeptical question mark. Before he could speak, there was a chime signaling someone had entered the front door.

"Hello?"

It was a female voice and from the way Liam jerked in his chair, he seemed to recognize it. I got up and put a hand out, showing he should stay where he was.

Chapter Nine

I found a woman standing in the middle of my mother's boutique shop, ignoring the priceless treasures. She had a long stream of dark chocolate hair tied back in a simple ponytail, with matching brown eyes. She looked to be in her late twenties. The pink box she held was vaguely familiar.

"Can I help you?" I asked.

"Oh!" She looked behind me. "I saw the lights on and thought maybe—? Is Liam here?"

"He's not available right now."

The feeling of emotional comfort gained from smelling fresh baking bread rolled towards me. Although they were rare, I had met these types before. My boss, Tony, was one. Truly nice people. Rays of sunshine and joy. An empath like me could get trapped in their marshmallow-caramel-goodness and never escape back to my land of witty sarcasm and dry, acerbic sadness. My talent jumped back like a startled horse.

"Could you give him this?"

I took the pink box. The top read 'Nelly's bakery.'

Before I could thank her or ask who she was, the door to Rosemary Thyme opened again. Crossing the threshold was one of my least favorite people in the world: Greg Easton, the former police chief of Grimsby and Reed's father. A man I had once thought might be a surrogate father until he betrayed me.

Easton ignored me, addressing the stranger. "Let's go home. My truck is outside."

She didn't seem perturbed by his abrupt tone. To me, she said, "Be sure to tell Liam I dropped by."

"And you are?"

"Nell of Nelly's bakery." She had a bright smile. "You must be his sister, Victoria."

"Call me Vic."

Mr. Easton grabbed Nell by the upper arm. The grip must have been fierce—she fell back a step, and I figured she'd have a bruise. Still, Nell showed more determination than I would have credited her for. There must be some steel under the cotton candy.

She gave Easton a warning look and pulled her arm out of his.

"It's better not to be involved with this family," he growled.

"Dating my mother doesn't give you authority over me."

"Dear me," I said to her, trying to redirect Mr. Easton's ire to me. "You certainly don't want to get involved with the notorious Rowans. We devour children like you. Like the witch in Hansel and Gretel, we might pop you in an oven."

Finally, staring directly at me, Mr. Easton said, "People around you get murdered."

Easton was exactly what you would imagine the retired police chief of a small town to look like. But the passing years had marked him. His black hair was now salt-and-pepper, and the grooves from his nostrils to his mouth cut deep. He emanated anger-fear-disgust-frustration in a bitter molasses mix.

"You do like to libel people, don't you, Mr. Easton? It's a good thing for Grimsby you aren't the police chief anymore."

"No thanks to your mother," he snarled.

Hm. Was his name in her book? How inconvenient for Reed if

it was. I couldn't stop myself from asking, "Have you bought a rug lately?"

"You think I care? Rachel got the city manager to force me into early retirement."

Ah, so probably the city manager had bought a rug. I stored that information away to discuss with the team.

"I have a lawyer friend. You might know him? Hunter Garrick? He eats guys like you for lunch. He might like to discuss your accusations. Your threats to my sister. Maybe in front of a judge."

The chime sounded again, and like a three-ring circus clown-farce, Reed entered. I told him, "Just in time to collect your lunatic father."

Reed said to his father, "Lottie told me you came here after Nell. She's waiting for you in the car. Let me deal with this, as we agreed."

For a moment, I thought Mr. Easton would disagree. I knew he was spoiling for a fight, but his son's presence deflated him. He gave me one last glare before he left.

Nell lingered. "Do tell Liam I said hi."

She handed me the box and went out the door, leaving me with my former boyfriend. *Fan-tas-tic.*

"Deal with me? How will you deal with me?" I asked, raising my chin.

He came right up to my face. Like a scene from a romance, I thought he might kiss me. Wasn't that what happened when you returned to your small town to reconnect with your old boyfriend?

Instead, he said, "Your mother was murdered."

The murder of one parent was a tragedy. Losing another smacked of a conspiracy.

"I didn't do it," I said.

"I know you didn't. You were still in the city."

Reed was so close to me I could feel his breath on my cheek.

"How do you know that?"

Before I could press him further, the door chimed again. My sister entered, carrying a box. I greeted her with, "Mother's death is a murder."

She blinked, her stare passing between Reed and me. I stepped away from him, distancing myself.

"That was a fast autopsy," was her only comment.

"Preliminary information," Reed explained.

"And you felt the need to rush down here and give us the good news?" I said sarcastically.

His eyes had never left mine. "It was the hyoid bone."

"What does that mean?" Phillipa asked. I told her what Reed had said about Patty's murder. "It's a bone in the throat that takes a lot of force to break. Someone broke Patty's."

Phillipa relaxed; I felt her alarm ease. "If the same person committed both murders, that leaves Liam out. He doesn't have a car. I doubt he called for a ride to the nursing facility to kill Mother after he supposedly murdered Patty behind the store."

Phillipa shifted her grip on the box she held, and Reed took it from her. The three of us walked back to the office.

"What's in there?" I asked.

"Mother's things from her room at the care center. I picked them up the day after she died, as they needed the room."

"Let's look. Maybe there's a clue in here," I said excitedly.

I wasn't sure I wanted Reed around, but he had shared some news. Phillipa greeted Liam, who was still sitting in the chair with his earbuds while he played on his phone.

There wasn't a clue.

Most of it was things to make a patient comfortable, such as a few romance novels, some magazines, and a collection of toiletries like cosmetics and shampoo. There was a catalog about an upcoming sale of antiques from a well-known auction house. I set that aside to look at later.

Lifting one bottle, I twisted off the cap and sniffed. Still the same perfume. It brought back memories of Mother entertaining, glamorous, her dress and jewelry sparkling. Us, displayed like trophies—her perfect children. After a sickly, perfumed kiss, she'd banish Liam and me to our rooms. Phillipa remained to play the piano for Mother's guests.

I quickly replaced the cap on the bottle.

Reed had idly picked up a magazine and was leafing through it when something fluttered out. He instinctively reached for it, but stopped at Liam's words.

"Don't touch that unless you want to die."

My brother returned to his phone game. After a stare at Liam, Reed bent again to pick the bill off the floor. I stopped him by grabbing his wrist.

"Don't." I shook my head. Reed stopped.

Phillipa bent over Liam and popped one of his earbuds out. "Care to explain?"

Exasperated at being interrupted, he pulled out the other earbud and gave us his irritated attention. "I can smell it from here. Death and decay. Nasty. I found one stuffed in the shop door."

Under our astonished eyes, he returned his earbuds. I yanked them out and slapped his phone down on the desk.

"We could use a little of your help in keeping you out of jail, little brother, so explain."

He gave an exasperated roll of his baby-blue eyes.

"The alarm company told me they were getting an error message on their system from the store. I came over to check it out and saw a hundred-dollar bill stuck in the door handle. You couldn't miss it. It was like this one. Smelly with death magic."

"Liam!" Phillipa cried, giving a warning glare from Liam and Reed. I touched her arm. "Remember? Reed knows about Liam's talent. *Thanks to Liam.*"

Reed asked my brother, "Just like this one? What did you do with it?"

"I sure as hell didn't pick it up. I'm not a moron." His gaze at

Reed clearly showed who my brother thought *was* the idiot in the room.

"Where is that other money?" I demanded.

"Contrary to what Grimsby town folk think, I don't wish anyone in this one-horse town ill. So I burned it. You can't leave something like that lying around, blowing in the wind. Anyone could pick it up."

Reed asked, "What do you mean by death magic?"

This was the problem with having normals around. They needed everything explained to them in baby steps.

I snapped out an explanation. "A curse, an ill-omened wish for another to experience harm. Hexes. Got it, Reed? Get up to speed here."

"I only ask for an explanation, Vic, because Patty was clutching one just like this."

Phillipa's mouth fell open. But Reed had given me ideas. "What day did the alarm company call you, Liam?"

"The night Patty died."

Reed was evidently thinking the same thing. "Did you find out what was wrong with the alarm?"

"Nothing. It was working fine from our end." Liam shrugged. "When I called them back, they said no one had called from their dispatch. Morons."

Pulling out a ruler from inside a drawer, I crouched over the death-curse bill. I flipped it over and saw the handwriting on it. "Hand me the magnifying glass, Sherlock."

Reed gave me the one sitting on the desk. We both got on our hands and knees to examine the piece of money, careful not to touch it.

Phillipa was back on her phone, and I heard her say, "Yes, I was there earlier this week to pick up Rachel Rowan's belongings. Right. I'm her daughter. Well, I found something curious in her things, and wanted to talk with the person who packed up her room."

Reed said to me, "This is what a death-curse looks like? It seems pretty ordinary to me."

"That's the point," I told him. "They usually pass these things off as something quite innocent. Something the target would innocently touch and keep. Look here."

I handed the magnifying glass to him so Reed could examine the handwriting. It was in dark ink. He read it aloud: "*Touch this bill, and join hands to find your friends.* I don't get death-curse from this. Sounds friendly."

"If you don't believe me, why don't you touch it?" Liam said sarcastically. He was rocking the wooden chair back and forth on its wheels. The creak-creak-creak would probably drive me crazy before we finished.

Standing up, I gave a gentle kick to Reed's bum. "If it said *touch this and die*, would you pick it up?"

"It's a hundred-dollar bill. Some people might risk it." He got back to his feet, probably to avoid more bum-kicks.

"That's why I burned it," explained Liam with the long-suffering air of someone having to deal with idiots.

Phillipa finished her phone call and told us what she had discovered. "The money was in Mother's pillowcase. The aide thought we would accuse her of trying to steal it, so she was very particular about remembering it. She put it in the book for us to have. Thankfully, she was wearing cleaning gloves at the time."

I laid out the facts. "So far, we know there were three similar bills. One with Mother, one found with Patty Maxwell, and another stuck in the shop's door, which Liam found. All with death-curses."

"The link between the three is your mother's antique shop," mused Reed, who was still lagging the three of us on the information highway.

I tried to use telepathy to ensure my siblings wouldn't blurt out anything about blackmail, but that wasn't my talent. Liam said matter-of-factly, "The blackmail links us together. I had no other connection to Patty Maxwell."

He seemed determined to get a prison sentence despite his sisters' best efforts.

"Blackmail?" Reed repeated blankly.

"Oops!" said Phillipa, giving a big, toothy smile and a playful flip of her long hair.

"Does no one here understand the concept of self-preservation?" I demanded, flinging my hands in the air in annoyance. I pointed at my siblings. "In case you've forgotten, Reed is FBI. A cop. You don't blab these things to the enemy."

"He's your friend," said Phillipa.

"He's her boyfriend," corrected Liam.

"He's not!" I contested hotly.

"We aren't," said Reed, with less heat and more humor.

"Our relationship was years ago. And Reed, you will not distract me from the fact that my siblings are disclosing information we should only share with our attorney."

"What information are you talking about?" asked Hunter Garrick from the doorway. In our excitement over the bill's discovery, we all had missed the door chime.

"Nothing," Phillipa, Liam, and I said all at the same time.

Chapter Ten

"I'm going to lock the front door," I told everyone. Passing Hunter, I added, "Don't touch the money on the floor. It could kill you."

After securing the entrance from any further drop-by visitors, I went back to the office. The air was full of tension. Hunter's emotions were very prickly, and I couldn't blame him. He was trying his best to protect us three idiots, who seemed determined to yell all their secrets to whoever wandered by.

For once, Phillipa looked helpless and uncertain of what to do. Liam was back to his earbuds and phone. Reed had a finger resting on his temple and was staring at the bill on the floor with his chin down.

I guess it looked like it was up to me to bring everyone together. I announced, "Reed brought us some news. Our mother's autopsy shows she died the same way Patty did."

Hunter's bland tone masked his annoyance. "That explains the police station. It was like a disturbed anthill. No one had time to speak with me."

What is vastly irritating to those of us with average looks who don't live in a bubble of fawning notoriety is how much coddling and high maintenance these high-flyers require. Egos have to be fed, or the star sulks.

Phillipa said, "Without you, Hunter, my brother would probably be in jail right now."

I was quick to add, "I'm sure Deacon Hayes wants to throw Liam in a cell. Only you can stop that."

Reed raised his head from contemplating the death-curse money. "Deacon wants Liam for Patty's murder. He keeps talking about arresting your brother, but the DA wants better proof."

"Do you mean Jack Ingram?" asked Phillipa.

"Your ex-husband is the DA now, Pip?" That might not have been the best thing to say in front of Hunter. The prickly bits from him got spikier. *Oh, lordy.*

Seeing Hunter's beautiful nose out of joint, Phillipa hastily explained. "Jack and I married right out of high school. Big mistake. It didn't last long. He's now remarried, with twins."

I tried again. "Don't worry, Hunter. Jack isn't in your league. And Pip's second husband was only a family doctor. Not a neurosurgeon or anything. No competition there."

Phillipa gave me an aggravated glare. "Alec Conrad caught me on a rebound. We didn't want the same things out of life. He's much better off married to Missy." She added brightly, "They have a baby on the way, and I bought the sweetest little bassinet for them."

"Can we stop talking about Phillipa's exes and discuss why people want your family dead?" Reed asked.

"I agree. The death-curse was an attempt on Mother, Patty, and Liam," I said.

"Death-curse?" Hunter asked. He didn't sound shrill, exactly —a man that handsome wouldn't ever sound like a schoolgirl— but his voice was higher.

I told him about the bill, how we found it, and that it would kill anyone who touched it.

Reed supplied, "Patty had a similar bill with her at the time she died. It's in the crime scene photos I examined."

Phillipa added, "Liam found another one sandwiched into the Rosemary Thyme door frame. It was the same night Patty died."

"That is a mighty big coincidence," Hunter said. "Did the money found on Patty have the same phrase marked on it?"

"No one mentioned that to me, but I'll find out," said Reed.

Whatever Hunter saw on our faces made him sigh. "Now, explain to me why anyone would think a death-curse could be real."

Reed surprised me by being the one to answer.

"Grimsby is a... unique town. Strange, inexplicable things happen. If you want to be here, or care about someone from here," his eyes met mine, "you have to reconcile yourself to understanding that there are some truths you'll never understand."

Hunter crossed his arms. He didn't appear to be warming to the idea. Reed persisted.

"This is a place where the odd and the unexplained happen every day. The city's gardener makes roses bloom for weddings in December. Grandma Sally knows when someone's pregnant before the mother misses her first period. Logic can't explain what happens every day here."

"Like a death-curse?"

"Like a death-curse. Or someone can touch an object and tell you its history, like Liam."

Hunter snorted in disbelief. "What a load of bull. Do you take me for an idiot?"

I made a suggestion. "Give Liam something, anything, from your pocket or your wallet. Something you know about. Let him show you."

Hunter opened his wallet and, after a moment of hesitation, took out a silver-colored coin. He placed it on the desk in front of Liam with a click. "Okay, magic-boy, tell me about this."

Liam put his phone and earbuds aside and looked at what

seemed to be an old silver half-dollar. His hand hovered over it, then slowly covered it, concealing it from our view, as he closed his eyes.

"An 1869 Seated Liberty half-dollar. This coin has been with your family for a long time. Three,—no four generations. It has an intense masculine energy, so I would guess it was passed from father to son or uncle to nephew. A close bond of some type."

While Hunter's face was inscrutable, I felt behind the facade. If I doubted Liam was right (I didn't), Hunter's emotions would have confirmed that he was correct.

"Whoever had it always kept it very close to them. The first person —" Liam frowned. "Worked with his hands. A laborer. He died in his mid-forties. A violent death. There's blood on the coin."

"Stop!" Hunter barked. "Hand it back. Who told you this?"

"No one," Liam said as he tossed the coin back to its owner.

"Vic told you about it, didn't she?"

"Nope, why would she?"

Hunter tamed his breathing and said reluctantly, "You're right. I never told her about it." He slid the coin back into his wallet. "It was the first half dollar my great-great-great-grandfather earned after being a slave. He had it on him when he was murdered. It's always given to the oldest son. Except once when my great-uncle didn't have any sons, and he gave it to my father."

Reed gave Hunter a moment to get over his embarrassment, then said, "It's clear someone is trying to send a threatening message to the three people connected with Rosemary Thyme, but why?"

Before I could stop myself, I said, "Probably because of the blackmail."

Hunter said sourly, "Yes, let's discuss the blackmail, shall we? Right in front of an FBI agent. Do any of you understand the principle of self-incrimination?"

"Don't worry, Hunter. Reed already knows about it. Now, the

important question is: why Patty? How much did she know about what our mother was doing?" I asked the room.

Liam was back to playing on his phone, the app's music chiming softly in the background. Giving an air punch for scoring on his game, he answered, "She knew everything. It's all in the notebook."

"The book you told us about?" demanded Hunter, while Reed asked, "What book?"

"As I told you before, Mother had a special leather notebook she used to record payments. That was the book she wanted Phillipa to get for her. But I imagine Patty stole it after she pushed Mother down the stairs."

Everyone in the room surely wanted to strangle him. I know I did. It was Phillipa who recovered enough control to ask, "What do you mean about Patty pushing Mother?"

Liam rolled his eyes at us again.

"C'mon, you didn't think Mother fell down the stairs without some help, did you? Patty argues with Mother over money. Patty visits Mother at the house, and suddenly she needs an ambulance? One plus one still equals two, as far as I know."

Phillipa asked impatiently, "Why was she arguing with Mother about money?"

"Patty was pushing Mother to increase the amount they were collecting from the clients listed in the book. Everything is in it."

Standing beside me, Reed said in a firm voice, "Describe the notebook, Liam."

"Brown leather, three inches by five. It has a ribbon band to mark the pages. A diagonal scratch on the back of the binding, two inches long. Coffee stain on page twelve."

"Do I understand that there is a missing black book somewhere that has incriminating evidence of your mother's blackmail payments? You think Patty had it? The woman your brother may have murdered?"

Hunter's voice rose in pitch almost to what I might call a

shriek, if he ever did something that undignified. Reed put a commiserating hand on his shoulder.

"Now you feel my pain, my brother."

"That's an excellent summary, except you forgot the death-curse," I said.

"And it's not a black book, it's brown." My sister raised her purse as if she was about to hit Liam, but she arrested the impulse in mid-strike.

"Deacon wouldn't understand what was in it. It's all in code." Liam's fingers flew over the phone screen. He scored again.

"Have the police found anything like that?" I asked Reed.

"Not as far as I know. They didn't find it at the crime scene."

Tucking his phone back into his pocket and putting his sunglasses back on his face, Liam said, "Probably Patty hid the book at her house. If you take me there, I'll be able to find it by listening to it."

I said brightly, "Anyone up for a break-in?"

Chapter Eleven

Our lawyer didn't want to be part of a criminal enterprise. Imagine that.

"Stop. Don't say one word more, Vic Rowan." Hunter held up a hand. "I do not want to know about any of your plans. It's already bad enough, between blackmailing and secret notebooks. As your attorney, I strongly advise you all not to do anything more. Let the police handle the investigation."

Hunter needed to protect his reputation and license. I shouldn't have been upset that he didn't want in on our investigation, but I was.

Hunter said to Phillipa, "A word with you outside? You seem to be the most responsible of this bunch."

The two left the room, and a moment later, I heard the front door chime, confirming their departure.

"I guess you won't help either?" I accused Reed.

Reed's eyebrows rose. "As an FBI agent, I will not take part in a break-in, if that's what you mean."

Why did he have to put it so bluntly?

Liam spoke up from his chair. "The book is Mother's legal property. We would only retrieve what Patty stole."

"A book of illegal activities," Reed pointed out.

"Hunter isn't here now. How do you know Patty pushed Mother down the stairs?" I asked my brother.

"In the hospital, she told me about it. She felt Patty had betrayed her. Went on and on about it. That evening they'd argued over the money and what had happened at the country club earlier that day. It's not surprising Patty pushed her."

Getting anything from Liam took a pry bar. I asked with the patience of a kindergarten teacher, "What happened at the club?"

"They went there for lunch. Mother put Patty in her place with one of her games."

"What does that mean?" asked Reed.

Liam explained.

"Patty wore a bridge to cover her missing teeth. She was a vain woman and embarrassed about it. After eating, they went to the bathroom together, and when Patty set it on the counter to clean it, Mother swiped it. There was some function going on with a lot of bigwigs. Mother made a point of introducing Patty to each one of them while she had a gaping hole in her mouth."

"At the hospital, Mother refused Patty's visit," said Phillipa. She had returned to the office unnoticed. I wondered what Hunter had to say oh so privately?

"Yep. Mother was furious with Patty for breaking her hip. It's why she gave you the sign-in to the bank account instead of Patty."

From behind Reed's back, I gave Liam a hand signal to shut up. I didn't want anyone to know about the offshore account except us. Liam folded his arms and shut up.

Reed said, "Like Hunter, I will not take part in any criminal enterprise. However, if you find, by chance, a blackmail book, I'll help you figure out the next step. After all, it's not my case, and Deacon has told me to butt out of it."

"What next step would there be?" I asked.

"If your mother were blackmailing people, it would provide a lot of potential suspects for Patty's murder. That could help

Liam's case, but since Liam knew about the blackmail, he could be criminally liable. I'd suggest you talk with Hunter. Help him get Liam a plea deal in exchange for information."

———

We three Rowans were sitting in Phillipa's car a few blocks away from Patty Maxwell's house. While I was the one who had suggested burgling Patty's house, I couldn't stop feeling edgy. Meanwhile, Liam was dead calm.

"You're sure you can feel the book once we get inside?"

Phillipa's question irritated Liam. "You've asked me this four times."

"Sorry. I'm rather nervous."

Using her connections and charm, Phillipa had discovered that the Grimsby PD was not keeping a watch on Patty Maxwell's house—they were only patrolling the neighborhood. So the plan was for Liam and I to case the joint while Phillipa, the getaway driver, circled the car and returned to the rendezvous spot.

Liam handed me a black knit hat. Only he would have balaclavas in the summer.

"Turn off your cell phone," he reminded me.

My sister whispered to us, "Be careful," as we slipped out of the back seat, gently closing our doors. I gave her a thumbs-up before we trotted off to commit our first burglary.

Patty lived in an older part of Grimsby that was close to the railroad tracks. Liam had touched the tracks and told us when a freight train would arrive. Right on schedule, I heard an engine in the distance. The noise would give us some additional cover.

Patty's neighborhood had developed from the original shanty part of Grimsby. The houses were simple one-story squares or rectangles with wood siding. Old, graveled alleys ran behind the houses. We were scurrying down one of these, which would give us backstreet access to Patty's house.

I tripped over a garbage can, and the racket set a dog barking. I grimaced. Stealthy, super-spy burglar I was not.

Back porch lights came on, but they weren't strong enough to penetrate the shadows of the alley. A few voices yelled for the dog to shut up, but no one came outside.

When we were children, we three kids had developed a silent language, mostly to help us evade our parents. Things quieted again, and I gave the old all-clear sign. Liam asked if we should abort our plan. I shook my head.

As we got closer, I heard something nosing around the back fence we were passing. Liam pulled something out of his pocket and tossed it over the fence. The snuffling turned into a happy yelp of discovery.

"Jerky," Liam whispered. I gave him a thumbs-up. My brother was pretty good at this. I'd have to keep that in mind if I ever needed a partner for another criminal enterprise.

Considering that she was a blackmailer, I don't know where Patty spent her money. It certainly wasn't on her property. The back fence was a wooden one, sagging, drunk and ready to fall. We stepped over it.

Packed with overgrown bushes, weeds, and an old car that sat on cinderblocks, the backyard had to be navigated. I started worrying about getting tetanus. However, the junk provided plenty of cover, and we got to the back of the house without being observed.

Burglar bars covered the windows. Peering through the dirty glass, I saw nails locking down the sash. Patty sure didn't like fresh air.

Liam tried the screen door. The screek sounded loud, but none of her neighbors alerted. The house on the left remained dark; mentally, I couldn't sense anyone there.

The other house was playing music so loudly that I doubted they could hear their own thoughts, let alone a squeaky door. The occupants gave off a boozy-weed cloud of happiness. I didn't think they would call the police.

Liam pulled out some tools from the bag around his waist. In a few minutes, he had the door open and motioned for me to follow.

Even in the dark, I could see that Patty's place was a hoarder's paradise. There was an overwhelming smell of animal feces and urine that made it hard to breathe. Thank goodness for the mask. Trying not to breathe through my mouth, I whispered, "How did you get the door open?"

"I studied some online videos."

Liam was quickly gaining skills for another line of work.

"How can we find anything in this mess?" But Liam wasn't listening. He'd frozen in a pose with all the alert attentiveness of a bird-dog. In a few minutes, he signaled for me to follow.

We made our way down the narrow walkway, cut through the towering piles of books, magazines, and old clothes on either side. It was pretty obvious why the Grimsby police hadn't found the blackmail book at Patty's house.

Eventually we found ourselves in a room at the front of the house. It was probably a living room, but there were too many boxes and junk to know for sure.

My foot crunched on something. I yelped, retreating backward in surprise, and my brother gave a low, cautionary hiss. In the dim streetlight streaking through the dirty windows, I discovered I'd stepped on a dead, dried rat. Okay, I was ready to abort this mission. Liam could rot in jail.

A flashlight beam flashed across the window. I ducked.

Outside, at the front door, I heard two familiar voices: Reed Easton and Deacon Hayes, police chief of the Grimsby PD.

"Why are you here, Reed?" demanded Deacon Hayes in a voice that did not sound friendly. I scoped out the police chief's emotions: aggravation-hostility with a slight, smokey tang of secrecy. Oh, so Hayes didn't want anyone to know he was entering the house of the murder victim, Patty Maxwell. I wished I could pass that information along to Reed.

"In the neighborhood," said the FBI agent who wasn't helping us with our burglary.

Reed's appearance stalled Hayes from opening the door. We should escape while we can. I tapped my brother's shoulder, but he ignored me. Instead, bent over double, my brother scurried off down a hallway.

I squatted there, helpless, wavering. Go after Liam, or sit still?

I waited. I wasn't familiar with the place and in the dark, would probably knock something over and start an avalanche.

Instead, I stretched my talent as far as it could go to the people next door. In their inebriated state, it was easy to nudge their emotions in the direction I wanted. I pushed my connection deeper, and my mind wobbled under the dizzying effects of too much alcohol.

"This neighborhood? Pretty far from your dad's place," commented the police chief. He was suspicious and hostile. He and Reed were clearly not friends, which was good news for us. I think.

"I wanted to see Patty's house and didn't get a chance earlier this week."

"At three in the morning?" Deacon was certainly distrustful.

"Couldn't sleep." Reed lied with ease. I would need to remember that.

"I hear you're back to being friendly with the Rowan girl. The one who looks like a young Rachel."

Drunk off the fumes from the neighbors, I almost stood to shout a stream of scorching words at Deacon, but I stopped myself mid-movement. Maintaining contact with the mind's next door made me feel dizzy. I hugged my knees and closed my eyes to concentrate.

I heard Reed's voice, even and strong.

"I only stopped by as a courtesy call to see if I could discover something to help the Grimsby PD. But it seems you don't need my expertise."

Deacon gave a disgusting half cough and a loud sniff of wet snot to clear his throat. "I'd steer clear of that family. They're poisonous. Your old man always insisted that Rachel killed Victor Rowan, and the kids helped."

Reed's answer was the warning rattle before a bite.

"My mother's illness distracted him. He wasn't thinking clearly at the time. You lost your wife last year, so you know what I mean. When you're grieving you don't think straight for a while."

Aw, Reed, thanks for the vote of confidence. However, there were often facts hidden within rumors. Rowan hands weren't completely clean.

"You forget I worked with your dad. He was a great man and a good chief, Reed."

The deep frost Reed's words provoked in Deacon almost made my teeth chatter.

"My wife isn't any of your business. I'd rather talk about you and Victoria Rowan. You dated her back in the day. Your dad even feared you'd marry her, and now, you both turn up in Grimsby when Rachel dies? Seems odd, doesn't it?"

"I'm on a quest to find the truth. The entire truth." Reed's voice was silky, the warning rattle gone.

"I'm warning you, don't barge into my interrogation room again."

The doorknob jangled again as it twisted in Deacon's hand. He could enter the house at any minute. *Ignore their talk, Vic, and concentrate.* Desperate, I pushed my talent as hard as I could.

A door slammed, and a slurred voice yelled, "Who's that on Patty's porch sneakin' about? I've already called the police—"

Deacon yelled back, "I am the police! The police chief."

"Likely story. Where's your squad car, then?"

Liam touched my arm. Surprised, I jumped up, only to make eye contact with Reed's startled face through the grimy window glass. Turned away to face the neighbor, Deacon didn't see me. I hurriedly ducked back down.

At my side, Liam signed success, and I nodded. We both started retreating, retracing our steps, while Deacon kept trying to convince the neighbor of who he was.

Out the back door, we ran through the yard. Just as I'd feared, I hit something, stubbing my toe. I staggered, and Liam reached for my arm and I felt the stone-like, stolid emotional strength of my brother. Both steadied me.

I was about to run down the alley, but he cautioned me in a whisper. "Walk. Running draws too much attention."

My brother and I would need to discuss his competence in conducting criminal enterprises. He could give me some tips.

Chapter Twelve

Back home, I slept like the dead. In the afternoon, I staggered downstairs like a zombie to see what there was to eat. The kitchen cupboards were mostly bare; I still hadn't gone grocery shopping, and Phillipa had stopped providing me takeout meals.

I did score a half-eaten box of ice-cream in the back of the freezer, though. I was eating a bowl of it when Phillipa came through the front door, dressed for work, the strap of a laptop bag over her shoulder. She dropped the bag in a chair.

"I've already sold a house, and you haven't gotten out of your penguin pajamas yet."

I licked the back of my spoon. "Jealous?"

"A bit. Is there any of that left?"

By that time she returned with a bowl, I had my ice-cream mashed into a thick, creamy soup. Seeing it, my sister asked, "You still do that from when we were kids?"

"It's good! Try it."

"Not without maple syrup." She came back with the bottle and mashed her ice-cream. Avoiding my gaze, Pip said, "Hunter made some appointments for Liam. To meet a few experts and get tested."

"That's a waste of time. Liam is what he is."

"The tests aren't to change him, Vic. The purpose is to help build a defense if Deacon charges our brother." Phillipa was using her superior, big-sister voice.

Irritated, I said, "Was that all discussed when you gave Hunter a sweet goodbye kiss at the station yesterday?"

"Yes, it was yesterday," Phillipa said stiffly.

"Has anyone asked Liam his opinion? Does he want to do this? Or are you running rough-shod over him, ordering him to do it?"

"I asked him about it when I picked him up from his apartment, and he said he was okay with it."

That wasn't the same as being willing. I snapped. "He's a grown man, Phillipa. Did you ask him how he felt about being a monkey at Hunter's zoo? Liam isn't Lennie Small from Of Mice and Men. He's not an idiot needing a babysitter to tell him how to live his life."

She drew back physically, her hands falling off the table to hide in her lap. "It's for his own good."

"Do you know how much that sounds like Mother?"

She blanched as if I had slapped her. Phillipa narrowed her eyes and became as chilly as her ice-cream.

"Don't you dare! You don't have any idea what Liam's life was like after you left Grimsby. He acted out in high school for fighting. Picked up for shoplifting. He barely graduated, and then only because I kept visiting the school, working my magic. Where were you? Living a perfect life, far away from us!"

"I'm sorry—"

"No one would hire him because of his reputation. I think that's why he started doing those jobs for Mother. To make money to buy groceries and pay his rent. He deserves all the help and support we can give him."

This was why I avoided human interaction. I always screwed it up. How had we gotten into this argument? I poured maple syrup onto my ice-cream. I needed more sugar.

"It's always about Liam with you, Vic. What about me?" I opened my mouth to answer, but Phillipa kept going, pounding away at me. "Have you ever thought that maybe I'd like to be part of the secret club you two have? Do you think I enjoy being shut out all the time?"

"We took you on our heist last night!" I protested.

She pointed her spoon at me.

"I was in the car! And now you've hidden the book and won't let me see it."

"Not yet. But soon, I promise. It's just not safe with Deacon Hayes sniffing around. I've also safely tucked that money bill away, and I didn't hear you protest about that!"

Phillipa wasn't listening to me.

"You're trying to hurt me because you think I'm on Mother's side, aren't you? But I'm not. I did the decent thing and cared for her while she was sick. If I didn't, who would have? Not Liam. Not you. That's for sure."

My sister stood up, picking up her portfolio bag. She said in a dry, emotionless voice, "You need to get dressed. We have an appointment in an hour to meet Mother's lawyer and hear her will."

"I thought you were the executor?"

"That was a Power-of-Attorney so I could pay the day-to-day bills and talk with her doctor. I'll pick up Liam and return for you. Do be ready, Vic. I want to get this done. I'm sure you want that too. After all, you have your life back in the city to get back to, don't you?"

In the silent ride over to the offices of Massey and Zimmerman, I imagined several scenarios. In the end, none of them were what I expected a will reading to be.

First, the attorney was not a character out of Dickens, with a round, beach-ball body and mutton-chop whiskers, dressed in tailcoats. Instead, we introduced ourselves to Rebecca Massey, a middle-aged woman with wheat-colored hair cut in a fashionable bob and wearing smooth makeup. She wore a modern, tailored teal pantsuit.

Musty old bookshelves stacked with thick tomes did not fill her office. No, it was in a Scandinavian minimalist style, with glass and steel furniture. There wasn't a book in sight.

Liam took the couch. He laid down, propping his head on the armrest, and with closed eyes, started listening to an audiobook on his phone. Since he was a beneficiary, his presence was required. But mentally? Mother couldn't force his attendance.

Phillipa and I sat together, facing Ms. Massey. The glass tabletop had a lot of surface area, so you could look right down and see her crossed legs and expensive stiletto shoes. The only thing on the desk other than a phone was a thick folder with the name *Rachel Rowan* on the front of it.

Her voice was smooth and cultured. Everything was under control, professional, non-curious, and bland as unbuttered toast. A bit more high-brow than what I would have expected from a Grimsby girl.

"Your mother changed her will after she broke her hip. I've seen other clients do the same. When death comes closer, it gives them a different perspective."

Rather a poetic image there, for a lawyer. While Massey didn't give any further details about the earlier version of our mother's will, I guessed Patty Maxwell's name wouldn't be on the legacy list.

My mother's lawyer continued. "Although I've discussed with Ms. Phillipa Rowan the broad strokes of your mother's wishes, there are a few things I would like to cover in the presence of all of her children."

She looked pointedly at our brother. Liam held up a hand as if he was in a classroom, acknowledging attendance but otherwise made no move to respond.

"It's fine," I told Massey. "Go ahead. Liam is paying attention. I promise."

"Bequeathed to Phillipa Rowan is your mother's liquid assets, such as her business and personal bank accounts, as well as her investment portfolio. I have a list of those cash assets here for you all to review, if you wish?"

None of us moved to take the paper. I gave a sideways look at my sister, but she was staring straight ahead. I was still being punished with silence. I reached with two fingers and slid the sheets of paper to me. A quick scan showed no mention of the off-shore account.

"The shop, Rosemary Thyme, and its contents become the property of Liam Rowan, her only son. She did not own the building. If Mr. Rowan wishes to continue the business at that location, he needs to contact the owner to negotiate the lease."

Great, Mother had dumped her criminal dealings on Liam and increased his motive for killing her or Patty. Especially if he knew of changes in the will. *Well done, Mother. Slow clap for you.*

"The house on Maple Street and its contents are for Victoria Rowan, her middle daughter."

I blinked. Really? I had fully expected to be disowned. Well, the old place had plenty of traps in it if she wanted to hurt me. Such as the closed door to Victor's blood-soaked room.

"The next step is that the will goes to probate. This means it will take time before the court releases assets. It's a legal formality. If no one contests it, the estate takes a year to be processed."

Thinking the business finished, I rose to my feet. Liam unfolded himself from the couch, and even Phillipa picked up her designer bag. But the lawyer pulled something else out of her folder, and we all froze. Massey laid out three shiny disks across her desk as though she were revealing the cards of a winning hand.

"Your mother left a personal message for each of you."

There went the trap door. Clang. Down into the crocodile pit we fell. In the distance, I heard the wail of a siren.

Liam walked over and picked up the disk with his name on it. Snapping open the case, he laid the sparkling circle flat on Mother's folder. He pulled a set of keys out of his pocket, then calmly gouged an X deeply across the face, careful not to harm Massey's table. Picking it up, he snapped it into two pieces, tossing them back on her desk before leaving.

"I guess Mr. Rowan doesn't want to hear his mother's last words," said the attorney to his sisters.

"Oh, I'm sure he's not missing anything." I picked up mine and handed the other to Phillipa. My sister said, "Thanks, Ms. Massey. I'm sure our mother wasn't an easy client."

"No, she wasn't. But I always found her interesting."

Curious, I asked, "How did you meet her?"

"I think it was at the opening of the library a couple of years ago. Your mother was sitting on the committee and the mayor introduced us. I found her in my office the next day, and she immediately became a client."

Massey uncrossed her long legs and rose. Her slim hand, with manicured nails, shook ours.

"Rachel Rowan was an astonishing woman. She seems to have known everyone in town—their birthdays, their children's names, and even the wine they preferred. It is sad to lose such a remarkable asset to our little community."

She either didn't know my mother or was being sarcastic. However, Massey's face had the solemnity of a funeral director's, and the only thing I received from her was the warmth of mild curiosity. "I hear you are at the Maple residence, Ms. Rowan?"

"Yes. Temporarily. I live in the city."

Her smile became solemn.

"Not to be intrusive, but I want to point out that your brother could lose his inheritance if they charge him with anything relating to the death of Rachel Rowan. Murder doesn't pay."

"He's innocent, so they won't," I said, narrowing my eyes.

"That's good to hear. Anything suspicious about your mother's death could delay settling the estate."

Like I cared about our mother's money or house! I was about to say something, but Phillipa spoke up first. "Liam is innocent of any gossip you may have heard around Grimsby."

Tucking the folder under her arm, Ms. Massey escorted us out down the hall to the front reception area.

"I'm glad to hear it. Massey and Zimmerman is an old firm, founded by my great-grandfather. We are old-fashioned here and are sometimes stuffy about our reputation."

She gave us another wide, white smile that had nothing behind it. I left before I punched her in the mouth.

Outside, I could breathe again.

"Are you going to watch it?" It was the first time since our argument that Phillipa had spoken to me.

"Maybe. I don't know yet. If I do, I'll need to be drunk."

Phillipa was uncertain. "It could have important information in it. Things we need to know."

"More than likely, it's only her last attempt to torture us from beyond the grave. If we were going to give her a grave. I'm thinking the city dump would make a good repository."

In the parking lot, Liam was leaning against Phillipa's car. I wondered what the vehicle was telling him.

"Aren't you curious?" My sister would not let this be.

For the first time, I realized the extent of the gap between how I dealt with my mother versus how my siblings did. My life was busy, and I had rarely thought about her before arriving in Grimsby almost three weeks ago. Liam breaking the DVD showed me he was moving onward; I would need to be there to help my sister do the same.

"Curiosity killed the cat. It's what Mother is banking on—that we won't let it go, won't release ourselves from her. She plans on getting the last word."

"I know you're right," said Phillipa as she pushed the button to unlock her car, "but what if there's something in them we need to know? Like who killed her?"

That was the problem with Phillipa—her relentless need to be responsible. Her survival skills weren't that great. She'd taken in Liam during his high-school years and looked after our mother. Even in her divorces, my sister was never ruthless enough. She had left both husbands giving the houses and bank accounts.

Pip needed to learn how to be greedy. I could teach her those life skills.

We headed back to the house in her car, but Phillipa pulled over to let a fire truck with its siren on pass by. "Something exciting is happening downtown."

I saw a black, roiling cloud in the sky coming from Grimsby's historic shopping district.

"I don't like this—" I said.

Liam shot over the front seat to tell us, "Rosemary Thyme is on fire."

Chapter Thirteen

Phillipa slowed and turned into a parking lot, but before she could stop the car, Liam flew out of the backseat. He sprinted towards Rosemary Thyme.

After we'd parked and locked the car, Phillipa and I followed him. When we got closer to the fire, we had to push ourselves through the crowd.

In the press, it was hard to avoid touching people; each person's emotions battered at my protective wall. A steady stream of smugness, dismay, fright, and uncertainty slapped me. None of the people I touched felt sorry.

Eventually, we found Liam. He was at the curb directly opposite Rosemary Thyme. Beside him was Nell from the bakery. As we came up, I heard him say, "Are you sure?"

"No, I'm fine. A customer smelled the smoke, and we all got out in a hurry."

Looking across the street, I realized that Nelly's Bakery was next door to Rosemary Thyme.

"Did it start at the bakery?" I asked. The nice baker, who was feeling like a deflated soufflé, told me, "No. It started in your mother's shop. A customer said she smelled smoke, and when we went outside, you could see the flames coming through the roof. We called the fire department, but someone had already called it in, and they were on their way."

I got a taste of worry from Nell – a slight bitterness on the edge of her sweetness. Well, no wonder, since her business was going to be extra crispy, deep-fat fried by the end of the day.

Liam asked her again, "But you're okay?" She nodded, her eyelashes growing wet from unshed tears.

Curious, I reached out to Liam. Hm. He wasn't as disinterested in the friendly Nell as he had pretended to be. I made a mental note to talk with my little brother and find out more about her.

From behind us, Deacon Hayes said, "Rowans destroying evidence of their crimes. What a surprise."

Before I could help myself, I snapped, "Whoever did it destroyed my brother's inheritance. We're all watching three hundred thousand dollars going up in smoke."

"Four hundred fifty thousand, three hundred twenty-two dollars and forty-eight cents, if you go by current auction value," corrected my brother. I knew Liam could not care less about the store going up in flames.

"Where's your high-dollar lawyer?" sneered Deacon Hayes, changing tactics. "I thought he'd be here, holding your hands while you burned the town down."

"He's busy looking for the actual killer," I shot back. At my words, Hayes' emotional landscape shifted, but it was hard to grasp the subtleties. Anger washed away less intense emotions, and Hayes was furious right now.

"Watch yourself, Victoria Rowan. Your father's murder might be a cold case, but Patty Maxwell and Rachel's are both active ones."

I hadn't forgotten Deacon's remark that I looked like my mother. He was going to pay for that. "You think you're smarter than your old boss? You certainly have a bigger gut."

My sister looked away from me, grimacing as if she had bitten on a sour lemon. Deacon's face flushed red, and he pushed by me to talk with the fire chief, who was standing beside one of his trucks.

"I don't have your talent at being nice," I told her. "Besides, it got rid of him, didn't it?" Turning to Liam, I asked, "What do you think about this? An accident?"

"No. I touched the ash. This was deliberate."

Why didn't that surprise me?

I hadn't been aware of how much emotion I had been drawing from the crowd. Now I was going to pay the price. Suddenly, I felt faint; the pavement was moving up and down under my feet.

Staggering, I abruptly sat down on the curb of the sidewalk. When you were an empath, being around people could give you a heady rush. The problem was, it never lasted. There was always a downside to the hill. And I was crashing.

It took me a few minutes to figure out that Phillipa was asking me a question. "Is that ice-cream all you ate today?"

I nodded, but that put my head back to spinning. I put my hands on my cheeks to stop the carnival ride.

Phillipa took charge. "Liam and Nell, stay here with Vic. Don't let anyone bother her. I'll be right back."

I closed my eyes, and Liam put a hand on my shoulder. That made things settle. At least I hadn't hidden the tainted money and the blackmail book in Mother's shop.

Phillipa shoved a wrapped sandwich into my hands, and the smell of a deli sub started me drooling. I ripped open the paper and took a big bite, the juices from the salad dressing sliding down my chin.

"Honestly, Vic, you just got out of the hospital. Take care of yourself," scolded Phillipa, as she tucked a napkin into the collar of my T-shirt. I garbled a "Sorry" as I crammed a second bite into my mouth. My sister cracked open a can of cold soda and put it beside where I sat.

With some food in me, I started noticing my surroundings again. I could hear people asking Phillipa if she knew what had started the fire. Was she safe? They told Nell how sorry they were about her bakery cafe. No one asked about Liam or me.

The crowd trickled away. Water puddles were all over the street as the firefighters started rolling up their hoses. Rosemary Thyme was a steaming scarecrow of a building with no roof. Next door, the bakery was burnt toast; the windows shattered; the roof only charred timbers framing the sky.

Over my head, the fire chief was now talking with Liam, asking for the name of the building's owner. Nell knew as it was the same landlord for her. He told them how to report the loss to their insurance companies and not to go inside the buildings until given permission.

The sky was back in its place, the ground firm under my sneakers. I wondered where Reed was. Surely he would have heard about this on his father's police scanner? I thought about calling him until I realized I didn't have his phone number.

Balling up the paper wrapping, I climbed to my feet. Streaks of soot from the blown ashes marked my clothes. I reeked of smoke, and my sneakers were wet.

"Let's go home," I told my siblings.

We started walking back to the car in pairs—Phillipa beside me, Liam with Nell behind us.

"You okay now?"

I had eaten so fast that I gave a rude burp. "Sorry. Yes, I'm fine now. Thanks for the food. It helped me a lot."

"You need to take care of yourself, Vic," she clucked, like a mother hen.

"Funny—earlier today I thought it was you who didn't take care of herself."

She gave me a rough sideways hug, letting me know she was sorry for fighting.

"I phoned Hunter when you were eating," she told me. "He

wants Liam in the city tomorrow for his appointments. I think he should go. Get away from here for a while. What about you?"

"Earlier I was in protection mode, not thinking clearly. If it helps with his defense, of course he should go."

"I've got clients to meet, so I was wondering if you could take him to town. Are you well enough to do that?"

"I'll be fine. Back there," I shrugged, "was because of too much emotion. Getting home for a few days to peace and quiet would help me."

"I told Hunter we thought the fire was arson." Phillipa wasn't precisely whispering, but neither was she speaking so loudly that Liam and Nell could hear us. It didn't matter. Liam was busy asking Nell questions about the bakery and what she would need to re-open it. The plot with those two was thickening. I'd have to investigate. Another reason to be alone for a while with Liam.

I replied, "I'm sure Hunter had a lot to say about that."

"He's worried about how this is escalating. First a thrown rock, and now this."

That made two of us. Two murders, a broken window, and a fire? This was getting nasty.

"Hunter has a hotel room for Liam so he can walk to the testing center. It will take around three to five days. Will that be okay with you? Or would you want him to stay with you?"

Neither of my siblings had ever stayed at my city apartment. I didn't want to set that precedent. "That's fine by me. Liam's a big boy, as you both like to remind me, and I need some downtime."

"That's what I thought. I told Hunter to book it, and we would cover the cost. Liam needs to get away from this for a while."

Forget Liam. *I* needed to get away from here for a while.

"Hunter doesn't know about Mother's special bank account, does he?"

"No. Neither does Liam. Only you and I—I want to keep it that way. We may need every cent if Liam goes on trial for murder.

I don't think you and I could pay for Hunter Garrick out of our own checking accounts."

I nodded, but didn't mention that if things got worse, we might have to pay for our own defense.

"Phillipa, you need to be careful, too. One Rowan is all Rowans to Grimsby."

"No one would harm me." She laughed in disbelief.

"Hm. Just don't take any chances while we're gone."

"I'm not a risk-taker like you, Vic."

"It would be easy to get you alone because you're a realtor."

"I promise, Vic, I'll be careful."

Phillipa dropped Nell off at her mother's salon, Liam at his garage apartment, and took me over to the house. We sat in the car, staring at its facade. Too many memories. Maybe we were sharing the same thoughts, for my sister said, "You could stay at my place."

I got out and leaned through the open passenger-side window to say, "What about you and Hunter? Is that going to get serious?"

"I like him. Is that okay with you?"

I searched through all my filing cabinets, sorting the index cards that labeled my feelings.

"Yeah, I don't mind," I said slowly. "I like him, but not in that way. He's not my type."

"You go more for law enforcement than the justice department, huh?"

I felt my face go hot. Phillipa laughed. She waved as she pulled away.

Chapter Fourteen

Mother's house didn't have Internet, so I used my cell as a hotspot. I emailed my boss suggesting a time we could do a conference call. The first thing to do was get the Madonna back to the university.

I also sent another email to a friend I knew at an auction house. Betz Zachary was an expert on European antique furniture. She owed me a favor after I'd spotted a forgery for them and saved her a lot of embarrassment.

Upstairs, I repacked my clothes bag. While I would be back, I wasn't leaving anything of mine in this place. I had no plans for any permanency here.

I didn't sleep well that night. The smoky fire scent had gotten into my hair; no matter how much I shampooed it, I couldn't get it out entirely. Lying there, replaying old memories, I kept imagining voices. I went downstairs to check the alarm several times.

It was my imagination. I thought it was. I hoped it was.

The next morning Liam and Phillipa found me sitting on the porch, my bags at my feet, ready to leave.

On the train, Liam rebuffed my attempt to discuss anything about the fire or Nell. I suggested I could siphon off some of his anxiety. He refused. "No. I can manage it."

I didn't know what he was thinking behind the sunglasses, since I was trying to be a politically correct empath and not peek. Perhaps sensing my restraint, Liam's mouth quirked under his beard.

"Anyway, you already took a load off when we were at the police station. I forgot how you could do that."

I said tentatively, "It's the least I could do. I would have done it sooner, but you didn't ask, and I didn't want to offer."

When we were kids, I had never asked. And therein lay one of the problems between us.

He said slowly, groping for the words as he looked out the window, "When Mother was still alive, I wanted that simmering anger and the self-loathing. But now I can let it go. Be free of her."

"If you don't want to answer, that's fine, but I was wondering why her keys upset you so much?"

"It reeked of all her cunning and meanness. It was as if she had walked back into the room."

That would be enough to give any Rowan child a nightmare.

Before I could ask any more, he pulled out a folded piece of paper from his jeans pocket and handed it to me.

"I want you to discuss this with Phillipa."

"What is it?" I asked, unfolding it to see a spreadsheet.

"It was our fault Nell's bakery got damaged. That's her livelihood. Her insurance has a high deductible and who knows when it will pay. I've made a list and a budget of all the things she might need. You can make Phillipa help her."

"I'm sure Pip would help her! Why didn't you ask her directly?"

"Phillipa's helped me a lot. I don't feel comfortable asking her again. From you, it would seem more business-like. You're good at that kinda stuff."

Liam's emotional output had grown too complicated for me to sort out. I reassured him. "Sure, I'll talk to her about it."

"It can't look like charity. Nell won't take money like that."

"I'll make sure it gets done."

As the train passed familiar landmarks, putting us closer to the city, I felt a strange anxiety. I first thought it was an emotional overflow from Liam, but it was my own baggage. For some bizarre reason, I worried that my carefully built life wouldn't be waiting for me when I arrived. That something had changed, and my life wouldn't be my own ever again.

I deliberately relaxed my shoulders and exhaled. Of course it would, I reassured myself. Mother's death had changed nothing. Grimsby would not get to me. I still had my work and always would have my city life.

Hunter Garrick met us at the station with a cab, ready to take us to Liam's hotel. He gave Liam a packet that included a schedule for my brother's appointments.

"Plenty of free time if you want to sightsee."

Scanning Hunter's emotional aura, I could tell that the Rosemary Thyme arson had put him on alert. He felt spiky, like a medieval mace. Hunter introduced Liam to the security guard at the hotel, slipping the man a hefty tip before we moved into the elevator.

We entered the suite, and my eyes widened. Hunter explained it was a VIP suite with a unique feature: a call button would receive a priority response. His firm kept it on retainer for their high-profile clients.

Liam turned on the massive television and started flipping through the stations. He barely gave us a goodbye when we left.

. . .

Hunter and I discussed schedules on the ride over to my place. I agreed to meet up late tomorrow evening for dinner. When he asked after Phillipa, the spikiness softened. He even asked me what perfume she liked.

"Ask Liam. He notices those types of details."

"I haven't hurt your feelings, have I?"

"Nope. But don't come crying to me if Phillipa hurts you," I warned him. He gave a light-hearted laugh, and I returned it with a silent smile. He might think he was the king of players, but this was a cage match. I wouldn't be laying any bets on him surviving.

I gave an inward sigh of relief as the car drew into the parking lot to my home. The brick warehouse had cracked pavement full of weeds, and even a graffiti-ed dumpster. It appeared to be an industrial factory without gentrification.

All of it was camouflage. My neighborhood wasn't that bad, but the seediness discouraged anyone from giving it a second look. I had learned at my mother's knee not to draw attention to myself.

During our brief relationship, I had never allowed Hunter inside. Today was no different. I waved him goodbye, punched in the security code, and entered my haven.

Inside, I reset the lock and the code. From there, I went up the narrow staircase sandwiched between walls to the top floor. You could see one camera, but not the other.

At the landing in front of my apartment, I entered a different door code. Entering, I locked the door behind me and threw my overnight bag onto the couch, shouting to no one, "I'm home!"

I enjoyed the echo of my voice through the loft. What a relief!

I kicked off my shoes, and in the kitchen, started coffee. From there to the bedroom, I stripped. After my shower, I dressed in my painting clothes. I wanted to work. I needed to work.

Grabbing a mug filled with coffee, I padded down the hall to my workroom. This locked area had a different security code. It had two hidden cameras. You couldn't be too careful when you handled priceless art.

I opened the door and entered my workroom, sniffing deeply. I was back. And best of all? No emotional junk from people.

Restoration work took extensive and painstaking concentration. When I got engrossed in it, I lost track of everything, especially time. It was only when I heard the buzzer at the intercom go off that I looked up.

Liam and Hunter were probably here for that dinner date. I laid my brushes down and went to the video-com and punched the button. Instead of my brother and his lawyer, I saw Reed Easton outside.

Chapter Fifteen

I froze for a moment before pushing the button for audio-only. "I gave at the office. Goodbye."

"Stop, Vic! I came to talk."

No, you came to mess up my life again. I felt desperate as my alone-time slipped away from me. I'd have to deal with people and feelings again.

Reed spoke quickly. "I want to tell you why I was in Grimsby. The real reason."

Hm. He had me. I was curious. I flipped the audio on again. "First tell me the fake one."

"I wasn't there to visit my dad. That was the cover story."

It was like I'd thought. Reed's appearance when I suddenly returned to Grimsby after fifteen years had been no accident. "Now tell me the real reason."

"Not out here. It's—complicated. And involves confidential information."

Oh, wasn't everything? I was about to turn off the door-com when he added, "It involves your family. Your mother. And brother."

He probably mentioned Liam because he knew I didn't give a hoot about my mother. "Wait there. I'll come down."

I knew my feelings intimately. As an empath, you had to. Otherwise, you didn't survive or stay sane. When Reed had come back into my life, old and new feelings became tangled. My childish resentment for Reed not leaving Grimsby with me so long ago vanished when I realized he had stayed because of his sick mother.

The familiarity of our high-school friendship had made it easy to slip back into confidences, and because of that, Reed now knew of my mother's blackmail scheme—something that could cause problems for all of us.

Even worse, I was far more attracted to grown-Reed than I had been to young-Reed.... which was odd, as I didn't think I knew who grown-Reed was. But damn, he was tasty as the first hot funnel-cake at the funfair.

I checked the wide-angle cameras to confirm the street and the blind corner were clear of anyone but Reed. As I opened the door, Reed slipped inside like an eel. The latch behind him closed, and out of habit, I pushed the button to activate the lock and alarm system.

"Why all the secrecy?" I demanded. He was standing so close I could feel his body heat.

"I heard about the fire, but I wasn't in Grimsby yesterday. Are you okay? "

"I'm fine," I said, growing irritated. "The fire only destroyed a bunch of very expensive antiques and a bakery. You didn't ask, but Liam and Phillipa are okay too. So is Nell. Now, tell me your oh-so-confidential secret."

Reed looked up the stairs to the door at the top landing. "Can we go up? I want to discuss this with you properly."

Before I could agree, he mounted the stairs. I followed reluctantly, all my mixed emotions thrashing around inside me. How had he gotten my address? Hunter? Phillipa? Whoever had shared it would get a punch in the nose next time we met.

Reed's breath was practically on my neck. I instinctively covered the numbers with my hand as I entered the code. Inside, he gazed curiously around my private sanctum. I crossed my arms. "Who told you where I lived? Phillipa?"

He ignored that. "The FBI's been tracking a contract killer for over five years. I think that's who killed Patty and Rachel."

I gave a short, impatient snarl of a laugh. "In Grimsby? You have got to be kidding me." He was bonkers.

"We got a lead that led to Grimsby. The bureau sent me because my family made a perfect cover for my visit. It all had to be done quietly. We've had him cornered before and poof—he vanishes."

I frowned. If this was a charade, it was an elaborate one. Reed barely passed creative writing in high school; his mind couldn't invent elaborate fantasy stories. I was the one who wrote them and Mr. Holly never guessed.

I indicated to Reed to take a seat on the couch while I opted for a chair. "Why do you think a stranger would kill Patty or my mother?"

"First, the blackmail. That type of crime thrives only in the dark, just like the Ghost Killer does. Also, how they died. Your mother's autopsy is finished, and the bureau has a copy. That's where I was yesterday, discussing it with my people."

Reed always had a reason why he couldn't be there for me.

"The original death certificate for Rachel stated she died from heart failure. However, the broken hyoid bone puzzled the coroner. Now they think, because of her age, osteoporosis weakened her bones, and that it snapped when the staff was trying to resuscitate her."

I blinked, trying to take in what he was telling me.

"Sounds like a cover-up by our favorite police chief, Deacon Hayes."

Reed spread his hands in a helpless gesture.

"Deacon doesn't understand the medical lingo, and he didn't care for your mother. I think he sees it as justice served." He leaned towards me, elbows on knees. "But you know how it happened, don't you, Vic?"

I stared at him blankly, showing my best poker face. I couldn't fool him. His green eyes narrowed. "Tell me how they conceal the rabbit during the hat trick. How the magic works."

"Magic? How would I know anything like that? You don't believe the Grimsby rumor Rowans are witches, do you?"

I squirmed under Reed's steady gaze and tried again.

"I don't see how a curse-wish on a piece of money has anything to do with a contract killer the FBI wants. That's ludicrous."

Reed explained, his bright eyes locked on mine.

"Whoever the killer is, the deaths always appear natural. But they're bizarre, often unexplainable. A young man in perfect health dies of a heart attack; another woman who won't take aspirin, overdoses. Someone with no suicidal tendencies jumps off a platform when a train speeds by. An expert swimmer drowns in calm water."

"That should rule out your mystery killer. Patty's death was obviously murder. Nothing mysterious about it," I countered.

Reed wouldn't give up. "One thing is key. The deaths always benefit someone: a business partner, relative, or maybe even a competitor."

I felt my face grow hot, my guilty thoughts going to the offshore bank account. Liam or Phillipa wouldn't pay a hitman to get their inheritance, but—? Of course not!

"Patty's murder doesn't fit, I grant you," admitted Reed. "But I think Rachel's death does. One of her blackmail victims was fed up with paying out. That's the reason Rachel and Patty died. Why your brother became a target. Either the blackmailer is the Ghost Killer or the GK organized it."

Oh. That made better sense.

"Some at the Bureau don't believe that the Ghost Killer exists at all."

"But you do?"

"I do. Too many coincidences. I finally found a person who would talk to us and while I was working out a deal for him, he died." Reed's voice grew stern. "This Ghost Killer is evil. If cornered, he will kill, and I believe your brother could be in grave danger. Maybe even you and Phillipa. Help me, Vic."

My brother's usual schedule would have placed him at Rosemary Thyme when the fire had happened. The only reason he hadn't been there was that he had been meeting Ms. Massey with us at Massey and Zimmerman.

"This is all speculation on my part," I began, and Reed nodded in understanding. "I think that when Patty died, it caused my mother's death because of a physical link made through the dirty money."

"So the person who strangled Patty knew Rachel would also die?"

"Someone physically strangled Patty. Did they know it would also cause the death of my mother? I'm not sure. But the death-curse money linked one death to the other. Someone gave them both those bills."

Reed put his forefinger at his temple, his chin lowering as he thought over what I said. "Someone made the spell, knowing Patty's death would happen soon. Either by their own design or by another's. And Patty's death jumped to Rachel because of the money."

"Yes. The spell uses contagious magic—the money is a correspondence, a magical link. If I took a ring, you once wore and worked a ritual over it, I could smash it with a hammer, and the damage to the ring would happen to you. Once in contact, always in contact."

"Go on."

"I'm guessing, okay? But I think the money connects to the

blackmail scheme. The spell would be stronger if they were a blackmail payment because it gives the bills a provenance—a confirmation of where they came from—that ties my mother, brother, and Patty together in the magic."

"That supposition would prove my theory that one of Rachel's victims was the killer or hired it to be done."

I could see he was getting excited, but it wouldn't work. I shook my head. "Reed, no one in court would believe this. You won't be able to prosecute."

"Continue." His tone was iron. I sighed.

"Remember what the spell said? *Touch this bill, and join hands to find your friends?* The killer collected them, death-cursed them, and gave them back. Patty had a bill when she died; another found under my mother's pillow. Liam failed to fall into his trap, since he destroyed the money."

"Voodoo."

I rolled my eyes and stood up, shaking my hands to the sky in sudden frustration. "Argh! This is why I didn't want to have this discussion! You've jumped to the wrong conclusion, like all normals do."

"Normals?" When I had left the couch, so had he. He started following me around the room as I paced. "What do you mean by that?"

"Look, this has nothing to do with voodoo. That's a completely different discipline. I think whoever did this was using ritual magic. A skilled witch, walking the Left-Handed Path."

"What do you mean by normals?"

"You, Reed. *You.* Haven't you figured it out yet? You know Liam has special talents. You think I do. Well, yes, and so does Phillipa. As did my mother. We know things; can do things." As the words spilled out, he came closer until I stopped pacing, my back against the wall.

"I've always known you can do things, Vic. I knew that long ago."

Why was I crying? This was stupid. I hiccuped.

Reed's expression was very serious. I saw the bad news coming a moment before I heard it. "I also know the truth about your father's murder."

At that moment, the audio intercom buzzed. To avoid facing Reed, I turned to see the video screen. It was Hunter Garrick, and Liam. Hunter held up a bag to the camera.

"We have Chinese food," Liam called. "I'm hungry. Let us in so we can eat."

Like a child, I wiped my eyes with the back of my hand. Reed's hand fell on my shoulder and squeezed it gently.

"We can talk about Victor later," he said. "Should we let them in?"

"Do what you want. I've got brushes to clean."

Chapter Sixteen

Because of Reed's arrival, I had forgotten the wet brushes sitting on my workbench. I took out my cleaning supplies, some old rags, and turned up the air purifier I had in this room. It helped to clean out the fumes and keep the dust down.

I heard the men's voices as they entered my home. I'd never asked Hunter to come back here, and naturally I thought he'd call. We'd meet at some restaurant. Now, he and Reed were where they didn't belong. I was quietly furious about the situation they had placed me in.

"This is your workroom?" asked Liam. He was standing in the doorway. I gave him a silent nod. A quick scan showed he seemed okay, despite having had a day meeting strangers who probably asked a lot of silly questions.

His attention immediately fixated on the Madonna that I had left on my easel. "I'd like to hear its song."

Yes, Liam would fully appreciate the painting on my easel. I pulled out a pair of light cotton gloves. "Wear these instead of yours. Don't touch any area but the back of the panel or the edge, like this. The front is still drying."

He might have big hands, but my brother's touch was feather light, his fingertips caressing the back of the wood panel.

"The tree didn't want to be removed," he said.

I pulled off the lanyard around my neck that held my magnifying loupe. I held it up, inviting Liam to take a look. "When the NAAR examined this area—"

"What's that?"

"Scanning macro-XRF and neutron activation autoradiography."

Liam filed it away in his head. "Go on."

"Underneath the paint, here, it showed that the artist removed some of the overhanging branches."

"Yes. The tree was first, and it was bigger than the sky. It changed the mood; made everything brighter, and put a glow around the woman."

"Exactly. Now look down here. What can you tell me?" I moved my magnifying glass to a fold of the Madonna's wrap around her waist. Liam frowned, his hand hovering over where I indicated.

"The shadows on the drape have a different feel. The person who did the tree and the sky didn't paint this."

"Hm. Well, some masters let apprentices work on some of their projects."

After the Madonna, I showed Liam another painting. It was a smaller piece—not an expensive one, since it lacked provenance, but one I personally liked.

"Oh, a woman painted this. It has a feminine feel, lively and gentle."

"That's intriguing. I'll have to take a second look."

We were on the fourth or fifth painting when I looked up to see Reed standing in the doorway. His shoulder rested against the jamb, and his expression seemed to be amusement. I hadn't felt him arrive, of course.

"Let's eat," I told my brother.

As I passed Reed to leave my studio, he said, "I'd like a tour one day."

"I do not give trespassers the five-dollar tour," I snapped, irritated all over again.

In the living room, Hunter had raided my kitchen. There were plates and silverware set out with glass tumblers. He was opening a wine bottle when we three returned.

"Maybe we can eat and discuss the case?"

The apartment didn't have a proper dining area, only a breakfast bar, so we sat around my coffee table in the living room, eating out of our laps. Taking a bite, I savored the spicy heat; I liked my food real, with color for my nose and tongue.

"Lucky Star?" I guessed.

"I know what you like." Hunter gave me a suggestive waggle of his eyebrows. Rebuffing Hunter's flirting, I asked my brother, "How did things go with the testing?"

Liam shrugged. "Mostly, it was boring. A lot of tests. Pick this or that. Tell me what this picture says, stuff like that." He fiddled with his fork, looking down at his noodles as he added reluctantly, "They want you to come and visit with one of my counselors tomorrow. At eleven o'clock. I told them I'd ask."

"Sure, I'll do that. When I finish, we can grab lunch together. There's a lot of great food trucks downtown and a park nearby. We could get out a bit."

"Okay."

I turned to Hunter. "What about the case do you want to discuss?"

Hunter laughed, flashing that smile. Good thing I was immune.

"The blackmail book! Did you find it or not?"

"I thought you didn't want to be involved?"

"Oh, not in stealing it, but it wouldn't hurt to look at something I had no idea how it got into your hands, right?"

I smirked.

"What do you think, Liam?"

"I don't care."

I set aside my plate and went to my bedroom. I had collected the mail when I came in the door, along with the box I had mailed to myself. When I brought it out to open it with a kitchen knife, Reed said in disbelief, "You mailed it? What if it had become lost?"

"Then I would have filed a claim on it. I bought insurance."

"You know mail becomes lost forever all the time?"

"Look, Reed, I couldn't bring it back in my bag. What if Deacon Hayes had a warrant to search it? And I couldn't leave it at the house for the same reason."

The notebook slid into my hands. I cracked it open, and both Hunter and Reed came to look over my shoulder. The entries were in my mother's graceful script, loops and o's perfectly formed. Except for the column headings, most of it was strings of numbers.

"Bank accounts?" I suggested.

"The numbers are irregular," said Reed. He bent so close to me I could smell the shampoo he used. His finger traced a row on the journal paper. "M, W, S? Married, widowed, and single would be my guess."

"Yeah, I think so."

The next column was a two-digit number, followed by another column with dollar signs. Like a restaurant review, someone had ranked the money into low and high scores by the amount of $ marks.

"The value of what they could pay to keep the secret," I said. I wished my mother or Patty were still alive. I'd like to smack them both.

Hunter shook his head. "The numbers, I don't know what they mean."

"May I?" Reed took the journal from me. "The first string of numbers has a break in between them."

"Like a bank account. But you said they were too irregular," I reminded him.

"Not a bank account. I think this is the first and last name of the victim."

Hunter asked, "And the other numbers, between their marital status and value?"

"We'd have to break the code to know for sure, but I'm guessing it's the reason they were being blackmailed. This book holds everything anyone would want to know about Rachel's illegal business. The secrets she discovered about people."

"I told you it was in code," said Liam with a bit of smugness. I noticed my brother had plowed through his plate and what remained on mine, including the eggroll I had been saving. Hadn't they fed him over there at the testing center?

Hunter snapped his fingers. "Let Liam work his woo-doo hoo-doo on it."

"The only impressions the notebook will give would be from Mother, and maybe Patty."

"But you told me about my coin," insisted Hunter.

"Sure. The feelings of people who owned it for a long time. But I can't tell you their names or where they lived. Now, if the victims wrote the book's entries, or if I had a pen they had touched, yeah, maybe I could tell you something about them."

Forget Liam's talent; there were other ways. "If it's a code, we can crack it."

"Find where the numbers repeat, and solve for the vowels, you mean?" suggested Hunter.

Reed frowned, still staring at the numbers on the paper. "Did Rachel have a computer?"

"No, she didn't trust them," said Liam.

Reed seemed to be thinking out loud. "So a computer program didn't generate the numbers. The numbers are sorted in triplets, with a comma in between. For example, the first group here is twenty-two, forty-three, sixty-eight, and the next group, for the last name, is much longer. But the long set still has a set of three numbers, spaced with commas, before you hit a dash with another set of three numbers."

"Like a social security number? Is that what you mean?" I suggested.

"Too long. I'm thinking this is a book code."

"What's that?" I asked, still clueless.

Liam, the encyclopedia, explained. "You use a book to find a letter you want to use. In the code, you use the page, the line, and the word's position in the line."

Reed added, "You use two identical books, one used by the sender, the other by the receiver. The problem is that it's impossible to break a book code unless we know the book and edition they used."

Liam immediately supplied the answer. "*Crime and Punishment*, Penguin Classics, published 1974. It burned up in the fire, along with everything else."

Hunter picked up his cell phone and started tapping the screen. "Online book store. We'll find a copy and get the code cracked."

My phone rang, startling me. I took it out, looked at the number, and told the others, "Sorry, I have to take this." Walking back to my studio, I greeted my caller. "Hey, Betz, thanks for getting back to me so quickly."

Her voice was husky and warm. "The photos you sent were intriguing. I forwarded them to an interior designer working with a client that wants authentic showpieces to pair up with a wine collection. But I'd have to see them in person before I could make an offer."

"They're at my mother's house in Grimsby. She's recently passed, and we want to get the house cleared out to prepare it for sale."

She gave the standard reply. "Sorry to hear about your mom."

"Yeah, thanks." I forced myself to put a little sadness in my voice. Always best to play the game people expected. "I thought you'd know someone. Hey, I also have a few mid-century pieces, but I didn't think you'd handle those."

"I don't, but I've got a friend downtown who might be interested. He runs a little hipster resale shop. If you're open to a commission situation, he'd probably be more agreeable. He's on a shoestring budget."

"That would work for me. I'm in town now, so email me his name and location. I'll check out his store. Would it be possible for you to visit Grimsby? It's a little spot —"

"I know it. We used to go up to a cabin off the lake during the summers."

Thinking of the lake, I tasted bile in my mouth. I swallowed it down, like I had so many things. "Maybe in about ten days? Check out what I've got? Bring a moving van."

"Girl, you are eager! You know that's not the way to get the best price?"

"Money isn't what I want. Convenience is."

"Okay, Vic, but I'm coming first to check out the goods. We can always arrange a van later once we work out the details."

"Deal. Be ready with your checkbook."

She laughed. "It won't be *my* checkbook, girl."

After we said goodbye, I returned to the living room and found the party breaking up. Hunter suggested to Reed that he take him back to wherever he was staying. At my glare, he agreed to Hunter's plan.

Liam hung back at the door. Sensing he had something to say, I let him pull me aside. He fiddled with the cuff of his shirt, pulling it down and back up over his wrist.

"You'll come tomorrow?"

"Of course. I said I would."

As he got into Hunter's car, I realized I hadn't asked Liam why his counselors needed to see me.

Chapter Seventeen

The next day, I took a cab over to the office complex where the testing center was located. I found them occupying over half the third floor of the skyscraper. It looked like they offered a wide range of services that dealt with learning disabilities.

The wall art was all cheerful. It wasn't reflective of my mood, which, after worrying all last night, was rather dour. My palms were sweaty in anticipation. I'd attended a few individual counseling sessions for my problems when the pain got too great, but never for someone else.

I told the receptionist I was there for an appointment with Ms. Murphy.

Parents and their kids mostly filled the waiting room. Worry was the prevalent adult emotion. Some of the kids sensed that and stayed huddled close by their parents. Others were working out their feelings by smashing toys or chasing other kids around the rows of chairs.

I usually chose not to spend time around kids. Their emotions were so flashy and quicksilver, like minnows, I could barely think.

Before I could go insane, they called my name. I followed the staffer down a corridor and was invited inside a private room where Ms. Murphy greeted me. She was about to shake my hand, but I avoided that by moving pillows on her couch to wedge myself into the corner against the armrest.

Ms. Murphy closed the door, sitting down in a club chair opposite. She didn't have a clipboard or a notepad in her hands. She was probably older than me by a dozen or more years, maybe in her late forties, with a friendly-curious texture to her emotions.

I licked my dry lips. "I'm Vic Rowan. My brother, Liam, said you'd like me to come by for a visit."

It wasn't quite a question, but she responded as if it was. Her make-up powder had shed a bit on the collar of her navy-blue dress, and her lipstick was wearing off. The imperfections made her feel more real; a next-door neighbor who asked if you had any eggs you could spare.

"Liam is a fascinatingly complex individual. At turns he is very open, perhaps even blunt with his observations, but he can also be very reticent. I thought you could help us paint a better picture of your brother's history and his current situation."

"He's super smart." It was a reflex to defend his intelligence. Too many had discounted his worth over the years.

She nodded her head in agreement. "Completely. He's quick to solve the puzzles we give him—although sometimes he does it in unconventional ways."

I don't know if she expected me to ask what she meant. If she did, I'd disappoint her. Like a wary cat, I would wait to find out what she wanted from me and not give her any more. Her aura of professional concern-curiosity increased as she watched me.

"Part of what we do here is learn about our clients' early childhood experiences. Especially their connections with parents, siblings, and school. It helps us understand how the client's background might still influence them. Getting a complete picture helps us decide how to proceed in helping them."

Oh, yeah, that's why I thought I was here. Time to rip off the bandage. See if we're all still hemorrhaging underneath it. Which trauma are we going to talk about today, Ms. Murphy?

"What do you want to know about Liam?"

"He seems very close to you." Was close, Ms. Murphy, but I threw him to the wolf and ran for safety. "Which made me wonder if you remembered an incident that took place when he was very young? Liam said he almost drowned. You look very pale, Ms. Rowan. Can I get you a glass of water?"

"No. No." I waved away the dense mist of her concern floating towards me. "I'm only surprised, that's all. That was a long time ago. I didn't think Liam remembered it."

"Liam thought it was around the time he started kindergarten, so around five."

I looked at the door. There it was. I felt the desire to run and squelched it. I had a debt to pay to my brother for leaving him at the mercy of our mother.

The air conditioning on my cold, sweaty neck made me shiver. My breathing became shallow. I cleared my throat.

"My father, Victor, met my mother at the Grimsby lake. Very picturesque place. My mother's family rented a vacation cabin there one summer, and they met and fell in love. It was a summer romance that became a marriage." I suddenly wished I had that cup of water. I was eating sand. "Because of that, my mother always held a fondness for the lake. We would go on a picnic there."

"I noticed Liam did that also—call your father by his first name. Do you call your mother Rachel?"

"No." Why call a man a father when he had never acted like one? He was like us, just another victim. My pause was too long. She prodded. "Would your sister, Phillipa, go with you?"

"Pip's eleven years older than Liam. So," I squinted, thinking, "I would have been around ten—Pip, sixteen. She didn't come with us very often. She took piano lessons and was busy with her friends. High school stuff."

"So that day when it happened, it was only you and Liam with your parents at the lake?"

I swallowed dry air before starting again. "I don't remember there being anyone there, but it was the middle of the week. My parents were in a mood that day; they were always fighting back then. Liam and I wandered off, glad to be away. We explored all around the picnic tables near the lake."

She gave me an encouraging nod.

"Liam was fascinated by the color of the fallen leaves. So I guess it was fall because I remember them being yellow, red, and orange shades. He made a stack of what he thought were the prettiest ones."

At ten, I'd been impatient with a younger brother who kept lagging. Liam became distracted by the acorns and pine cones, and stuffed them into his pockets. I gave a smile that vanished as I remembered it all.

"Liam told me he was going to become a tree. That was his plan. To be a tree." I said nothing more, images flashing through my mind's eye, and I was jumping too far ahead mentally. I shook my head roughly to stop it.

"He was too slow. I left him and went back to the car to find Victor packing the car. My mother was folding the picnic blanket. It was a red and black plaid. They call it a Buffalo check."

Her "Go on" was so soft that I barely registered it. I was so wrapped up in my own emotions, I didn't feel hers anymore.

"Mother started getting impatient that Liam hadn't returned. She kept calling, but he didn't answer, and she started yelling at Victor about it. He yelled at her that she could deal with it and got into the car. The driver's seat. Only he drove that car. He loved it, you see."

"When did you find Liam?"

"We didn't. He finally showed up. And he was a mess. He had used mud to glue leaves all over himself. His hair, arms, clothes. For a moment, he looked like a tree—or a walking, four-foot bush."

The mental picture of Liam stuck all over with red and yellow leaves had been funny for about one minute. I choked back a nervous giggle, and from feeling cold, went hot. My face flushed. I felt feverish. The dam broke, and the words rushed through the breach.

"When Mother saw him, she told Liam he'd been bad. Bad for not coming when she called. Bad for messing up his clothes. She shook him and then dragged him down to the lake to get him clean."

My pause this time was quite long. I looked at the clock hanging on the wall. There was too much time left. I licked my lips again.

"You saw this?"

"I was in the back seat of the car. She put me there to wait, and I could see them through the back window. Victor had backed the car into the parking slot to unload things easier, so it faced the water."

Lost in memories, I didn't realize I told her the rest.

Mother grabbed Liam by the upper arm, her grip so fierce that she lifted him half off the ground. The more he fought, the colder her rage became. I felt it searing me, freezing me in place. At the water's edge, she waded in, oblivious to how cold the water was. Carrying my brother as he kicked and screamed.

"With Liam?"

"Yes. She had to get him clean, you see. He was dirty. She kept pushing him down into the water. Holding him under while she scrubbed the leaves and mud off."

"Victor was still in the front seat? Didn't he hear what was happening?"

I frowned, trying to remember.

"I think... I think, he turned the radio on in the car."

When I didn't continue, Ms. Murphy asked me gently, "What did you see?"

"Liam stopped fighting. Stopped struggling. Mother brought

him out and dropped him on the ground. She came to the car, got the red and black check blanket out to dry herself. I remember the sound of her throwing her muddy sneakers down on the car floor. Ruined, she said. The day and her sneakers were ruined."

I took a deep breath, forcing air into my lungs.

"She told my father she had dealt with the problem. He was to put Liam in the car."

The clock hands seemed frozen.

"Is that all that happened?"

Wasn't that enough? But to those who open the wound to look inside, it is never enough.

"Victor did as he was told. He put Liam next to me. Cold and blue, next to me. I thought Liam was dead. That he'd drowned. But when we pulled out of the park, he choked. Vomited the water up. On the blanket. On the red and black blanket."

I sighed, releasing my breath in a quiet flutter.

"That's when I knew he was okay."

"But he wasn't, was he, Vic? He was never okay again."

"No. He wasn't."

Chapter Eighteen

I left the room and walked down the hall. With each step, the distance ahead seemed to recede from me, the passage getting longer. The surrounding voices sounded like a foreign language.

Somehow I was standing in an elevator, Liam beside me. It wasn't until we passed through the office lobby and into the fresh air, and I said, "Why did you tell them that?"

Liam shrugged. "They wanted to know about my family, my upbringing. That seemed to be an important thing to tell them."

The sidewalk light changed to green, and people moved around us as we stood, immobile, facing each other.

"You didn't have to tell them that."

Liam took off his sunglasses. His eyes were very blue, shining.

"Don't you see, Vic? You needed it. Not me."

I was speechless.

My brother's hand on my arm guided me safely to the sidewalk. "How do we get to the park?"

. . .

We took the path around the duck pond, along with joggers and mothers pushing strollers. Moving gave me an excuse not to look at Liam, but after about five minutes of silence, I couldn't stand it any longer.

"What do you mean by that? That you did it for me?"

Liam was wearing a baseball cap, and even in the warmth of the last week of August, a thin, long-sleeved shirt. What I could see of his face through his shield of beard and sunglasses was inscrutable. I tried to reach across our bridge, but smacked myself against a closed door.

At my astonished expression, my brother said, "You need to stop that, Vic. Stop taking my emotions. How I'm feeling."

"I only meant to help."

"Yes, I know. But we're not kids anymore."

"I'm sorry. I don't want you to be hurting."

Liam went back to walking. The cloudless day caused the sun to sparkle on the surface of the water. I wished I had a pair of sunglasses too, and not only because of the brilliance of the sunshine.

He spoke so low I had to lean closer. "It helped. In the beginning. Not to feel anything. Not to care about all the casual cruelties. It helped me endure her, and I'll always be thankful to you for that."

Since he didn't want my comfort, I stuffed my hands into my jean pockets.

"But when you left, I had to deal with all of my emotions by myself. It overwhelmed me to feel everything again, to have the numbness gone. I didn't have any experience with knowing myself. Confused, I got into trouble. Acted out. Vandalism. Petty theft. That cop, Hayes, got to know me pretty well."

Liam lengthened his stride, making me run a few steps to get beside him again.

"After Victor's death, people finally paid attention to what she did, and not just her words. They saw below her fake face. It wasn't long before she was screaming and ranting about how everyone in town was snubbing her. When I was sixteen, I moved in with Phillipa. Of course, Mother threatened us both, but Pip had Jack, so she didn't dare touch us."

Phillipa had eloped with Jack Ingram at her senior prom dance. He was another summer visitor, a college student who fell hard for my sister.

"I figured me living with them is why Jack filed for divorce."

Liam surprised me. Usually, he was astute about situations. Almost uncomfortably so.

"Liam, those two were a mismatch from the very beginning. Jack was always about himself and what he wanted. He was ambitious, but only for what he could do. Remember when he dragged Pip away so he could attend law school in Virginia?"

Maybe I should have stayed quiet. Pip had been in Virginia when Victor died, and all hell broke loose. I pushed that memory away.

"What I'm saying is, don't blame yourself. Jack felt threatened by Pip getting her real estate license. She was finally doing something for herself, and he couldn't handle it. He wanted her to stay at home and have babies."

Liam grunted. I wasn't sure I had convinced him, but the conversation had strayed from what I wanted to discuss.

"I should have stopped Mother that day at the lake."

Liam shook his head. "Don't be stupid. What could you have done? It was Victor who should have done something. We were only kids."

"Still, I should have tried. Done something. Distracted her."

"You couldn't do anything when she was like that. Not when she had crazy eyes."

Walking around in the park, we passed kids and families, and couples walking hand-in-hand. How many of these others had pain we couldn't see? Tragedies and trauma they were all hiding? I didn't reach out to discover them. I had enough of that.

"So what do we do now?" I asked him.

"We heal."

After grabbing something to eat from a street vendor, we made our way back to the testing center. Liam had about another hour of things to do there. Afterward, he planned on visiting the aquarium and museum of natural history.

"Do you have money?" I asked, sounding like a parent.

"I have what I need," he replied. "Tomorrow, come to the hotel after six. I've rented a kick-ass virtual reality game system we can try."

I promised I would. Standing at the curb, waiting for my ride, Liam told me the testing would cover another two days at least. In a few weeks, they would contact us to make a return appointment to discuss their results and suggestions.

His hand fell on my shoulder.

"Don't worry. I won't discuss Victor's death, no matter what. That's your secret to tell when you want."

I gulped. I hadn't wanted to ask Liam that point-blank, but was grateful for the reassurance. "Thanks. I appreciate that."

On the drive back, I checked my voicemails and returned a call to Phillipa. She wanted to know when we were returning.

"The house got egged. I've contacted a firm in Berryville to come over and power-wash the exterior. No one in Grimsby would do it. I had to pay my fix-it guy double just to replace the broken glass."

"Sorry you have to deal with this."

"No problem." After a moment, my sister asked, "How's Liam doing?"

Phillipa didn't need to know what had happened today. She had enough on her plate. I said cheerfully, "He's sight-seeing tonight, and tomorrow I'm going over to play some video games with him at his hotel suite. You should see it; very luxe. They told us they would do a follow-up with an evaluation and recommendations in a couple of weeks. I thought you might like to be there with us?"

"Yes, I would. Let me know the date as soon as you can, and I'll clear my calendar."

This time the pause was on my side. Finally, I muttered, "Er. Well, Liam thinks he's the reason you and Jack broke up."

Phillipa gave a tinkling laugh. It was her fake one.

"Don't lie, Pip. I won't tell Liam, so tell me the truth."

"Yeah, having a brother who was getting himself into trouble all the time while he was living with us was a strain. That's true. But the real reason? Jack didn't like me being gone in the evening, taking that real estate course. When I brought home my first check, my first commission, he hit the roof. You'd think he'd be happy. No. He started yelling he'd never have a wife that earned more than he did. It wasn't Liam, Vic. We had problems that weren't going away, unless I rolled over and agreed to be subordinate to him in all things."

"Okay. Thanks for telling me, Pip. I'm sorry."

"It was a long time ago. Jack has a simple-minded woman who worships him now. That was never ever going to be me." Another pause. This time her laugh was genuine. "I'm not pining away, Vic. Don't worry."

Why was everyone telling me not to worry?

The van from the university arrived to pick up the Madonna

painting the next day. Tony Wells, my boss, called me an hour later to tell me the work was exceptional.

"That's what I like to hear," I told him over the video call. After paying me more compliments, my boss grew serious. "You look tired, Vic."

"Thanks, Tony. There's a lot to do to clear up my mother's estate, so I'm returning to Grimsby the day after tomorrow."

"Understandable. Let's talk about your calendar. There's nothing high priority, but we have an opening of a new building before Christmas, and the president wanted some pieces on display. I have a couple in mind, but one has some smoke damage, and the other has a small tear on the corner."

On my computer screen, some images popped up, showing the two pieces in question. Much of the problem seemed to be dirt.

"Let me look at that right lower corner." Tony zoomed in to show it better. "Okay, that might take some time, but overall, I think the first one needs only a good cleaning. Once I see them in person, I can give you a better idea whether I can have them ready in time."

We agreed the university would deliver them tomorrow. Before I could end the call, Tony reminded me again to take time to grieve. "I know you pride yourself on being self-sufficient but depression can sneak up on you."

"Thanks, Tony, for being concerned, but my mother and I weren't close. We hadn't spoken for well over a decade."

Before he could say anything or ask any further questions, I added, "I have a few small commissions to take care of, so I need to get going."

"Oh, right. Sure. Again, great job on the Madonna."

I had two other projects. One was the simple job of strengthening the back of a canvas that was sagging. I could finish it before I left town.

The other painting needed an estimate on a repair cost. It wasn't an especially valuable painting, but had been in the family for some time with sentimental value. I emailed them details on what I could do to repair the tear. They agreed, and I gave an estimated date for when I could finish the job.

I tidied up my workshop and did the laundry and dishes. Remembering Phillipa's reproach, I also got my driver's license renewed.

This return to normality could not last.

Chapter Nineteen

I got a text from Liam around six p.m. that he wanted to meet up, so I headed over to his hotel. I was still somewhat awed by how stylish the suite was. Not a place I imagined Liam would be comfortable living in, but he seemed to take it all in stride.

The last time I was here, I did a quick look around, but now Liam gave me a grand tour. The bathroom had a tub for two and a separate shower, with more showerheads than I had fingers on my two hands.

"It's a rain shower," my brother told me as he turned on all the jets. The bathroom quickly became a sauna. "Pretty cool, huh?"

I had to agree. Everything was very luxurious. I almost wished I had an excuse to book the room for myself.

Liam, though, was still the same, no matter the setting. We ended up ordering pizza and hot wings with liters of root beer. He showed me the virtual reality game on loan from the hotel. While I gave it my best shot, it was clear Liam knew the system far better than I did, and I lost. Repeatedly.

Seeing me getting red in the face over losing again and again, he suggested a card game we'd played as children. After I won three times in a row, I told him to stop. "You don't have to humor me."

"I'd forgotten how to play," he protested.

"Hm. Why do I doubt that?"

As we enjoyed the view of the city lights seen through the expansive wall of glass, we reminisced. Thankfully, our stories were not about the horrible side of our childhood.

"Remember when we snuck into that abandoned building? That warehouse place? We were going to hunt ghosts."

"Oh gosh, Vic, you kept whining about how we shouldn't be there. When a skunk knocked over a beer can, how you screamed! You almost got us both sprayed." Liam rolled around on the carpet, laughing.

By this time it was early in the morning, and the lack of sleep made us a little high and giggly.

"Have you forgotten when you set off the library alarm by going out the wrong door? When I got nabbed at the door, I said I did it. Mrs. Crackenberry revoked my library privileges for a month."

"Remember how we used cardboard sheets to sled down Farmer's Hill?"

"You cried about losing your mittens, and I gave you mine."

"What about that summer we rode our bikes, miles, and miles, so we could get to that spot to pick blackberries?"

"And the birds had eaten them all!"

Giddiness gave way to more serious confidences.

"How did you meet Nell, Liam? I'm curious."

"It was a few weeks after she opened her bakery. It was one of those nights I had difficulty sleeping, so I went for an early morning walk. Before the world gets busy with people. I was standing outside Rosemary Thyme, talking to one of the new street lamps. They aren't really old. It's a reproduction, but many people stop there to cross the sidewalk, so it picks up gossip."

"I'm sure you two had a fascinating talk, but I was more interested in Nell," I reminded him.

"Nell comes early to the bakery, before it opens, to start the baking. She saw me standing outside and invited me in for coffee. I think she mistook me for a bum."

I could imagine how my giant of a brother with his full beard, scruffy clothes, and conversation with an inanimate object had appeared. She'd probably thought he was crazy. Come to think of it, maybe no one was crazy. Maybe they only saw the world differently, like Liam did.

"When I walked in, I was dumbstruck." He became quiet, thinking back on the experience. I sipped my root beer, waiting so as not to spoil the mood. "Everything inside spoke of love. The chairs, the table, and even the air loved being there. It was a place of joy. I took a seat, and she brought me a coffee before returning to do her bread. I watched her for hours while she hummed and sang, making donuts."

"Sounds perfect."

"It was."

"What happened next?" Because I knew something had spoiled this joy. Otherwise, my brother would be sharing this deluxe room with Nell, not his sister.

"I was eating a cinnamon roll when one of her customers got upset that I was there. Told her to get rid of the weirdo. When she wouldn't, he yelled at her, making a scene, before leaving. A couple of other people left too."

"There are always some jerks like that. Ignore them, Liam."

"When it's only me, I do, but I hurt her business. Nell's better off without me hanging around her. I won't ruin her life."

"Nell is an adult. Talk with her. Let her make that decision."

"I don't want her to lose her happiness because of me."

"Meaning you don't think you deserve anything good. Have you ever thought of leaving Grimsby? Starting someplace else?"

"Leaving doesn't change what I am."

"No, but it could give you a chance to be seen differently without all the old prejudices. No Deacon Hayes breathing down your neck because you were a wild teen."

"Hayes is only doing his job."

"You're more generous than I am," I said, angry at my brother for passively accepting abuse from the police chief.

Liam shrugged. "He's got his own problems. Don't let the tough, old-boy, wild-west sheriff-act fool you. His wife died last year. In a car crash."

"Oh. I remember Reed mentioning that."

"Don't get me wrong, the guy's a pompous jackass, but he's gone a bit off the deep end since she died. No warnings, only tickets, or worse, a night spent in a jail cell."

Liam gave me a speculative look, his curiosity increasing. "What about your cop? What are you going to do about Reed Easton?"

"Do about him?" I echoed his question.

"You asked about Nell, so turnabout is fair play."

"I haven't decided yet," I blurted. That didn't seem to fool Liam.

"He's still stuck on you as much as ever."

"Reed said you told him back in high school you heard things sing. Why did you do that? You didn't tell anyone else, did you?"

"You were hanging around him, and he seemed okay with you. Why not me?"

Liam, Liam.

"Reed says he knows the truth about how Victor died."

Liam looked at me curiously. "Do you think he does? Or is he bluffing? Mother was evil, but also smart. They'll never find out what she did with the gun unless I tell them."

Chapter Twenty

The following day, we checked out of his hotel room. We would swing by my place to pick up my suitcase and take the train back to Grimsby. Our plan changed when our cab pulled up to my apartment building. Reed Easton was leaning against a slick black car, reading a book.

He greeted us with a wave. "Hunter thought I could take you two back to Grimsby."

Before I could protest, Liam climbed into the back of Reed's car, forcing my hand. "Fine. Wait here, and I'll get my bag."

I cursed as I stuffed things fiercely into my bag. I secured the studio and my apartment. Nothing else would breach my defenses.

Liam sprawled sideways in the back seat, forcing me to take the front. While Reed navigated the city traffic chatting about unimportant things; I looked out the window, ignoring him.

In about half an hour, we left the city behind and were passing fields of cows.

"I found a copy of *Crime and Punishment*. Maybe we could go over the codebook tonight?" Reed asked.

I spoke for the first time.

"Liam and Phillipa should be there. This concerns them, too, if you haven't forgotten."

"I haven't forgotten."

As he stared ahead, I traced his profile. I liked his nose. His chin. The lines in his forehead, with the eyebrows that had a slight arch right before they ended. His mouth. Those lips.

It was far too close in here. I cracked the window and said hastily, "We can do it at Phillipa's condo. Let me ask her if that's okay."

I texted Phillipa, and she agreed to the plan. With that settled, I should have felt at ease, but I didn't. Something was circling me, trying to pry me open. I felt uneasy.

We passed a traffic sign showing the miles to Grimsby. This ride wasn't going as fast as I'd like. To distract myself, I asked Reed, "Who's Lottie?"

"Lottie?" he repeated, surprised at the change of subject.

"You mentioned her when your dad came into Rosemary Thyme."

"Oh, yeah, I did. Lottie Danbury. She's Nell's mom and owns a hair salon in Grimsby."

"And?"

Reluctantly, he said, "She's my dad's girlfriend. They've been off and on again for about three years now."

"I'm truly sorry about your mom, Reed. I didn't know."

"How would you? I didn't tell you. My parents didn't want anyone to know she was terminal. Back then, cancer was a dirty disease people didn't talk about." His fingers tightened on the steering wheel. "I think my dad was half out of his mind."

Inside the car, the atmosphere grew deathly quiet. The snoring from the back seat had stopped. In the stillness, I froze. Something was coming down the tracks; I could hear the warning whistle. But I couldn't evade the hit.

"After I broke up with Darcy, my fiancée, I thought about you,

Vic. It got me wondering what happened back then. I requested Victor's case files."

I could hardly breathe. Liam was sitting up in the back seat, his sunglasses masking his face. But Reed kept talking, shattering me. "I couldn't believe it at first. How could my old man mess it up so badly?"

"What did he mess up, Reed?" I whispered, my voice a thin thread, too easy to break.

"Your dad killed himself, didn't he?"

"Pull the car over! Now!"

Reed said, "Don't run away again, Vic. It's time we talk."

"I need to vomit, you idiot!" I shouted.

Reed quickly pulled onto the shoulder. My hand fumbled on the door handle until I finally got it opened. I stumbled out, almost falling to my knees. Halfway down the slope, I retched.

Someone was holding back my hair. That was Liam. Reed was patting my face with a napkin soaked with water from the bottle I had brought with me.

"I'm sorry, Vic."

"You shouldn't be sorry," Liam told him in his customary flat tone. "It's way past when this should be out in the open."

My stomach had little left in it. I rinsed my mouth again and spat out as much of the sick flavor as I could, then tried to walk back up the hill, but my legs were jelly. Reed's hand came under one arm; Liam held the other. They guided me back up to where I leaned my butt against Reed's car, looking up at the sky.

A car stopped, and the driver rolled down his window to shout at us. "Are you alright?"

He gave my brother and Reed a suspicious glare. I waved and shouted back that I was fine. I was heartily tired of hearing that phrase. The Good Samaritan slowly pulled his car back onto the road.

"Why do you think Victor killed himself? They didn't find the gun."

"How would you know that, Vic?" asked Reed gently. "In the police statements, your mother and brother swore you had left for college the night before?"

Anger was better than weakness. "You know those statements were false, Reed. You know I was there when it happened, so stop the game. It doesn't suit you, Mr. FBI."

"Lucky guess. I thought you might have been, but I wasn't sure until now."

I was so weary. So tired of all of this. I should never have come back to Grimsby. Reed would never give up until I told him the story of what happened.

It was Liam who persuaded me.

"Tell him. Mother's dead, and she can't hurt us for telling. Even if he was a rotten father, Victor deserves the truth."

I shivered, suddenly cold. Liam had told his story to his counselor. I guess it was my turn now. I blinked rapidly, my lashes wet from tears, and rubbed my sweat-damp hair from my forehead. I started slowly, trying to squeeze out the words from a dry throat.

"I never told you, Reed, but my father helped me do the paperwork to apply to college. Since I was a dependent, I needed a parent's signature, tax returns, all sorts of stuff. It surprised me when he agreed to help me, because it would be against Mother's wishes, and Victor never did that."

When I didn't continue, Reed shook his head. "Why? Your family has plenty of money."

Liam inserted in a matter-of-fact tone, "It wasn't about the money. Mother was still angry that Phillipa had eloped with Jack and escaped her. Never would she let that happen again."

I patted my forehead with the napkin, trying to cool myself down. My body couldn't decide if it wanted to be cold or hot.

"Who knows why Victor helped? It's a mystery." I exhaled and resumed my tale. "Everyone was on edge for weeks. Mother was fighting over the phone with Phillipa about being with Jack in

Virginia. She was after Victor all the time. Either about his medication or the car."

"He loved that car," Liam said. It had been a family story you learned by rote: Victor loved his car more than anything. More than his children. More than his life.

Liam took up the story. "Mother wanted him to get rid of the car, you see—sell it. She wanted something flashy. The day before Victor died, our mother sold it when he wasn't home. For junk. I remember the guy with the wrecker. He let me sit in the front seat of the truck cab as they cranked Victor's car up onto the ramp."

"That must have been the last straw," I murmured. "School was out for the summer. I gave you money to chase the ice-cream truck. Remember, Liam?"

"It was a red-white-blue, Bomber push-up one."

"Mother was at her library committee meeting. The house was quiet. I thought it was a good time to talk to Victor. Let him know I had gotten the paperwork confirming my acceptance and the scholarship. That I had the money to go. I went to his bedroom, but I was too excited to read him before—"

I wasn't eager to continue. Liam explained to Reed, "My parents had separate bedrooms. I never realized how strange that was until I lived with Phillipa and Jack."

Reed handed me the bottle. "Take it slow. Have a sip."

In my long pause, the only sound was the rushing by of the traffic on the road. Say it, Vic, tell them the truth. I licked my dry lips and swallowed some of the water.

"We'd never enter our parents' bedrooms without an invitation. I don't know why I broke that rule on that day. Too excited, I guess. I opened the door, and he was sitting on the bed, the muzzle of the shotgun pressed to his chest. I—ran forward. Stupid. So stupid. I think I startled him."

I gulped. A couple of semi-trucks flew by and I could feel their gassy exhaust brush my face. On the road was a normal life, with normal people. I wish I was in a truck, going somewhere, anywhere.

"I couldn't move. Then I heard the ice-cream truck going down the street. My first thought was that Liam would be back. He'd see this—*this mess.*"

I stopped talking, thinking about what I had done. Locking the bedroom door. Rushing to strip off the bloody T-shirt and taking a fast shower; the detergent smell of the clean clothes as I pulled them over my head.

"When Liam got back, he helped me pack, and we both went to the bus station. I don't think anyone noticed us because it was the rush hour on a Friday before a holiday weekend. And I left."

"You left," repeated Reed.

"I didn't want Liam to stay, but he refused to go with me. He was a minor. He thought Mother would force me to come back if he was with me."

"I found places to be other than home," said Liam. "Alleys to explore. Interesting garbage to touch. Mother needed to discover Victor without me around and decide what she was going to do."

I blinked, surprised at his vehemence. Reed stalked down the hill, staring into the woods. Liam, remaining at my side, said, "He doesn't get it."

"No."

Reed Easton, a product of a normal family, would never understand.

Having a husband who had killed himself was worse than one being murdered. Rachel Rowan would never let the town know her life was imperfect. No—a husband who died during a home invasion or protecting her jewelry made a much better story to tell her friends at the next ribbon-cutting. In the end, it was a futile endeavor. When Grimsby rejected her, she punished them.

Reed came back to the car. He was calmer. "Why did she do it?"

"If you think cancer is a dirty thing, imagine a suicide in the family."

Reed sighed. "It was your father's prescription bottle that led me to the truth."

"How so?"

"He had an empty pill bottle of antidepressants in his bathroom which had expired. It made me wonder why he was taking them."

Liam told us both. "Mother destroyed the pills. Said it was a weakness."

"I didn't know that," I said.

"They had a scene about it one day when you were at the public library."

We all had pieces of the puzzle, seeing events from different angles.

Reed asked me, "How can you stay there?"

He meant the house.

"She's dead."

"Murdered."

"Not by us," I told Reed, hoping that what I said was true.

Chapter Twenty-One

We dropped Liam off at his garage apartment, understanding that we'd meet up tomorrow at Phillipa's. I wasn't up to doing spy stuff tonight and had rescheduled with my sister.

When I got to my parents' home, I found that egg yolk was still plastered all over the front porch. While I put the key in the lock, opened the door, and shut off the alarm, Reed said, "You shouldn't stay here by yourself. I'm staying."

I was too tired to argue.

"Suit yourself." Reed's visit last week had been the first time he had been inside that house. It felt strange, but he knew all my secrets. What did it matter anymore?

There was only one bedroom door open; the others on the second floor were still locked. Walking into the guest room, I put down my bag. Reed wrapped his arms around me. I should have bristled, but it had been a long day. As he stroked my hair, I melted against him.

"There's nothing here for dinner. I still haven't gone grocery shopping."

"We can order takeout." His chest rumbled in my ear, pressed against his chest.

"I don't think any Grimsby delivery driver will come to the witch's house."

After calling a few places that hung up on him, Reed finally ordered by giving the neighbor's address. When the delivery car pulled up across the street, Reed rushed out bare-footed. It took a flash of his badge and a big tip to get our food.

By the time he returned victorious, I was laughing.

Food helped the conversation go smoothly. Reed also seemed to want me to think about something else, because he began talking about his college years, the pranks he had done at the FBI, and some stories about his work that didn't reveal classified information.

"How did you meet Darcy?" I asked.

"Who? Oh, you mean Darcy, my ex?"

I nodded.

"I'll tell you if you tell me the back-story between you and Hunter Garrick."

"Okay." We did a pinky swear, and Reed began first.

"Darcy and I met at Quantico, the FBI training academy there. I was fresh out of school. It was an exciting time, and we hit it off."

From Reed's casual shrug, I guessed he wasn't that upset about her.

"But as time went by, the Bureau assigned us different offices, and we found out that maintaining a long-distance relationship wasn't easy. By the time we got back to the same region, we were different people."

Reed and I hadn't seen each other for fifteen years, yet time didn't seem to matter to us. Take that, Darcy.

"She didn't think I was ready to get married—she believed I was still mooning for a girl I'd known a long time ago. I wondered if she was right. It's why I got Victor's case files. Why I tracked you down."

"Hm. I wondered when you were going to fess up to that," I said around my noodles.

"I found out where you went to school—that you studied abroad in Paris and the Netherlands. That the university employs you, but you also do freelance jobs."

That seemed a lot to me. It was far more than I knew about Reed's life. But I couldn't be angry anymore about his nosiness; after all, I was the master snoop, groping everyone's feelings.

"Now, you tell me about Hunter Garrick."

"Not much to tell," I said, scrunching my nose, recalling. "We met at an art gala where my boss, Tony Wells, introduced us. Hunter was the attorney for a billionaire accused of killing his girlfriend."

"The Hammerby murder trial?"

"The same. Tony knew I had a knack for discovering what people wanted hidden. I helped him interview some job applicants and stopped him from buying paintings from some dishonest people."

"Because of being an empath?"

"Yeah, but Tony doesn't know that. He calls it my lucky guess. Women's intuition. Anyway, Hunter was starting his depositions in the case, and Tony thought I could help give some insight."

"And you did?"

I gave Reed a grin. "I sat in on an interview and helped Hunter discover that Hammerby's girlfriend, Millicent, had a secret lover. A lover who didn't like sharing and had a choking fetish. Hunter got enough evidence to convince the DA to drop the charges and pursue Millicent's boyfriend. They found some pretty incriminating evidence at his apartment."

"I know you put a lot of money into remodeling your apartment five years ago about the same time."

I smirked. "Hammerby was very grateful. He didn't fancy life in prison."

"I remember seeing Hunter on the news. He was everywhere.

But not you. Why did you let him take all the credit? He could have said you were his assistant or something."

"He deserved it. I'm not a lawyer, and I can only be a human lie-detector sometimes. I can't guarantee whether a hunch is right or if I'll even sense anything useful. It took Hunter to put all the pieces together."

Reed pressed. "That isn't all between you and Hunter, is it?"

I shrugged. "We had a one-night stand. Short and fun. Nothing serious and long over. He's pursuing Phillipa now."

A banging at the front door made us both jump.

"Are you expecting anyone?"

"No."

Walking into the hallway, I heard Reed exclaim, "It's my dad!"

He must have opened the door, because I heard Mr. Easton say, "I was driving by and saw your car outside. What are you doing here?"

"I'm with Vic Rowan. What are you doing here, Dad?" He had a good point. The Easton house was in a neighborhood about five miles away. An easy drive, but not a route that would make you pass my house.

I heard an unfamiliar voice, a woman's, say, "Your dad always drives by here, Reed. Several times a day. To check on the Rowan house."

"Check on the house?" Reed repeated in a dumbfounded voice. By this time, I was in the hallway. "He's checking up on the Rowans, Reed. Don't you understand? Waiting for us to kill some-one. Or looking for evidence against us—isn't that so, Mr. Easton?"

Reed's father, Greg Easton, couldn't hide his feelings from me. His suspicion-distaste-fascination was all rolled up in a nasty sticky ball. As tall as Reed, he had a bit of a gut (but not as much as Hayes'; I had to admit). His hair still boasted a military buzz cut, even if he hadn't worn a uniform in over a decade.

His companion was a woman in her early fifties with dark hair, a heavy foundation of makeup on her round face and thick black eyeliner highlighting hazel eyes. Her feelings were open and honest: irritation and exasperation. She was out of patience with Greg Easton.

Reed did the introductions.

"Vic, this is Lottie Danbury, Nell's mom—Victoria Rowan, Liam and Phillipa's sister. She's visiting from the city."

"Pleased to meet you," she said, giving me a perfunctory nod before turning back to Mr. Easton. "Can we go, Greg? You promised me a movie after dinner."

But tugging on his arm would not budge Mr. Easton. His eyes fixated on me as he told his son, "Leave this girl alone. She's trouble."

"Better go, Reed. I might bewitch you," I snapped, my anger rising to match Mr. Easton's.

"You still haven't explained why you're here, Dad."

I wasn't sure why Lottie stirred the pot. Maybe she was tired of being dragged around to the Rowan place on date night.

She told Reed, "Your dad does this once a day at least. Maybe twice. He's—what d'you call it? I heard it on a daytime talk show —compulsive. He's compulsive about checking on the Rowan house. Can't help himself. Swears there are clues still to be found about Victor Rowan's murder."

I shook my head at Reed in warning. I wasn't ready to discuss Victor's death tonight with this has-been, even if he was Reed's dad.

Instead, I taunted Easton. "If you come by here so often, why didn't you see the house being egged by vandals? Or who threw a rock in my window? Or are only Rowans guilty of committing crime?"

Easton pointed his finger at me; it was trembling with fury.

"This girl tells lies, my boy. Lies. I've known that for a long time. When she lived here, she came to me with some cock-and-bull story that she and her brother were being abused. I came around and talked it over with Victor and Rachel."

My body stiffened as I made my face blank. No one would see how Easton's words affected me. Yes, the year before Victor had killed himself, I had asked Greg Easton for help. A man of authority, of justice, who would finally make things right. Fix things.

"I never knew you talked with my parents, Mr. Easton." My voice was deadly. No one moved.

"I sure did. Both of them told me all about you. An experienced liar and delinquent, just like your brother became."

"Dad, you need to go." Reed took his dad's arm, trying to get him out the door, but the man was stubborn.

"One of you Rowans killed Victor. I'll discover the truth one day and expose you all."

"Stop!" Reed's exclamation landed like a grenade, making me jump backward. Lottie released her grip on the glass door and it banged in the frame, rattling the old house.

"I am sick and tired of hearing about how the Rowans are guilty." Reed was furious. "It's nothing but an excuse, Dad. Your crutch. To protect yourself from the knowledge that mom was dying."

"Now, look here," Reed's dad protested feebly.

"No. You look, Dad. Into your heart. Solving some imaginary case that exists only in your head will not bring mom back. It will not change that you failed her when she needed you the most. That you failed *me*."

Reed was truth-telling. Each word was a cutting swing from the sword of justice. Easton's shining knight act had received the death blow.

"I've had enough. Tomorrow, at mom's grave, you will beg her forgiveness on your knees, or I will never see you again. You will tell her how sorry you are. What a mistake it was that you didn't go with her to her doctor's appointments. Sorry that you didn't fix her meals. That you weren't there, holding her hand, when she passed."

Reed spared a glance at the woman standing beside Easton.

"Then you will apologize to Lottie for all the crap you've put her through, chasing this fantasy of blaming Rowans. It wasn't Rachel Rowan who convinced the city manager to retire you. It was Craig himself. You weren't taking care of the community any longer. Instead, you were hanging at the station, talking about the glory days. Not returning phone calls, not investigating complaints."

Reed came to stand beside me, taking my hand in his.

"And now I learn you failed Vic when she needed you the most. You heard a child was suffering, and you did nothing."

Reed's eyes were hard and soft at the same time.

"Whether or not Vic was lying, as a law enforcement officer, you should have informed child protective services. They would have investigated. As a cop and a man,—I don't know if I can forgive that."

The old police chief had somehow shrunk. His shoulders slumped. Lottie stroked Mr. Easton's arm, like the comfort you gave an old dog right before you put it down.

"Get out of here. And I'd better not see your truck passing by here again. This is done."

Chapter Twenty-Two

The next morning I awoke to the sound of rain. It wasn't until I rolled out of bed that I realized the sound of water pounding the window was a crew power-washing the house.

When Greg Easton had left, Reed had taken a shower while I read a book. He'd insisted on bunking downstairs on Mother's uncomfortable antique couch. The whole thing should have been funny, but it hadn't been.

As my stomach growled, I looked at the bedside clock. It was almost noon. I dressed and brushed my hair, pulling it back into a workable ponytail. My shoes were downstairs. Mother didn't allow shoes upstairs and it was hard to break old habits.

Like I expected, Reed was in the kitchen. But instead of preparing a meal, he was pulling everything out of the cabinets.

"How much of this do you want to keep?"

I looked at the stacks he had made.

"You can dump all the food. Well, not the salt and pepper. I imagine that's okay, but my mother hasn't been here in about six months. I'll go grocery shopping today. Keep some plates and glasses we can use. I'll trash or donate the rest."

He went back to his chore of sorting, his back to me. The muscles in his neck, above his shirt collar, were taut.

After Mr. Easton's visit, the evening had soured, and we didn't return to the easy companionship we had been enjoying. That's the reality of letting people into your life. Messy emotions.

Thinking of last night's dinner, I took the foil box out of the fridge. Eating the leftovers cold, I watched Reed work his way through all the kitchen cabinets. The counters became full, so he started stacking plates, saucers, and teacups on the dining room table. There looked to be at least five sets of dish patterns.

I dumped the empty container into the trash. Washing my hands, I told him, "You need to go see your dad. Or was that an empty threat about your mother's grave?"

He threw a glass jar of spaghetti sauce into the trash bag so hard it broke. "Are you telling me to make up with my father?"

"Look, I get it. He acted like an ass. It hurts. But he couldn't deal with your mom dying."

Here I was defending Greg Easton! That was the problem with being an empath. You absorbed so much of another you started seeing their side.

I tried again. "You're a man now. Maybe you can get through to him. Tell him what happened to Victor. I don't want to be there when you do, but maybe that will help you two mend fences. See if he's ready to listen to the truth."

Reed's mouth was a thin line, and the area around his lips was white, but his cheeks were flushed. He came over and put his hands on my shoulders, holding me in place while he looked down, meeting me eye-to-eye.

"You haven't thought this thing through, Vic. Revealing what happened to your father is going to open a big can of worms. Before you do that, you need to get on the phone with your pet lawyer. Find out what type of statement you want to make to the police. Ask him if you could be charged."

"Charged?" I said, surprised.

"Concealing how Victor died. Making a false statement to the police about not being here. What about Liam knowing what really happened? If my father got vindictive, he could drum up some charges that would make you or your brother's life seriously uncomfortable."

"Oh." Reed was right. I hadn't thought it through. "Okay, I'll talk to Hunter today."

"I'd recommend you bypass the Grimsby DA and go to the state's attorney general. Bring Hunter and make a statement. Play on your young age at the time and that Rachel pressured you to lie."

"But she didn't pressure me to lie. I ran away on my own."

His mouth thinned with aggravation. "You were in shock, scared."

That part was true.

"But he killed himself, Reed. I didn't do it. I just ran. How can that be a crime?"

"Promise me you'll talk to Hunter before doing anything about it?"

I nodded.

Reed reached over my shoulder and picked up the rock sitting on the windowsill. It was the one I had decorated with my scribbles. "What's this?"

"I'll take it. Sentimental value." He handed it over to me, ignoring the brief contact of our hands. He was going to be a real pig today. I couldn't stop pushing. "Talk with your dad. I think he has regrets."

"You think? Is that your emotion-detector picking things up?" He folded his arms across his chest, hip against the counter.

I didn't like Mr. Easton, but he still held raw pain and guilt over his wife's death. And sadness towards Reed. Sure, he's messed up, but all of us are to some degree. Besides, I didn't want to be caught between father and son.

"He knows he didn't do well by your mom, Reed." Reed gave me a look of cold, angry disbelief.

"What he said last night about you going to him. About you and Liam being abused as kids. He didn't help, and probably made things worse, didn't he?"

"This isn't about me—"

"Isn't it? Isn't all of this about you, your mother, Liam? Why did Victor kill himself? Why did someone murder Rachel? That's a lot of Rowan chickens coming home to roost."

I shrugged helplessly. He gave my shoulder a little shake and demanded, "What happened between you and my dad?"

I floundered and stuttered.

"You and I had b-become friends. When you had m-me over for dinner the first time, I couldn't believe it. How normal your family was. Your mom was like one you see on television—baking cookies, wearing an apron. Your dad in his uniform, wearing his gun in that shiny black holster."

How to explain to him the wonderland his home life had seemed to me? No Alice had seen a more bizarre world than walking into that of the Easton household. Where parents sat down for dinner and had a discussion. Someone did not portion food out to your plate. Where Reed could sass his parents, and they view his words as a joke.

"At first I wanted to be a part of that. It was like entering a fantasy world where everything was perfect. I believed that your family was perfect, and that was my mistake. Not Greg Easton's."

Reed gave a grating laugh. "My family is certainly not perfect."

"None of us are," I said in a small voice.

He frowned down at me, both of his hands back on my shoulders now.

"Why didn't you come to me first? Tell me?"

His questions revealed the source of his hurt. He wanted to have been my confidant, the hero, the savior. But I always knew that a kid couldn't take down Rachel. I bit my lip so hard that I felt the sweetness of blood in my mouth.

"Rachel was dangerous. I thought another adult would be the only way things could get fixed. Kids are told that if we report abuse to a teacher or cop, something is done. But it didn't work the way the PSAs say. When nothing happened, I thought he ignored what I told him."

I hadn't realized that Mr. Easton had talked with my parents until last night. That made an old incident in my senior year make sense. Coming home from school, I'd found everything personal in my room removed. Gone were the art posters I had bought from museums, using my carefully hoarded money. Small knick-knacks of keychains, ticket stubs, and school photos of friends that one collects, all missing. The debris of a child was all gone. Vanished as if they had never existed. As if I had never existed.

I knew I was being punished, but I didn't know what for. Rachel only gave me a smug smile over dinner and never explained. I took it as another one of her casual cruelties, but it must have been because of Mr. Easton's visit. The timeline made sense.

Reed's question broke into my thoughts. "Why are all the doors upstairs locked? Locked from the outside?"

Instinctively, my fingers curled over the rock. My hand rose.

"How would you know that? Did you try the doors?"

"I was curious—"

I stopped myself in time from striking Reed with the rock. The intensity of wanting to defend myself made me take a step back from him, putting my back against the wall. *This is why I live alone. Work alone. People.*

I warned him in a bitter voice, "Don't go into those rooms, Reed."

Reed knew he had overstepped. "I won't, I promise. Unless you invite me."

"That's unlikely."

If I could burn the house down, I would. Maybe I could?

Donate it to the fire department for a training exercise? Ugh. No, it was a historic home, so I doubted I could do that. Too bad.

"I thought that maybe your father's room could hold valuable evidence."

My hand with the rock came up again. I forced it down. I said tersely, "You said he killed himself. Remember, great detective?"

"There could be evidence in the room to explain his death," Reed explained.

I frowned. Why was this all getting so complicated? Why would I need to prove a truth that I hadn't wanted to tell anyone for fifteen years?

"Or we could stay quiet and let Grimsby believe the Rowans covered up a crime."

"You can't do that, Vic. The lid is off Pandora's box. You can't keep it shut now."

Chapter Twenty-Three

I battled with the grocery cart and its wonky wheel. I could go back and get a different one, but I rather enjoyed fighting it, forcing it to go straight against its mechanical desire.

At my insistence, Reed had dropped me off at the local grocery store. I told him I would call later for a cab, so no need to wait.

I picked up boxed meals I could quickly make. I wanted nothing complex, because I didn't plan to stay in Grimsby any longer than I needed. If Reed extended his stay in my house of horrors, he could pick up his own damn food.

I leaned over the handle of my cart, pinning it in place, to read the back of a box and figure out how many extra ingredients it would require. Someone behind me said, "You still haven't returned those library books, Victoria Rowan."

Turning, I laughed and greeted the Grimsby librarian, Mrs. Crackenberry, with her nickname. "Crackers! I think you can forget those books."

She was smaller than I remembered, and thinner. Her hair was now white where once it had been a sandy red, and veins marbled her hands, but her faded blue eyes were still as knowing as ever. "If they are lost, you need to pay the fine, Victoria."

The vague emotional cloud of my fellow shoppers I ignored, but now, addressing one person, my empath abilities narrowed their focus to taste Mrs. Crackenberry's mood. Her overall flavor was tart like a pomegranate, tempered with the earthiness of dark chocolate.

"You've made quite a name for yourself in the collectible art circles."

"I'm surprised you noticed. I'm usually behind the scenes, and only mentioned in technical magazines."

Crackers carried one of the store's small hand baskets. There wasn't much in it—a few little cans of tuna. She felt uncertain, and was trying to be brave about something. Meeting me made her anxious, so I gave a reassuring smile.

"Are you back in town because of your mother's death?"

"Yes. Wrapping up the house, and a few other things." Like murder-for-hire, blackmail schemes, and rooms soaked with old blood.

I felt Mrs. Crackenberry's anxiety sharpen as she said nonchalantly, "A pity about your mother's shop burning down. Do they know what caused it?"

Oh, Crackers. What drove you to that?

"Arson, it seems. The fire department is investigating it. I don't know much more than that."

"It's good no one was hurt."

"They got a call to 911 early on, so they contained it mostly. The store's a total loss, though."

Sometimes you get hunches, and when a certain emotional output backs it up, suspicion grows to a certainty. I wondered if Crackers had researched arson at the public library. I hoped she was smart enough to clear browser histories and hadn't used her log-in.

The old librarian looked down into her basket and rearranged the three cans. "I was thinking, my dear. So difficult, you see. I was wondering—" She cut off and began again, her faded eyes finally meeting mine. "Do I give my next payment to you or Liam?"

My mouth opened, but nothing came out. *Mrs. Crackenberry? My mother was blackmailing Crackers?* Not for the first time, I thought of killing my mother; good thing the hag was dead.

"No. I am not taking over my mother's business. And no, you will not be giving any payments to me, Liam, or Phillipa either. All that is over."

The dizzying relief she felt washed over me so quickly that I had to use the shopping cart to keep my balance. I was a punctured balloon, spinning about as everything inside me released.

"There are so many rumors swirling about, I wasn't sure. I'm glad you aren't carrying through with your mother's activities. Not a nice thing. And it isn't healthy to use someone else's secrets against them."

Wait. Crackers didn't murder Mother and Patty, did she—? No. It was a casual acknowledgment that blackmailing didn't make friends.

A shopper standing behind the librarian was interested in the shelf we blocked.

"Look, Mrs. Crackenberry, can we go next door? There's a coffee shop, and I would like to talk with you about my mother." Her tension returned, so I quickly added, "I want to make things right with whoever Rachel victimized. I thought you might help me with that."

She agreed, but was still wary of me and my intentions. I abandoned my cart and insisted on paying for her basket at the checkout. It came to less than ten dollars, but you'd think I had given her a birthday present when I handed my debit card over to the cashier.

She ordered a simple coffee, while I got something more elaborate. We were past the lunch rush and easily found a private corner. The bored barista went back to scanning his phone. The new Grimsby, with a boutique coffee shop, continued to surprise me.

When we settled across from each other, I began.

"I didn't know what my mother was doing until I returned home," I reassured Mrs. Crackenberry, trying to put her at ease. "Phillipa didn't know either."

"Your brother certainly did." Crackers was smart.

"Yes, but let me reassure you, he was as trapped by my mother as you were. He wasn't a willing participant and will not be continuing with it."

Mrs. Crackenberry sighed. "That is a relief. The last time I saw Patty, she told me she was taking over Rachel's business. Your mother was in the nursing home."

My iced coffee arrived. When the barista left, I leaned over the table and said confidentially, "I think that's why Patty Maxwell died. Can you tell me about her? I never knew her."

"A stupid woman," Crackers said scornfully. "Greedy. Not necessarily for money but for position, wanting to be someone."

"She craved status?"

"Patty admired how your mother, as an outsider, had married Victor, a descendant of a founding family. You see, Patty was also an outsider."

After stirring in the creamer, Crackers laid her spoon to the side of her saucer. "By being with your mother, Patty basked in that reflected glory. She was an expert at being a toady, and she wasn't too bright. I'm sure those qualities are why Rachel kept her after the town turned against her."

"Against my mother? Because of the blackmail?"

"No, dear. This was before Rachel started her business of secrets. After your father died, the Grimsby social set didn't appreciate how she stole the presidency of this-and-that committee. They took the chance to put her in her place. But Patty gave

Rachel all the adoration she was missing. A dull tool, but useful."

I leaned forward, closing the distance between us. "But, in the end, you thought Patty was taking over for Mother. Why?"

"I made my payments on the fifteenth and the last day of the month. I would go by Rosemary and Thyme to pay it in cash directly to your mother. Sometimes if you paid her a compliment and groveled enough, she'd cut the fee, you see."

A sip of my drink helped to cover the taste of bile that comment produced.

"But that changed after your mother broke her hip. Patty came to me and took my payment. She told me it was unlikely that Rachel would leave the nursing care facility and that she would take over the operation. Patty said she had Rachel's blessing."

"That doesn't sound like my mother."

"Yes, Victoria, that's what I thought. It sounded more like Patty was seizing an opportunity than being given one. The next week I visited your mother and told her what Patty had said. She was livid."

"Do you think Patty knew your—?"

"My secret? Oh yes. She always made a point of dropping little hints about it. Especially when she met me in town, like at the store or the library. She wasn't a subtle person. Crude, really."

"Do you think she did the same to others?"

Mrs. Crackenberry took another sip of her coffee, her lipstick leaving an imprint on the white china. "I would imagine so, but I haven't discussed it with them."

It took me a while to get control of my voice. "You know others?"

"Some. Of course, anyone seen walking into Rosemary and Thyme was a possible victim of Rachel's spite. It's why the back alley doesn't have a camera. Some wanted anonymity about their sins—otherwise, why pay?"

She gave me a slight smile, the lines around her eyes crinkling.

"I can tell you want to know what my secret is."

"You don't have to satisfy my curiosity—" I began, but Crackers interrupted me by raising a hand bent with arthritis. "Your mother wasn't blackmailing people over family recipes, Victoria. These are things that could ruin someone's standing in the community, destroy marriages, or overturn wills."

I swallowed. She was going to say it. I could feel it.

In her gentle but firm voice, the one I had trusted as a child to show me all the best and latest books, Mrs. Crackenberry told me her secret.

"I had an affair with a married man when I was a young woman. He no longer lives here. However, the situation is delicate, as he is a powerful man on the political stage."

"If he's so powerful, he should be the one who paid my mother, not you," I protested.

"Thank you, Victoria, but I wasn't paying the money to protect him. I paid to protect the identity of my child. I gave my baby away to a sweet family, but they never revealed to him that he wasn't theirs."

I wished my mother were alive so I could punch her in the face.

"Rachel discovered my secret, and I think it was because of a book club meeting at my house. She went to the bathroom, but I found her exiting my bedroom with her purse in hand. Rachel had a smug look on her face."

"You think she took something?"

"A baby photograph. It's the only one I had of him."

The photograph was one that Liam probably touched.

"I'll look for it."

Crackers waved away my concern.

"Soon after that, Rachel invited me to lunch where she revealed she knew I had a child out of wedlock."

"I'm so sorry, Crackers—"

She looked at the window, her thoughts elsewhere.

"He was such a lovely baby."
Apart, but together, we wept in silence.

Chapter Twenty-Four

Phillipa was quick to remind me I was late to her place.

Flustered, I told her, "Grocery shopping took longer than I thought."

Liam and Reed talked about some television show and how the arc of the story made no sense. Each was citing the same evidence, so I didn't understand why it sounded more like an argument than a discussion.

Pip saw the direction of my gaze and said in a hushed tone, "Did you two fight? He's been testy ever since he got here."

"Not a fight exactly. Family problems with his dad."

Phillipa had a buffet where you could assemble sandwiches, sides, salad, and a drink. After piling my plate, I took a seat around her coffee table, where the others had gathered. It put me at the furthest point away from Reed. Things felt brittle between us. I suspected that he and his dad had not resolved things.

"How do we go about solving this book code thing?" I asked, snapping a carrot stick in two.

Reed pulled the book out of his bag and handed it to Liam. "I'll call out the number, and your brother will find the corresponding letter in the book. We'll see if we get anything that resembles names."

"I met one of Rachel's victims. It's Crackers."

Phillipa's mouth gaped open for a moment before she quickly shut it. "Mrs. Crackenberry? What in the world would Mother have on her?"

I didn't answer directly. "I think we should find a line that matches the length of her last name. Twelve letters. She made payments twice a month in the amount of two hundred dollars."

Reed quickly flipped through his photocopies. "These two might be her."

He called out the numbers, and within moments, we had pinned it down to one entry. By the time Liam had found all the letters, the entry decoded to the line: *Crackenberry—child.*

"That proves we have the right edition," I said.

"Crackers has a child?" asked Phillipa, astonished.

"Illegitimate and adopted away," I confirmed. I told them what Crackers had said about Patty trying to take over Mother's blackmailing business.

"My theory is that Patty was lording it up over the victims. When Mother found out, Cracker said she was in a towering rage. Probably the push down the stairs didn't endear Patty to Mother either."

Reed said, "Seems to me, that taunting blackmail victims could cause one's murder."

Phillipa agreed with Reed.

"With Mother ill, likely to die, probably someone thought they would finally be free. Then Patty comes along, bragging she'll be the new queen. They can't have been happy about that."

"Sometimes jailers let prisoners escape to give them the illusion of freedom before they get recaptured. It breaks their resistance." That contribution was from the FBI agent. Made me wonder what they studied at Quantico.

Suddenly Liam spoke up. "It was a photo of a baby, wasn't it?

Mother asked me to read it. I didn't know it was Mrs. Crackenberry's, only that the baby wasn't with his mother any longer. A sad photo. I only get impressions, residual feelings, not names."

I said, "Mother always could sniff out secrets. Something about Crackers made her curious. She took the photo, and Liam's talent confirmed it, or his reading gave her an idea of what Crackers was trying to hide."

Liam went on describing the things Rachel had brought him. "A wedding ring, a card from a florist bouquet, a man's wallet, a woman's high-heeled shoes—"

He would have kept going, but Phillipa put her hand on his shoulder. "It's not your fault what Mother did."

Liam wasn't wearing his sunglasses today, and it was easy to see his grimace, despite the beard.

"Not my fault—but I aided and abetted to get money to live on my own. I'd already messed up your first marriage, and I would not do that to your second."

"I've told you before, you did not mess up my marriage with Jack. He couldn't stand me making my own money. And Conrad? He wanted kids, and I didn't."

Liam picked up his story again. "I moved out, but no one wanted to hire someone with no skills and a dodgy high-school past with 'juvie criminal' stamped all over it. Mother told me she would pay me for each item I analyzed for her. Being Mother, I knew there was another agenda, but my rent had to be paid."

"You should have come to me," insisted Phillipa.

"You've done enough."

And what did Vic do for her brother? Left him with a dead father and a crazy mother. Seeing my discomfort, Reed cleared his throat and changed the subject. "It looks like about thirty names in Patty's book. Let's see how much we can get done, okay?"

We worked through a few sheets. No page repeated any of the numbers for the same letters.

"That's why a book code is so secure," Reed explained. "You

can't crack it by looking at the most used numbers. Each string is unique and you need the right book and the correct edition to decode it."

Reed and Liam established a routine and were the best team, so Phillipa and I retreated to the snack table. I wasn't hungry; there was something I wanted to discuss with her.

"Did you talk with Nell?"

"She won't take the money," said Phillipa.

I looked at the back of Liam's head. He wouldn't like that.

"I have an idea, but you and Liam would need to be okay with it." Pip gestured with her wineglass for me to go ahead. "Mother's will didn't mention the off-shore account, but you have access?"

"She gave me the login info a few weeks ago. I'm not sure why. It seemed too generous for her."

I gave an unhappy laugh.

"Mother wouldn't give it to Patty after the stair push. Certainly not after hearing how Patty bragged to Crackers. Besides, by giving it to you, she smeared you with her filthy business."

Mother had loved tying her children to her. As soon as she'd given that password to Phillipa, she'd made us her co-conspirators.

Phillipa said, "As long as you have the right info, you gain access to the money. They keep things very anonymous."

"Right." I lowered my voice. Reed didn't know about the money, and I had no plans to inform him about Mother's loot. "This was what I was thinking. Set up a foundation. A non-profit. We'll give help to those Mother blackmailed."

Phillipa gave a lovely wide smile, showing off perfect white teeth. "And we offer Nell something from the fund?"

"Bingo. Tell her we're investing back into Grimsby, and she'd be doing us a favor if her business was the first guinea pig for our program of benevolence. What do you think?"

"I think it could work. She wants the bakery to be taken seriously. She'd expanded the menu to a lunch cafe about a month before and had bought new equipment. The insurance is stalling about paying until the question of it being arson is cleared up by the police."

"Well Liam may need some money. He lost his inheritance when Rosemary Thyme burned to the ground. What's the situation with the insurance on Mother's shop?"

Phillipa sighed. "It's the same company Nell was using so we are on hold also. But there's a bigger problem. I looked over the policy and Mother never inventoried everything that was in there. Probably trying to cover her tracks."

"Well I don't want to keep any of the money. It's dirty. What I do want is Mrs. Crackenberry to be paid back everything Mother took from her." At my sister's expression, I cocked my head. "What?"

"I wondered if Mother went after Crackers because of you. She knew you hid at the public library after school. I think she was jealous of Mrs. Crackenberry."

As I digested the ramifications of what Phillipa said, she put her hand on my arm, positioning herself so her back was to Reed. "Have you watched the DVD from Mother yet?"

"No. Have you?"

This close to my sister's face, I could see the faint lines at the edges of her eyes, and the grooves on either side of her nose. She smelled of lilacs. I needed to get Hunter back down here. Make her happy.

"It was—" Phillipa blinked. "...Hard, but I got through it. I think Liam did the right thing by not listening to her. If yours is like mine, it's a personal message of how you screwed up her life. How you're not good enough, will never be good enough, and are utter trash."

I gave a hoarse chuckle. "Well, how perfectly charming. I'll watch it when I'm plastered. Seriously though, she's dead, Pip. She can't control us any longer."

"Maybe so, but she's not done with us yet, Vic. Be careful and don't let your guard down. Like with Reed. Rowans destroy who they love."

Her words gave me a sudden idea. "Is that why you looked tired? Did you tell Hunter no?"

"It wouldn't have worked out. He's a big city guy, and I'm a Grimsby girl." Before I could argue, she brought the conversation back to Reed. "Do you think it's a coincidence that he's down here now?"

No, it wasn't a coincidence. Reed was hunting a person who arranged mysterious murders, who might have targeted our mother and Patty Maxwell. But that was information I wasn't ready to tell my siblings yet.

Chapter Twenty-Five

eed and I stood outside Phillipa's condo, both of us looking different ways. Eventually, he said, "Let me drive you home."

In the car, the conversation took an oh-so-polite turn: was the air conditioner too cold? But before I could blurt out a question about his dad, Reed's phone rang. It was Lottie, Nell's mom, and Greg Easton's girlfriend.

"Wait a sec. I'm driving."

Reed put his phone in a dash holder, selecting the speaker option.

"—what can I do to help?"

"Do?"

"About your dad? We got into a fight, and Greg left in that old truck of his, and he won't answer his phone, and he's not at home either, because I went over there, and the house is dark, and I—"

"Hold on, Lottie. I'm sure he's fine. Let him blow off some steam."

"He was drinking, Reed, and I don't feel good about it. Did you talk with your dad today?"

Reed gave me a sideways look, which I ignored by looking at the window and pretending I didn't exist.

"Yes, I did."

"He said all sorts of hurtful things—" Lottie started crying over the phone. It wasn't small, discreetly sniffling, but a wrenched-from-the-heart sob of pain. "I don't know what to do!"

Reed's shoulders dropped with a sigh.

"I'll come by, Lottie. Don't worry. But I'm sure he's okay. He's just in one of his funks. You know how he gets."

She choked out a thank you before hanging up.

"Would it be okay to drop you off?"

"No problem."

He pulled up beside the house, and I stared up at the dark facade. I had forgotten to leave the porch light on. It was fine. I didn't need Reed.

He kept the engine running while I unbuckled my seat belt. As I climbed out, he said, "You understand, Vic? I'll be back later? I promise."

I didn't speak, but only gave him a nod through the window before walking to the front porch. The cleanup crew was long gone, but there was still the faintly damp smell on the front porch.

The problem with emotions is that they distract. I was so inwardly focused on thinking about Reed that I didn't scan my surroundings.

I opened the door and turned to switch off the alarm, but it wasn't on. Had I forgotten to switch it on when I dropped off the groceries earlier in the day? That wasn't like me.

Before I could hit the light switch, a hand came over my mouth. A sweaty man's hand, smelling of nicotine and perfumed soap. An aggressively male emotional taste of smoky-hungry, burning-battery-acid that I was familiar from my first night in the house.

Within seconds he had slammed me face-first against the wall. Something cracked, and my nose started bleeding. Wrenching my hands behind my back, he zip-tied my wrists as he whispered hoarsely into my ear, "Let's go upstairs, baby."

I acted on animal instinct: struggling and thrashing, trying to bite anything I could. But at a slim five feet six, I was over-matched. With ease, he wrenched my head backward and wrapped his arm under my chin, pinning me against his chest.

"If you want to fight, let's do it in bed."

With each step up the stairs, he threw me forward. I tried to grab the railing, to hold myself in place, but I couldn't stop him. My hand slipped away, my grasp not strong enough to stop his movement upward.

A palm of his hand over my mouth prevented me from screaming. The smells made me dizzy as I realized it was the person who threw the rock.

He didn't speak again until we were on the first floor. "Now, which bedroom should we use?"

No! I bucked and thrashed against his iron grip. I had no room for feeling anything but blinding fear. I only stopped when something cold and sharp came under my shirt, pricking my skin.

"Go ahead, baby, try me," he growled.

He was powerful. With his arm still around my neck, he half-lifted me off my feet while he kicked the door of the nearest room open. The lock couldn't hold against his boot, and the door spun away so hard it struck the wall, revealing a room filled with Liam's childhood collections.

This must not have satisfied him, for he went to the second door. Again, the lock splintered under his boot. The door bounced, hitting the wall with a whack.

This one was Phillipa's room, decorated like a dollhouse in pink, purple, and white.

"Pretty, but I want Rachel's room," he grunted. His breath was hot and moist against my neck, the searing burn of battery-acid in my mind-taste.

We were coming closer to Victor's room. I started fighting

again. I couldn't imagine going into that room of blood and gun smoke.

The tip of the cold steel blade hooked my bra before moving down to slide into my side with the ease of a knife into warm butter at a summer's picnic. Wet flowed down my side. I gasped in shock.

Bam-bam. The third door gave way to his kick. It was my room. A bare four walls, stripped of personality. Hysterically, I thought of the three bears and a rapist Goldilocks.

The next was Mother's room. Once more, the door was no match for his violence. As we entered, I smelled my mother's perfume. Confused, not able to think, for a moment I thought she was still here.

He tossed me forcibly down on the bed, making my body bounce on the mattress. Ignoring me, he stalked around the room, examining her trinkets, photo frames, and the jewelry left on the dresser.

He was a big man, broad in both shoulders and waist. He wore a blue work shirt, like a mechanic's, and worn jeans. Dark thick hair like a bush on top of a long face with a receding chin and a thin, cruel mouth.

"You won't be telling anyone now, bitch."

Drawing his arm across the top of the dresser and nightstands, he sent everything shattering to the floor. He pulled out drawers, shook them, and tossed them aside to where they crashed against the walls. He threw a small table against the wall. The leg broke off as it slid limply down to the floor.

With each blow, I shook harder, shrinking back from his rage. When he came back to where I lay, my panicked breathing made a whistling sound through my nose.

He stood for a moment, towering over me, but instead of touching me again, he dropped to the floor. From under the bed, he yanked out storage boxes, throwing aside Rachel's winter clothes.

"Where did she hide it? Her little book of secrets?"

I closed my eyes. Reed said he'd come back, but when?

Desperate, I sent out my empathetic senses, trying to reach anyone, a neighbor, a passerby. But I couldn't get past the emotions of this raging monster in the room with me. His storm of rage and excitement was impossible to breach.

Frustrated by not finding what he sought, he turned his attention back to me. He pressed his knee into my spine as he hissed, "Your mother found me out and thought she could keep me on a chain. Like some little *dog*. Where's the book?"

Fingers in my hair, he jerked me backward. His knee was a fulcrum, and my back arched like a crescent.

My choked cry got me a shove down into the mattress where I couldn't breathe. He pushed me down deeper, and I gasped for breath. A vision-memory of Liam held down in the water by Rachel surfaced.

I was my brother. I was drowning.

In my panic, I thrashed. I tried to get up, away from the crushing weight on my back.

"Not trying to get away, are you, baby?"

The monster's hand went to my jeans. Feeling his fingers on the bare skin of my waist, I reached the point where I would do anything to save myself.

Even become a monster.

My talent reached for my attacker's mind. I grabbed onto it like a life preserver—but one thing they teach you in First Aid is that you never hold on to a drowning person. It will drag you under to your death.

Sensing this man's deeper self made me retch. I tried to manipulate, change what he was feeling, but I couldn't. He had no kinder feelings to work upon, no pity, no compassion. Unlike my experiences with others, where I had drained off the excess or manipulated emotions, there was nothing for me here. He was a block of evil. I could gain no foothold.

I needed absolute control.

Domination of this man, to make him obey me like a puppet.

I removed my protections, let go of all defenses, lowered the castle's drawbridge, and allowed the enemy in. Reaching out, I took in all of what my attacker was.

His rampage of anger and cruelty became mine. His appetite for control and frustrated desires were mine. I welcomed inside even that secret that he tried to hide from himself—that he would never be good enough, that he was a nothing.

I would make him nothing.

Crush him. Like a bell, the words rang in my mind. It sounded like my mother's voice. Strange how I could remember hers, but not my father's.

This monster flooded my sense of self, like water breaching a dam. The rushing tide of him destroying a child's sandcastle, flooding rooms, sinking me. I was a small vessel facing a hurricane.

I steered myself into the storm, bracing.

I will take it all.

His passionate madness came over the top, and my consciousness capsized.

I was lost.

I awoke to something whimpering. It took me a moment to realize it wasn't me.

Pushing up from the bed, soaked with my blood, I saw him mewing in a corner, curled in a fetal position. I staggered to my feet, and with my hands still bound behind me, stalked over to him.

"Shut the hell up!" I screamed.

Inside me, his rage gave me energy. Something inside me, a serpent, demanded that I kill him. Punish him for violating my room, my things.

Crush him.

I started kicking him in the head. He raised his hands, trying to shelter from my blows. As each kick landed, I felt euphoric, more complete and whole. His self became more integrated with my own.

Destroy him. Let me show you how.

I saw the knife, stained with my blood, lying on the floor. I picked it up, but the handle slipped. Determined, I shifted my hand on it to gain a better grasp. I sawed at the zip ties around my wrists with grim determination as I shouted obscenities at the man crouched before me.

The ties fell, released. I brought my hands in front of me, flexing my fingers to get circulation back.

I was going to kill the bastard.

"Vic!"

Barely human, with little of Vic left in me, I turned to stare blindly at Reed. He and his father were standing in the doorway of my mother's room. Mr. Easton's horrified face over his son's shoulder.

"Give me the knife, Vic. Let me take care of this."

I brought my hands in front of me and pointed the blade at him. "Don't come any closer." The hoarse snarl wasn't my own voice.

Reed didn't listen. He was too close. I couldn't let him get close, or he'd destroy me.

I stabbed my hand forward, trying to reach him with the knife. He sidestepped me and grabbed my wrist. Turning me around, he wrapped his arms around me, my back to his chest.

I screamed.

Chapter Twenty-Six

I was in an ambulance. Someone was shining a light in my eyes. I winced.

"What's your name?"

I mumbled it.

"Do you know what day it is?"

For a moment, I couldn't remember.

"Wednesday—" I croaked hesitantly, panicking that I had the wrong answer.

Behind the paramedic, I saw Reed. It was probably the harsh lighting inside the ambulance that gave his face that queer green color.

"You left," I whispered, my throat raw.

"I'm sorry, Vic."

"How—?"

"I was going to Lotties when I passed my dad going the opposite direction. I followed him here to your house. We were shouting on your front lawn when I looked up and saw someone's shadow in the window of your mother's room."

The paramedic asked me other questions. I thought she gave

me something for the pain; everything around me was rotating. A soft glow bathed the world. Words seemed far away.

"We found the front door unlocked. You didn't answer."

The ambulance stopped. The doors opened, and we were now out in the cool night air. Voices shouted something, but I chose to forget it all.

The surgery and recovery I didn't remember.

I awoke to see Phillipa standing at the window of my hospital room, her face in profile. She was on her cell phone, and her voice was sad and strained. I felt nothing.

"If you can come down, I think it would help. Vic hasn't woken yet, but the police have all sorts of questions for when she does. I think she should have a lawyer." Pause. "Yes, someone attacked her. But the guy involved—they're saying he's not competent." Pause. "It's too hard to explain over the phone, but Reed says the man is catatonic. Not aware of anything going on around him. I haven't seen him, though. He's actually in the same hospital here, but in a different wing, thank goodness."

At her last sentence, I moved. As Phillipa met my eyes, she said goodbye and hung up. Coming to me, her hand hovered over mine. "God, Vic, you've given us a scare."

I licked my lips. They were as dry as my throat. Taking in the hospital surroundings, I had a strange feeling of déjà vu. I whispered, "Sorry. I'm sorry."

"Here, take a sip of water. Don't sit up."

I sucked on the straw of a mug she held for me. Between sips, I asked hoarsely, "Was that Hunter?"

"Yes. I want you to have a lawyer."

Not a bad thing. I couldn't remember what the state's home invasion law was. "Is Deacon Hayes throwing a fit, ready to arrest Rowans again?"

"Nothing we can't handle." Moving a book off the chair, my sister sat down beside me. I could tell she wanted to ask me what happened, but Rowans were great at ignoring the elephant in the room. It would be easier if I told her. "He wanted the book. Mother's blackmail book."

As she grimaced, the lines on either side of her mouth grew more pronounced. Looking down to where my battered hand rested against the white sheets, she said, "Deacon hinted that the guy who attacked you—Kirk Wagner—could be wanted for other crimes. Other girls. Reed told me Wagner has a rap sheet for peeping Tom stuff and burglary."

Why wasn't I feeling the aftereffects of what had happened? Why wasn't I scared? Or upset? Instead, my emotions were flat. Did that IV have drugs in it? If it did, they were mighty good ones.

"He didn't seem inexperienced," I said. There had been no hesitation when he'd taken me with that blitz attack at the door.

"But he didn't—?"

"No."

She sighed. "You must have been so scared."

"I was."

We sat there in silence. Neither of us wanted to talk more about my experience. Not meeting my eyes, my big sister said, "You should leave Grimsby."

"I will. But not yet." I coughed, and Phillipa helped me raise my bed before giving me more water.

"Really, Vic, don't be so stubborn. Please, go home. You'll be safe there."

"And leave you and Liam? Like I did before? No. It's one for all, all for one." That got a laugh. She may have been older than Liam and me, but she still remembered some of our childhood games. I told her, "We face this together."

"Okay, Vic. But we do it with support. I've told Mrs. Crackenberry to spread it around that Mother's book was destroyed in the

Rosemary Thyme fire. I don't want anyone thinking we know names or have any intention of carrying on with Mother's business."

"Good idea."

Conversation stalled. I said hesitantly, "It's good that Hunter agreed to come down."

"Yes."

With no sixth sense of her emotions, I was operating blind. I couldn't feel the best thing to say. Exhausted, my side hurt, so I asked bluntly, "Do you like him?"

"I do. But Hunter was one of your boyfriends, Vic. I won't poach."

I gave a weak chuckle. "Is that what he told you?"

"No. But it's obvious you two have a history."

I thought about that history.

"Do you know what the worst part of being an empath is?" Before my sister could answer, I told her, "When you feel everyone else's emotions, you doubt what you truly want. Their desires get muddled with yours. Sometimes you wonder what's yours and what's the other guy's. Do you actually like someone, or only feel like it because he wants you to?"

I couldn't take a deep breath. My side hurt too much.

"Hunter and I had a very brief, one-night stand that fractured a budding friendship. Not that I had ran from something promising, but that I avoided a natural disaster."

I took another sip of water. All this talking was straining my throat.

"How could you not like him, Vic? He's successful, confident, and sexy. Perfect in every way."

"He is all that, Pip, but I don't like notoriety, and Hunter's entire world is about being in a fishbowl. He feeds off the excitement of being the showman. Being on display. That life would kill me."

I was growing tired, but I wanted her to know my thoughts.

"He's far more your type. Go-getter, overachiever. Best of all, unlike your other two husbands, Hunter likes strong, confident women. He wants a woman as a partner, not a doormat."

I yawned. It was hard to keep my eyes open.

"You look horrible, Vic." Phillipa took the water mug from my limp hands and readjusted my blanket. "Go back to sleep." So I did.

It was my third day in the hospital, and I was feeling more alert. I had bandages on my wrists and some of my fingers were taped. My nose had a minor fracture, so I spent the day lying in bed with an icepack over half of my face.

The knife had missed anything vital. Where the wound had been stitched, it still felt squishy. That wasn't a medical term, but it described how yucky it felt when I tried to move.

My brother was filling me in on what Reed had told them about my attacker.

"If you'd ask me to read the rock, I could have told you that the energy behind it was a serious threat. Why didn't you let me touch it?"

"I thought it was a kid's prank. I didn't know it was Kirk Wagner creeping around the house."

Liam was back to sunglasses and gloves. With his arms crossed, his fingers tucked into his elbows, he said, "I could have helped, but instead, you treated me like I'm still a kid, Vic. Stop it."

"I'm sorry."

"He should have attacked me. I was the one who helped Mother."

"I don't think you're his type, Liam."

"Was that supposed to be a joke? If so, it was lame."

Since I was losing the discussion, I switched subjects. "Phillipa said she talked to you about my idea. About the business loan that isn't a loan. Have you talked with Nell yet about it?"

"I was going to but haven't had the time." To anyone who wasn't Liam's sibling, he would have sounded irritated. But he was only speaking the truth, so I didn't get mad.

"Go see her today," I urged. "I'd like to turn that money into something good."

"Helping Nell won't prevent another attack," he warned.

"I know who started the fire. That person won't do anything more. And this creeper? I hear he's a vegetable now." Liam's eyebrows rose over the top of his eyeglasses. I said lamely, "I overheard Pip telling Hunter."

Liam, ever pragmatic, said, "Not that he didn't deserve that, or worse. I found him in Mother's ledger listed as a molester."

Thankfully, this time in the hospital, I didn't have a roommate who might have heard Liam's slip.

"Jolly. Well, I don't feel generous enough to return any of his blackmail payments." I didn't want to talk anymore about Kirk Wagner. Each time I thought of him, my mind went to dark places.

I wanted to talk about something fun and happy.

"I think you should ask Nell out for a date."

Whatever I had done to Kirk Wagner had drained my empathic batteries, and I couldn't feel my own emotions, let alone anyone else's. Between Liam's beard, glasses, and hat, his expression was well-shielded.

He replied, "She can do better."

I knew the subtext of what he was saying. "You and Pip are still buying into Mother's script. That we're all worthless and unworthy. You might be happy with Nell if you gave it a chance."

"I might be happy. But would she? I don't think she deserves to be tied to a Rowan and all of our baggage. It's not like any of us are normal."

"I think it's time we set aside the idea that we're all crazy mutants not worthy of love."

"That's brave talk, sis, but have you spoken to Reed since all of this happened?" My expression must have answered him. "I thought not. He's been sleeping in chairs and eating vending machine food, waiting to hear news of you. You could throw the guy a bone."

"Uh. Oh. I didn't know that," I said weakly.

His eyebrows climbed again.

"Before you arrange my love life, sort out your own."

Chapter Twenty-Seven

My interview with Chief Hayes was a crowded event. I should have sold tickets.

Hunter Garrick stood next to my bed, Phillipa at his side. They made a good-looking couple—a far better match than we would have made. Hunter had met me earlier and given me advice ahead of the meeting.

Liam stood in the corner, as far from touching anyone or anything as he could manage. Still, he had a clear view of me. He gave me a hand sign showing me support in a time of trouble. He also thought I should cut and run back to the city. Considering the state I was in, there would be no running today.

It was the first time I had seen Reed since the ambulance ride. He was standing next to his father. Both men were making a point of fixing their attention exclusively upon Chief Hayes.

I still didn't like the new police chief, but he had a job to do.

"After putting away the groceries, I must have forgotten to turn on the alarm when I left. I realized that when I entered. He grabbed me at the door, inside the house."

Hayes grunted. "What next?"

"He tied my hands and forced me upstairs. He had a knife."

My pause was too long. Deacon Hayes asked, "And after that?"

"I must have blacked out. I don't remember much more until Reed and his father arrived."

Mr. Easton came to my defense, surprising me. "Look, Deacon, the girl is the victim here. This is a simple case of someone breaking in and assaulting the poor kid. She's lucky to be alive."

The police chief shrugged. "She could have invited him over. A bit of fun and games that went wrong."

Reed said in that deadly, quiet tone he had, "It was a break-in and assault, no doubt about that."

Hayes said with a slight sneer, "Out of all the houses in town, Kirk Wagner picks the Rowan house? What a coincidence."

Hunter didn't want me to say anything, but Hayes irritated me. "I think he was watching the house. Someone threw a rock through the front window the first night I was there. Ask Phillipa. We had to get someone to replace the glass."

Phillipa nodded in agreement.

"Could be." Hayes wasn't buying it.

I wished I could have read him, but my talent right now was about as bright as a dead bulb. Any time I reached to use it, the knife wound seeped blood through its bandage. It was hard being deaf to people, and it made me wonder how normal people maintained relationships.

"Do you know how he got in the house?" Reed asked.

"I came by at lunch and forgot to turn the alarm back on. I think."

Hayes mouth made a sour grimace and said reluctantly, "The company shows the alarm was on but Kirk used an override code to get in. He works for the people your mother used."

It was some small comfort that I hadn't forgotten the alarm after all.

Mr. Easton said, "Why, Wagner was probably cutting alarms to enter homes. Didn't you tell me her nursing home was having trouble with their alarms?"

Hayes looked irritated by his old boss's remark. He didn't want to discuss how my mother had died.

"The manager wasn't happy because the alarms kept going off in the middle of the morning, scaring patients. Kirk Wagner was the tech the company sent out to discuss the problem with me. He blamed electrical surges."

So Kirk Wagner was on the spot where Rachel was recovering from surgery. *Hm. Not suspicious at all, I'm sure.*

"The nursing facility has security cameras everywhere. Rachel Rowan's last visit was by a nurse for the nightly check-in. That was hours before she died, and no one saw him entering. Her death was natural."

I played my last card. "Kirk Wagner said he hated my mother."

She had plenty of enemies, even without blackmailing half the town.

Hayes' dark eyes brightened. "What did he say about Rachel Rowan?"

"Just that he hated her. Had some grudge against her."

"Did he mention your mother's associate, Patty Maxwell? Make any reference to the fire at your mother's business?"

"No. I blacked out. Remember?" I was getting tired, and the room was stuffy. I reclined back on the pillow. I hoped I looked pathetic with the two fading black eyes that my broken nose had caused.

Hunter said sternly, "I think my client has supplied you with enough information."

Hayes shifted his weight, edging towards the door. "We're still in the early stages of the investigation, but when we searched Wagner's apartment, we found some interesting evidence that might connect him with Patty Maxwell."

At our eager faces, Hayes said, "I'm not saying anything more," and left.

Reed met my eyes for the first time. "Vic is tired. It's time for us to let her rest."

No denying, I was happy to see everyone leave.

Hunter told me he would discuss our next legal move with Phillipa. I hoped Pip had gotten over her reluctance to pursue him. They looked good together.

Liam didn't even wave goodbye. I hoped he was off to see Nell.

Reed said something to his dad, showing they were at least back on terms that involved speaking in normal voices. When the door closed, it left me with Reed, who clearly wanted a talk.

I leaned back in bed and grabbed my ice-pack. It was a handy device to hide behind. I waited, but Reed said nothing. He was the type who didn't feel the pressure of silence, but I couldn't stand it.

Right before I was about to open my mouth, he asked, "Can I touch you?"

My bottom lip trembled. "Yes."

He leaned over and kissed my clammy forehead. I pulled the ice pack off and stared up at his concerned blue eyes.

"It was scary."

He knelt beside my bed, his hand sliding under my wounded one, cupping it lightly. "It must have been."

"You weren't there," I said accusingly.

"I should have been there," he agreed.

My lip trembled harder. "I'm a monster."

"No, you aren't."

"I heard Phillipa say on the phone that he was catatonic. You told her that. You don't know, but I did that. I made him a zombie by ripping away all his emotions."

Reed didn't seem as surprised as I'd thought he might be by my revelation. "You took all of his hate into yourself. I saw it on your face when we came into the room."

I couldn't help myself. "How did I look?"

"With a bloody face, a broken nose, two black eyes swelling shut, and your shirt soaked red? Not so good."

"I didn't want you to touch me."

"The knife rather clued me in on that."

"I was afraid of giving Wagner to you." Well, the part that was Vic had thought that, but mostly I had only felt like killing whoever was close.

Reed's forefinger tapped his cheek in thought. "You tried that once before, didn't you? That day I was visiting your house when you got mad at me."

"How do you know that?"

"I felt something, faintly. Like hearing the horn of a train late at night, far away. Or the brush of a breeze against your cheek right before the wind dies. It faded away. Your face looked utterly crestfallen; you expected something to happen, and it didn't."

"I can take people's emotions—remove them."

He nodded. "I knew that. You've said some things."

I tried to think back on all that I had said around Reed, but it was too hard.

"I used to do it to Liam when Mother attacked him. But with my brother, I only took a little. Or I tried to. I was a kid, but now I wonder if I took too much and that's why Liam is how he is. Because of me—"

"That's between you and Liam. Don't confuse an act of sacrifice to save your brother in the situation with Kirk Wagner. One was done for love and the other for survival."

I couldn't see for a moment because my eyes had tear bubbles. I blinked, and they slid down the side of my face into my hair.

Reed kept talking. "What Hayes didn't tell you is that Kirk Wagner is shaping up to be a suspect in half a dozen sexual assaults and rapes. A few here in Grimsby, but also over in the neighboring county, at the college. He was a violent man, Vic. He wouldn't have let you go unharmed."

It's hard to sniff with a hairline fracture in your nose. I fumbled for a tissue from the box at the side of my table. Reed handed me one.

"I can't undo what I did," I said to him, blinking rapidly to clear my vision. "He'll be like that forever. A vegetable. I'm a monster."

Reed gave me a look that wasn't seeing a monster. I gulped.

"I was once on a raid. It was at an old, abandoned warehouse. A warren filled with human rats. My team thought we'd cleared the area and found everyone."

He broke eye contact, looking first out the hospital window and then down at his hands. "I was the last one out. I turned a corner, and there was a gun in my face."

Reed grimaced, flattening the line of his mouth, his nostrils tightening. "I killed him before he killed me."

"You had to!" I cried, rushing to defend him.

"Still, he was a human being. Like Kirk Wagner. A man who had a family. Maybe some that loved him."

I fumbled for his hand and covered it with mine. He continued, "I'll never forget what I did or wonder if I could have done something differently. Do I regret it? Yes. But it happened, and I will deal with it."

"But I'm not a cop," I protested.

"He attacked you, Vic. You used the weapon you had at hand."

I lay there, thinking over what he said. He made me feel a little better, but I knew the guilt would stay with me forever.

"I acted like my mother. Ruthless."

He chuckled. "In no way are you like your mother, Vic. Do you think Rachel would give a damn about Kirk Wagner's mental state?"

I stared at the ceiling, hoping his words were true, but I didn't want to think about it any longer.

I told Reed in a voice that was teasing, so he wouldn't mistake my words, "You should have been there. You owe me."

"You're right, I do. What can I do?" He leaned closer, his eyes growing bright. Oh, I bet he had thoughts about how he could do that—but they weren't the same as mine.

"Do you have any male cousins? Some big, hulking brutes that have a lot of muscles?"

Chapter Twenty-Eight

Some logistics needed to be put in place—such as getting out of the hospital. That took a day longer than I had hoped, so I had to delay my plan.

Phillipa invited me to stay at her place, but Reed told her I would be with him at his hotel. She seemed relieved at that, which made me wonder if Hunter Garrick was still in town.

I didn't protest. I wasn't ready to return to the house, and I was too sick to go back to the city and be alone. Between nightmares replaying the attack and recovering from the hospital's disruptive sleep routine, I was a mess.

It was easier to let someone else decide.

Reed brought my bag from the house to the hospital so I could pick fresh clothes. On exiting, they gave me a sealed bag filled with the top and jeans I had worn that day. I stared down at them dumbly. The pattern of blood splatter on my shirt was visible through the plastic. I handed it to Reed.

"I don't want it."

In the parking lot, he threw it into the trunk of his car before helping me get into the front passenger seat. I closed my eyes the entire trip, sinking into an abyss of tiredness.

"We're here."

I blinked several times, bringing the hotel into focus. It was a modern affair. A new place to serve the tourists.

Reed's room had two queen beds, and he gave me one, the furthest from the door. I gave a passing glance to the weapon resting in a holster on his nightstand. I got the message: he'd be between me and anything that came through the door.

"You're staying? Right?" Why was my voice trembling?

Reed nodded.

"Get some rest. I've got work I can do here."

I woke up a few times and immediately sought him out. Mostly he was on his laptop, once on a phone call that sounded like he was talking to his boss, and another time on the bed, photographs laid out in a pattern across the bedspread.

That night I woke up again, still unsettled from the hospital routine. There was noise, laughter from a group passing in the hall outside the room. Once I thought I heard a baby crying, but it was only me.

Feeling my restlessness, Reed would speak quietly from his bed. "It's okay, Vic. I'm here."

My shaking quieted, and I fell back into a dreamless sleep.

In the morning, Reed brought me a blueberry muffin and some orange juice from the hotel's breakfast buffet. He asked, "You sure you don't want more?"

"No, this is enough."

I sat in bed and watched him devour three slices of bacon, two waffles, and a yogurt. If this was his daily fare, I don't know how the guy didn't gain weight.

"When do you need my cousins with muscles?" he asked.

"I called a service when I was in the hospital and they are delivering a trash container to the house tomorrow. I want to empty the house. The sooner, the better."

Around another forkful of pancakes dripping syrup, he asked, "Can you do that? Phillipa said your mother's will was in probate."

"Pip is the executor appointed by the probate court."

"Is that why we need my cousins?"

I looked out the window and saw a cloudy sky, misty with rain. I told Reed, "Be sure they bring their sledgehammers."

The next day, I was up early brushing my teeth. I had taken sponge baths in the hospital and upon leaving was told I could shower with the dressing. But I didn't trust it to stay on, and I certainly was in no shape to see underneath it. I opted to take another quick sponge bath, avoiding the battered face in the mirror.

When Reed and I pulled up to the house, it surprised me to see a small crowd. There were three of Reed's cousins—corn-fed farm boys who probably lifted cows for exercise—and Greg Easton, Lottie, and Nell. Phillipa and Liam walked straight over to the car and helped me get out.

"Are you ready to do this?" asked my big sister.

"What she means is, you look like crap on a cracker," said Liam.

"I want it done." I lifted my chin, setting my jaw. Nothing was going to stop me.

Sensing my resolve, Phillipa and Liam fell in on either side of me as I walked up to the porch. I stopped at the steps and handed Reed the key.

"Can I put you in charge? I want the furniture in the living and dining rooms on the lawn. Liam won't go in, but Phillipa can help tell you what I want."

Reed nodded and, taking the key, took the porch steps two at a time. He greeted his cousins, and with his dad, they all entered the house.

Lottie leaned over the porch railing. "You should sit down, dear. You look peaky."

I trudged up the stairs, my side aching with each step. There was a lounger on the porch. I dropped into it. After tucking a pillow behind my head, Lottie stepped away, going around the corner of the house towards the backyard.

With her gone, Liam asked, "What's the plan?"

My talent was slowly returning. I could feel the sour tang of Phillipa's nervousness, and Liam braced against pain.

"I don't want to sell anything that has a taint. But I have an idea of how we can clean the furniture of any emotional residue that might mess with its future owners."

Liam asked curiously, "What idea?"

"You'll touch the item and read it with your talent. When you're holding all of its past, let me know. I'll lift the emotional part of it from you and pass it to Reed. He'll make it all disappear."

"Reed?" asked Phillipa, surprised.

"When Wagner attacked me," I swallowed hard before pushing through, "I grabbed his emotions. When Reed showed up, I gave it all to him, and he threw it away. I don't know how Reed does it, but he's a black hole. A sink. Anything I give him vanishes."

The guys were carrying out the sofa, my mother's prized possession. If there was a haunted piece of furniture in the house, it was surely that. Seeing it, Liam nervously licked his lips. I didn't ask what memories it aroused in him, but I could feel his fear from three feet away.

"Reed!" I shouted. "You're needed."

He appeared quickly. I had explained my plan to him on the ride over. He helped me up from the lounger, and we all went down to the front lawn. We circled the couch as if it was a tiger. I reached over and took Reed's hand and placed the other one on my brother's shoulder.

"You want me to touch it?" I felt Liam's reluctance.

"When you're ready. Don't worry. You'll see." I said it confidently, even though I didn't know if my idea would actually work.

He pulled off a glove and tucked it into a pocket, then reached out a trembling hand, using the tips of his fingers to brush the polished wood.

When he made contact, I didn't receive the information he did from his talent, but felt the ghost of old feelings stuck to the couch. I didn't bother examining them before whipping them away to Reed.

Like scoring a basketball through the hoop, Reed sank the mass of energy into oblivion. We three had hit a home run with all bases loaded.

Liam's mouth dropped open in surprise. He took off his sunglasses, revealing his baby-blue eyes.

"What—what just happened?"

"Can you feel anything from it?" I asked him, pointing to our mother's couch.

Liam removed his other glove and swept both bare hands over the back of the couch, the seat cushions, and finally the pillows.

"No. It's blank. I can feel the history of it, but no emotions from it. No fear or anger."

I gave my brother a wide smile. "We're going to clean this house from the cellar to the attic."

However, even this little activity had left me shaking. The spirit was willing, but the flesh needed rest. Reed's arm came up under my elbow and helped me back to the lounger.

Phillipa came out the front door, followed by more guys carrying furniture. I waved her over to me.

"I'm cleaning house. Is my sister, the executor, okay with that?"

"We aren't out of probate yet," cautioned my sister.

"I'm not chucking anything valuable, but Mother bought only junk for our bedrooms because she knew no one outside the house would ever see it. I want to give you a chance to pull anything you want, but I won't stop cleaning."

"I guess we could donate it," said Phillipa doubtfully.

"No. I want the satisfaction of seeing it in the dumpster. You okay with that?" She nodded. "Take some boys upstairs and take what you want from your bedroom and the guest room. But don't go into our parents' rooms. That's not for today."

I closed my eyes and leaned my head against the chair's back.

"Do you want me to do your room?" It was Reed. He had been standing there during my discussion with my sister. Without opening my eyes, I told him, "There's a lamp on my desk I'd like. But the rest? Into the dumpster."

Reed left, and Liam took a chair beside mine. I told him, "Your room has a lot of stuff in it. I was thinking of having them box it up and bring it out here. No need for you to go inside."

"You don't think that's a cowardly move on my part? You sent in Phillipa."

"You don't see me going in there, do you?"

A female voice said behind me, "Would you like a coffee or lemonade?" I opened one eye and saw Nell, her question directed at us both.

Liam explained her presence. "Nell and Lottie set up a table in the back with food."

"Oh. Does that mean pastries somewhere?"

Reed found me juggling a mug of coffee and a cinnamon roll when he returned with my lamp. "This one?"

"Yes." It took a moment for the three of us to clean it. I set it beside my chair. I would give it a new home with new memories.

"What's that?" I used my sweet bun to point at a notebook Reed held under his arm.

"Oh, this? I found it in the drawer of your desk. There was a stack of them."

I licked the sugar from my fingers and took the spiral pad. I flipped open the cover and gave a snorting laugh. They were my old drawings—sketches of people I knew, or models from magazines. Hand and eye studies I had done back in high school.

"I particularly like the one near the back," said Reed, looking over my shoulder. Of course, it would be a sketch of a teen Reed, all slim and gangly, his young face softer than the man next to me.

"Your ego, sir," I said. "Has anyone mentioned it before?"

I flipped through more drawing pads. It was a miracle my mother hadn't disposed of them, but maybe she'd sensed a bit of magic in the pencil lines and was wary of what they would do to her.

Behind Reed, I saw my furniture being pitched into the dumpster. I smiled with satisfaction.

"Reed, could you go to Liam's bedroom, just have the guys put everything that isn't furniture into boxes, and bring it down to us? The furniture goes into the dumpster."

The afternoon flew by. Liam was happy going through his things, finding old treasures he had forgotten. It seemed Mother hadn't touched his things; she'd probably seen his collection as worthless junk.

Phillipa soon joined us. She held only one box, which contained a few porcelain ballerinas. I had forgotten that Pip had collected figurines for a while.

"You were right, Vic. There isn't anything else I wanted."

"So the boys can do your room?"

She nodded.

Phillipa's bedroom soon joined mine and Liam's in the big dumpster.

Afterward, it was time to break for a late lunch. Nell supplied the crew with homemade sandwiches, cans of soda or beer, and an assortment of cookies and brownies.

They left me alone, and I started nodding off when Greg Easton walked over to me. He cleared his throat. Looking up, I had to shield my eyes from the sun to make out his face. He was uncomfortable, both inside and out.

"Mr. Easton," I greeted him cautiously.

"When we were clearing your bedroom, we found this under a

loose floorboard." He was holding out a rectangular tin. I sat up, reaching my hand out to receive it. "Oh my, I completely forgot this. Thank you, Mr. Easton."

I set my childhood treasure box next to my lamp. I'd go through its contents when I could be private.

Reed's dad cleared his throat again. He was going to apologize. But a man had his pride, and I figured Reed had already chopped him down to firewood, so I thought I'd help him save some face.

"I told Reed some information about the death of my father. I feel you should be the one to get the credit for solving the case. What do you think?"

Easton became excited at my question, but he surprised me by not jumping at my suggestion. He scratched the back of his sunburned neck and looked over to where Reed was standing in a huddle with his cousins as they ate sandwiches.

"I don't know if that would be right," he said.

"After all the time you've invested in the mystery of Victor's death, and you mean to tell me you don't want the truth?"

"If you want to tell me."

Boy, Reed must have really sliced and diced his dad.

"I'm not up for it today or even tomorrow, but I would like you to be there when we open Victor's room. Liam doesn't think anyone has entered it since the police did, way back in the day. It seems my mother acted like the room didn't exist."

Easton's emotions jumped all over me like a happy puppy.

"Would Monday, after the weekend, work for you?"

He nodded, trying to conceal his eagerness.

I wondered who would be most angry with my decision—Hunter, or Reed?

Chapter Twenty-Nine

The second day of cleaning the house brought a local audience. The neighbors who yesterday had watched from windows now braved the sidewalk. I overheard them ask Mr. Easton what was happening.

"Spring cleaning," he told them.

Some asked him if the house was to be sold. He admitted he didn't know our plans, but didn't think any of us would live there long term. Damn right.

Some time before mid-morning, they discovered an old croquet set in the basement. They set the hoops up, and played a few rounds over lunch. The corn-fed cousins could shoot a deer at twenty paces, but they couldn't hit a wooden ball through a hoop.

Nell completed the course first and announced to everyone, "Poison!" before savagely eliminating her opponents one by one.

I rather liked this ruthless side she displayed. It probably made her an excellent businesswoman.

She eliminated Liam's ball last. True love.

. . .

We went through more of the furniture, separating Mother's antiques from Victor's mid-century pieces. By late afternoon, furniture littered the lawn.

Around three, Betz Zachary arrived in her bright red sports car. I came down from my throne on the porch to meet her on the sidewalk.

She was a black woman in her mid-thirties, a few inches shorter than me, with a round face boasting apple cheeks and full lips. Her curvy bosom and hips were part of her fortune. It made some in the antique business lose their head; they paid too much as a buyer, or sold too low. Her cunning had made her an underground legend in the art dealership world.

"I see you've been busy." Her dark eyes scanned the front lawn. Knowing her, she was probably running a calculator in her head on each piece.

"Any trouble finding the place?" I asked.

"No trouble at all."

I spread my arm behind me. "You want to prowl?"

"I certainly do."

While Betz worked for one of the better auction houses, she also had private clients—people who liked the idea of snatching a deal no one else had seen. She pulled out an expensive phone from a designer purse and started taking photos.

"Hm," she said. Her face might be inscrutable to others, but I could tell from the creamy-eggnog-with-rum taste of her emotions she was pleased. Her fingers stroked the wood of my mother's display cabinet. "Nice display of marquetry in the panels."

"I thought so," I said humbly.

"Your collector liked French pieces."

"I guess she did."

"Are you selling the lot?"

"Once the estate is out of probate, yes. For now, I'd like you to examine the pieces and give us some estimates of their worth. Of course, we'll pay your fee for the evaluations. When probate completes, I'll be sure you get the first pick of whatever you wish."

A police car pulling up behind Betz's interrupted our conversation. Chief Hayes got out of the driver's side and Ms. Massey out of the other side. I guessed a neighbor had complained about something. Grimsby was a small town, after all.

"Destroying evidence?" asked Hayes, as he came over to where we stood. He was in uniform. Despite it being a Sunday, our attorney wore another tailored pantsuit and jacket.

I gave Hayes a syrupy smile. "Evidence of what exactly?"

Looking between us, Ms. Massey warned me, "You realize the estate is still in probate? You can't sell anything."

Betz raised one carefully groomed eyebrow at me. Even without empath abilities, you could see her interest in the drama. I reassured them all. "We aren't selling. Yet. Betz Zachary is here to evaluate the estate as a professional appraiser."

"So what about that stuff in the dumpster?" Hayes pointed to the trash container parked in the driveway.

I cocked my head. "Why don't you dive in there and find out, Hayes?"

"From what I can tell," said Betz, narrowing her gaze towards the garbage container, "it looks like garage sale leftovers. The junk that folks won't buy for a dollar, and the owner has to mark free to get it out of their driveway."

"Maybe it would make good firewood," I suggested.

Ms. Massey turned to the chief of police and said, "Look, Deacon, I don't appreciate you dragging me over here on my day off. If this woman is evaluating the estate, the executor may do that." She asked me, "Is your sister here?"

"In the backyard. She's playing croquet or eating a brownie. Feel free to go find out which."

Ms. Massey gave us all a curt nod. Without losing her balance on those stilettos, she glided up the drive.

"Go ahead, Betz," I encouraged her. "Take plenty of pictures, and if you need anything moved to see the bottom or want to pull out drawers, ask one of the guys to help you." I pointed up to the porch where my helpers were.

Taking in the eye-candy, she said, "Hm-mm. You know, I might need all three of those boys. After all, I wouldn't want to break a nail."

She went up to Reed's cousins, who were lounging on the porch. They were all wearing tight T-shirts over their bodybuilder chests and faded blue jeans over lean hips. They might have been a bit sweaty as well.

From somewhere else, Reed appeared with his dad.

"Hey, Deacon," said Mr. Easton. While the two men shook hands, I knew that even if Deacon pretended he was glad to see the former police chief, he wasn't happy with Easton's appearance.

"I was telling Ms. Rowan here that it would be best not to disturb the crime scene until we complete the investigation."

"I haven't done one thing to my mother's bedroom. Cross my heart and hope to die." At my words, the intensity of Deacon's dislike of me launched sky high, like a bottle rocket. He asked in a frosty voice, "So what are you doing?"

"My siblings may go through their bedrooms and dispose of their personal possessions. But the house is filled with highly collectible furniture. You may remember the Rosemary Thyme fire? Well, that burned up a valuable lot of antiques that were my brother's inheritance. I don't plan on that happening again; these pieces are going to be safely away from Grimsby."

Deacon Hayes switched tactics.

"Do you have a permit for that dumpster?"

"I sure do."

Reed must have sensed how tired I was—or maybe it wasn't a good idea for me to spar with the Grimsby chief of police. He told me, "Vic, I think Liam wanted you to see something in the garage. Let me show Deacon around."

Sure, whatever, it was only my life. I turned my back on them and went to talk to Betz, who was finally examining furniture and not beefcake. I asked her, "What do you think?"

"Lovely items. Kept in excellent condition mostly."

"But is there a market for it?"

"There's a market for anything if you know how to find the buyer. Are you thinking an auction or wanting a private buyer?"

Her gaze went past me to take in Hayes talking with Easton and Reed. "What's going on, Vic? This isn't stolen, is it?"

"No," I reassured her, though I didn't tell her it might have been bought with blood money. "My mother died. The house and the contents will come to me once probate completes. The cop over there resents my family. It's an old story... all about small-town politics."

Accepting my explanation, Betz got down to telling me the amount she'd charge for an appraisal and the percentage she would want for any sales she arranged to private buyers. Or I could choose to go through her employer's auction house.

I told her, "What I'd like to do is have you take anything you want to your warehouse. My mother's antique business in town had a fire, destroying some valuable stuff. I don't want to risk anything like that happening here."

"A fire? And your face looks like a punching bag. What are you getting me into?"

"Nothing that would harm you or your boss. I promise you."

When Betz left, I made my way to the backyard and collapsed in a recliner. Even the littlest things were taking the stuffing out of me. I closed my eyes against the sunshine.

In a fog, I heard Rebecca Massey speaking with my sister.

"Yes, I'm sorry about that. Deacon is a distant relation, so when he heard about your house cleaning, he rushed over and dragged me with him."

Phillipa asked what I had been wondering. "But how did he know you were our lawyer?"

"I think the entire town knew I was your mother's lawyer."

"Did you know my mother personally? I was curious why she picked you."

"Oh no. We didn't have a personal relationship, even though Rachel often invited me to the house. But as I explained to her, I keep my personal life separate from my business one. We met at one of the Chamber of Commerce meetings."

Hm. I needed to check and see if Rebecca Massey's name was in Mother's little book. Was Massey a victim, accomplice, or provider of information?

"How is the probate going?" my sister asked, and the conversation became technical. The court details were boring, and I drifted away.

"If you need a nap, let me take you back to the hotel." Reed's voice made me open my eyes. He was back-lit, so that I couldn't see his face. I put my hand up to shade mine and pulled myself to a sitting position.

"I'm a little tired, but I would like to get things wrapped up today, if that's possible. Betz will schedule a truck to come to pick up the antiques, but until then, I need the ones we've cleaned back in the house. Can your cousins manage that?"

"No problem. I'll tell the guys. But have you eaten anything?"

I hadn't. Reed went to fetch me food. He had been hovering around me since Wagner's attack; he always seemed to know where I was. The only time he left me alone was when I was in a group like now. While it comforted me, it also made me nervous. He was back to wearing his gun all the time. Was he expecting something else to happen? Why the guard duty?

I squinted and looked up at the second story of the house. From the backyard you could see the drapes over the window to Victor's bedroom. I had already told Hunter my plan on telling

Greg Easton the truth. As my lawyer, he had insisted on being present.

I had yet to tell Reed.

Chapter Thirty

Reed didn't take the news well. There was some shouting that became a punishing 'silent treatment.' Since I had waited to tell him until we pulled up to the house Monday morning, the entire scene didn't last too long.

"I don't think you should do it so soon after—"

I knew what he meant. I hadn't entered the house since the attack.

"I don't plan on living in Grimsby. I will sell or destroy the house so this needs to be done."

This last exchange happened when we were standing outside, in full view of Mr. Easton and Hunter Garrick standing on the porch. When we reached the steps, Hunter said loudly, "My client is providing this information voluntarily to assist the police."

"Mr. Easton isn't with the police or any law enforcement, as far as I know," I said.

Reed's father nodded in agreement.

"I'm purely here as John Q. Citizen."

I let Reed use my key to enter the house while I struggled to maintain the emotional numbness to block thinking of Kirk

Wagner's attack. It wasn't working out well; my hands were trembling.

Everyone felt the strain. Hunter was almost as tense as I was. He was in lawyer mode, ready to defend or attack. Meanwhile, Greg Easton was quivering like a bird dog before the hunt.

I said, "Before we go up, I'd like to sit in the dining room and discuss some things."

At my suggestion, we took seats opposite each other at the dining table. The furniture was back in place, awaiting Betz and her moving crew. The dishes that Reed had removed from the kitchen so long ago, Philippa had packed away.

The Eastons took one side, and Hunter and I faced them on the opposite side of the table. I wished Reed were beside me so I could touch him and give him my fear, but no—I needed to deal with this.

Hunter put a notebook on the table along with his phone, which he set to record. He started by identifying who was in the room, the date, what our purpose was, and that he was representing me.

I cleared my throat. My hands rested on the table's polished wooden surface as I found a spot to stare at between Greg's and Reed's shoulders.

"At the time of my father's death, Victor Rowan, I made a statement that I was not at home. I said I was already at college and knew nothing about his death. That was not true. I was here in the house and witnessed the shooting."

Greg Easton didn't exactly gasp, but the intensity of his interest had the smoky heat of a bonfire. I swallowed before beginning again.

"In the months leading up to Victor's death, he assisted me in applying to several universities. I did this without my mother's knowledge. We both knew she would disapprove of me leaving Grimsby and would try to stop me."

Hunter had a pen in hand and a pad opened, but he made no notes. Yet.

"Why would she not approve?" Mr. Easton's question startled me out of my self-reflection, disrupting the rote phrases I had practiced repeatedly in my head.

"My mother, Rachel Rowan, was upset when my sister Phillipa left Grimsby. Phillipa's first husband, Jack Ingram, attended law school out-of-state before they returned to Grimsby. Everyone in my family knew my mother was very upset about her being gone. Mother said she would never let me or Liam get away. You can confirm this with my siblings."

There was a pause, and when Mr. Easton asked nothing else, I continued my narrative.

"While I waited to hear if I would be accepted, I made sure I was the one who collected the mail. I didn't want my mother discovering any letters from the colleges I was applying to."

My mind was going back, back to a day I didn't want to remember but could never forget.

"The day my father died, I found an acceptance letter in the mail. I was standing at the curb, reading it, when an ice-cream truck passed me. Liam was with me and asked if we could get some. I gave him some money, and while he ran after the truck, I went inside the house."

My pause was long enough that Reed got up to get me a glass of water from the kitchen. As he handed it to me, he gave me a quick touch on my shoulder. With my nervousness eased, he returned to his seat.

"To my knowledge, no one was in the house except myself and my father. Liam was chasing after an ice-cream truck, Phillipa was four states away, and my mother was at a committee meeting. I believe it was the Friends of the Library, but—"

"It was the library group. We verified that," said Mr. Easton.

"Upstairs, my father had a bedroom across from my mother's. Both are at the end of the hall, on the second floor. When I came upstairs, his door was closed, but I heard someone moving inside. I knocked. No one answered, so I opened the door. It was unlocked, you see."

I licked my lips and swallowed. I kept staring at that valley between the shoulders of the men sitting opposite me.

"When I entered, Victor was holding a shotgun. He didn't hunt with it. It was his father's, and he kept it for the memories."

"*His* shotgun?" said Mr. Easton. I ignored his surprise. I had to get it out. Now. Get it out before I couldn't.

"I—well, t-t-the gun went off, killing him."

I heard again the shot, the blast that shook my world.

There was a long pause before Reed asked the first question.

"Did you touch the gun at any point?"

"No."

"Did you touch him when you were in the room?"

"No."

"Didn't you want to check to see if he was still alive?"

My eyes saw only the past. "He wasn't alive."

"Why did your father have the gun out?" Reed's voice was calm, although not particularly sympathetic. Neutral. It was easier for me to hear him speak without showing concern.

"In the years since, I've often wondered. My only guess would be that he planned to kill himself."

"Why would you think that? Perhaps he had it out because he feared an intruder."

I shook my head.

"No one else was in the house. Why would he have a gun out in the middle of the day? No. I think he wanted to die."

"You're doing fine," said Hunter, giving my back a soft pat. I nodded, emitting a shaky breath before continuing.

"You see, the last few months before his death, my parents had been arguing more than usual. It was over nonsense stuff. My mother wanted him to sell his car and buy a new one. When he wouldn't do it, she had a tow truck come and collect it. That was the day before this one."

Greg Easton spoke for the first time.

"If Victor's name was on the title, she wouldn't be able to sell it without his permission." I could feel him wrestling with understanding what I had just told them. He was a surprised-shocked-angry mix, tasting of hot-black-bitter-coffee.

"I can't explain that. Liam remembers the tow truck. He might recall the name of the company. He has a knack for such things. I don't."

Hunter interrupted us. "My client has made her statement. She is not here to do the work of the police and explain how they mistook a suicide for a murder. That's not her job."

Greg Easton bridled at Hunter's words, but I didn't want him to be angry. I wanted Easton willing to listen and believe. I put a hand over Hunter's; his vibration was too much, causing me to remove my hand quickly away.

I said softly, "You can check what I'm saying later."

I selfishly wished Phillipa or Liam were here to support me, but I had kept them both in the dark about this meeting. I had to do this alone. Face up to what happened. And to what I hadn't done.

"I think he was thinking of killing himself. When I opened the door, Victor was removing the gun from his mouth." I swallowed hard, and my lips were salty. "I must have startled him, causing the gun to go off by accident."

I felt a flash of those old emotions from my father right before he shot himself: surprise-deep-sorrow-guilt. His last feelings flooded me again, and I couldn't stop myself. I started crying. I put my hands over my face as a shield, trying to hide Victor's pain and my shame.

"I think this interview is at an end," Hunter stated.

"Wait. We need to know what Vic did afterward."

Oh, Reed, how can you be this way? He held me up even as he made me talk. I ground the heels of my hands into my eye sockets. *Stop crying, Vic. Get this out. Get this done here and now, so you never have to go back. Back to that room and the smell of gunpowder and blood.*

"I fled the room, locking it behind me. I was in a panic when I heard the front door. It was Liam. I told him to come up to my room."

"Did you tell your brother what happened?" asked Reed.

"By the time he got to my room, I had changed shirts. The T-shirt I had been wearing had blood on it. I stuffed it in a laundry bag I had. I didn't tell him about Victor, but I told him I was leaving for college and that there would be a big fight about it. When I suggested he run away with me, Liam refused, but he came to the train station to see me off."

I was back under control again. Thankfully, Hunter had brought some tissues.

"What did you do for money?" asked Mr. Easton.

"When he'd helped me, Victor had set up a bank account for when I would leave. It was in my name only."

"If Liam didn't know, why didn't he return home after you left on the train?" asked Reed.

"I warned him there would be a big blow-up once Mother discovered my escape. That he might not want to be home when that happened."

"No more questions," said Hunter. He reached over and shut off the phone recorder.

I tucked my hands under the table between my knees, hugging them. I was shaking. My secret was out in the open. People other than family now knew my deepest fears. I didn't like it.

Still, I knew Greg Easton didn't believe me. He started arguing with Reed about the crime scene. I paid them little attention.

Hunter leaned over to me. "You did well."

"I want to take them up to the room."

Chapter Thirty-One

The Eastons were still squabbling in the hallway in front of my father's bedroom. I realized this was the way they communicated. Since there wasn't any acid in the bite, I didn't understand it.

Mr. Easton was still insisting I had to be wrong.

"There were signs there was an outsider in the room at the time of Victor's death. The man left a glove and boot-print in blood."

I ignored his disbelief; instead, I kept my eyes on the closed door. The longer we waited, the more I was losing my courage to walk in there. It didn't help that Hunter was also trying to talk me out of it.

"—subjecting yourself to this trauma all over again."

He was right about that. The gun smoke was stinging my nostrils; my T-shirt was still wet with blood.

I said faintly, "I'd like to get this done."

Reed immediately agreed. "I'm sorry, Vic. We're here to do it your way."

My hand was shaking so hard that it took a moment to get the key into the lock. Reed had found the key to it in the kitchen junk drawer on the clean-out.

Reed reached out as if to do it himself, but I waved his hand away. I didn't want my feelings muffled, swept away. I had been doing that for fifteen years. Taking away the pain had only crippled me. Liam was right: it was time to heal.

Maybe he was wrong about Mother keeping the room the same after Victor's death... But that forlorn hope died as the door swung open.

I swayed and became light-headed. Reed didn't touch me, but he came closer, ready if I wanted him.

Festering wounds didn't heal until all the poison was drained away.

I took one step inside and moved away from the entrance so the others could enter. Mr. Easton pointed out things to the other two men, but I couldn't process what he was saying.

My mind spun through the movie reel it had recorded all those years ago. I was standing here. Victor was at the foot of the bed. Maybe he had been sitting, and he'd stood up when I entered? I wasn't sure. My entrance startled him, and he was in motion. The gun exploded, ringing in my ears, the gun-smoke cloud in the air, the blood smelling like steel.

As my first panic passed, I realized the room was a mess, but not precisely in the way I remembered.

Gone were the blood-soaked bedspread and sheets; probably taken by police. On the wall and ceiling was blood splatter, but now it looked more like black mold than blood.

The dresser drawers were open; scattered clothes lay all over the floor. The closet door was ajar. Cardboard storage boxes were upside down. The smashed bedside table lamps lay on the carpet.

"Did the police do this?" I asked in a hollow voice.

All the men turned as one to look at me. "What?" asked Greg.

"The clothes, the stuff all over the floor. The lamps."

"The intruder did it," said Mr. Easton.

I blinked. Intruder? Oh, right—the story Mother had created to explain Victor's death.

"We have a boot imprint in blood. A man's glove. Another man was here when it happened," insisted Reed's dad.

I swayed and had to lean against the wall to stand up. The wound on my side throbbed. In a flash, Reed was at my side.

"You're hyperventilating, Vic. Take slow, deep breaths. Look at me. Slow, deep breaths."

I stared at him, trying to do as he said, but the room was slowly tilting. He moved closer, blocking out my view of the room. "C'mon. You can do it."

"I think I want to leave, please," I said in a tiny voice. Reed tucked his arm under my elbow and steered me into the hall.

"Can you make it down the stairs?"

"Yes."

With Reed's arm around my waist, it was hard not to think about Kirk Wagner dragging me up the stairs last week. The visceral reaction I felt almost made me shove him away. As my stomach heaved, I was thankful it was empty of any breakfast.

"Deep breaths, Vic," Reed reminded me. "We're almost at the door."

As we walked out of the house, a breeze revived me. It was cooler now, with a sprinkle of rain touching my cheeks. I leaned into it.

Reed was holding me lightly, and I could hear the thump-thump of his heart. Yes, I wanted this. But as I sensed the turmoil of my emotions slipping away into his void, I pulled back. Removing my pain wouldn't help me.

He stroked my hair, kissing the top of my head. "You did great back there, Vic, but let me and my dad take it from here. We're the investigators, you know."

I protested, wetting his shirt with my mouth, mumbling against it. "If there was an intruder, maybe he was after the notebook?"

"There wasn't a notebook then, remember? Or a blackmail scheme."

"You're right," I said. I was finding it hard to think.

"C'mon, girl. You need to sit down for a while."

We ended up sitting on Greg Easton's truck tailgate, swinging our legs under us as if we were kids. His arm was around me as I nestled against his side.

"If it isn't too much right now," he said gently, "tell me what you remember about the room that was different."

"Mother must have trashed his room to make it look like a burglary. Victor kept things tidy. He liked everything in its place and was always picking up after us, washing a glass after he'd used it. He'd hate what she did to his room."

"What about the gun? Where did it go?"

"Liam said she did something with Victor's gun. Disposed of it. He'd know, maybe."

"Let me go over the case notes with my dad. You're done with this. We'll get it figured out, don't worry."

I persisted, trying to figure out the puzzle. "But... if your dad thought there was a man at the scene when Victor died, why did he think one of us murdered Victor?"

"He thought Rachel planned it and had someone else commit the crime. An accomplice. Or a lover. It didn't help that your father had a substantial life insurance policy."

Hunter and Mr. Easton exited the house. Hunter must have collected the keys from the dining room table, for he locked the house up before the two made their way down to where we were sitting.

To me, Hunter said, "I'll get this transcribed"—he held up his cell phone—"into a statement. We can go to the state's DA office together, as we agreed."

"I'd like Mr. Easton to come with us. I want him to have the credit for solving the case."

Greg Easton looked down at the ground. He was uncomfortable taking credit for something he didn't believe.

"That is, after he's had time to go over the case files with Reed. They'll have to pull all the puzzle pieces together. Verify the car sale, and talk with Liam and Phillipa."

Before we could discuss anything more, the sprinkle of rain became heavy drops. We said hasty goodbyes and ran to our vehicles.

As Reed drove, I watched the beating swish-swish of the windshield wipers. With my confession done, I felt better, but I wouldn't be able to escape Grimsby completely until we solved my mother's murder.

Afterward, I crashed at Reed's hotel room. I spent much of the next few days sleeping, waking only to stagger to the bathroom or eat a muffin that he put into my hands. My sleep was heavy and without dreams.

Reaction. I was a bear hibernating. But even bears eventually emerge.

When I fully awoke from my waking dream, I realized I smelled. I was rank. I sat up and saw Reed sitting at the desk, crouched over his laptop.

"I'm taking a shower."

He looked up, surprised. It was the first time I had spoken since we had left the house.

The hot water felt good. I shampooed my hair not once, but twice. When the strands were squeaky clean, I finally vanquished all remains of Kirk Wagner. I let the dirty water take him down the drain.

It was past the date I could have removed the bandage. I did that now. Pulling gingerly at the corners, I wrinkled my nose at the smell from the padding. But it was from old drainage; my skin underneath, while red and puckered, was healing.

The problem with hotels is that they have full-length mirrors in too many places. I had lost weight and could feel and see my ribs. The bruising on my face was fading to yellow, and while my nose was still tender to the touch, it looked almost normal.

I cracked open the door and saw my suitcase resting outside. I thanked Reed as I dragged it through. Digging through, I pulled out clean underwear, a bra, a scoop-necked green T-shirt, and a fresh pair of jeans.

There was a tap at the door.

"You want breakfast?"

I sure did. Through the door, over the sound of the hairdryer, I shouted, "Let's go to Vincent's."

Chapter Thirty-Two

It was a weekday and near the end of the breakfast rush. We had to get a tired waitress to clear a table for us.

As I dug into my stack of syrupy blueberry pancakes, I said around a mouthful, "Tell me about what's been happening."

Reed put his coffee cup down.

"Liam's been filling in the blanks. Before she called the police, Rachel hid the gun, a pair of your father's boots, and some old garden gloves. A few weeks later, she duct-taped them in a weighted blanket and dumped it off the railway bridge."

The railway bridge was actually for cars, but it ran parallel to a train bridge that crossed a leg of the Grimsby lake.

I dipped a piece of crunchy bacon into the pool of syrup. "How did Liam know that?"

"Rachel made him sit in the back of the car while she did it. Told him it made him an accomplice."

"Hm. Sounds like her."

The waitress returned. I asked her for a Belgian waffle with strawberries and a side of hash browns. After she left, Reed continued. "On Liam's evidence, my father got the dive school instructor to check it out. He found it yesterday."

"Dive school?" I started on my second glass of orange juice. Food had never tasted so good.

"A new place. Seems the lake is good for bass fishing and diving. I've been looking over the crime scene data with my dad—" Reed stopped as I started pouring ketchup over the hash browns which had just arrived at our table. "Are you sure discussing this won't disturb you?"

"As long as you don't show me photos, I'm fine."

"We think Rachel used a pair of Victor's boots and garden gloves to make it appear someone else had been there. From the committee minutes she attended, it looks like she arrived about a half-hour after it happened."

"I've always wondered why no one reported the gunshot"

"Fourth of July weekend."

Oh, that's right. Anyone hearing it would have thought it was some neighborhood kid with fireworks. My waffle arrived. I asked for more whipped cream. As I cut it up, I asked Reed, "Your dad believes me now?"

"Yes."

"When can we get Victor's case closed?"

"Your lawyer is ready to make an appointment when you are."

"Good. I'll text him later today. What's the latest about Kirk Wagner?"

"Hayes charged him with your assault. He remains catatonic, and his doctor says he's experienced a psychotic break. He won't stand trial."

I shivered but reminded myself not to feel guilty about saving my own life. Reed interrupted my dark thoughts. "Deacon Hayes thinks Kirk Wagner killed Patty Maxwell."

"Why?"

"Turns out Wagner was out on a false alarm call for his employer that night. He was in the area around the time Patty was killed."

"Do you think Wagner killed Patty?"

"He certainly had a motive, since he was one of Rachel's black-mail victims."

"But Hayes doesn't know about that, right? You haven't told him? No? Okay. So why does Hayes think Wagner killed Patty?"

"Hayes thinks it was another opportunistic sexual assault. They searched Wagner's apartment and found a collection of trophies from his victims. There was a gold cross with small rubies, identified as something Patty always wore."

Creepy.

The waitress came and cleared our plates away, and Reed requested a refill on his coffee. We were the last in the restaurant now.

"Do you think Hayes is trying to cover up my mother's murder, or is just incompetent?"

Reed shrugged. "He can't explain how it happened, so he's ignoring it. Like so many of the Ghost Killer victims, her death is strange, but stretching the facts can explain it. Kirk Wagner is being tied to multiple crimes, and that has the chief's full attention. Discovering a serial rapist and solving cold crimes is getting Deacon a lot of attention."

"That doesn't bug you? You thought I should take credit for the Hammerby murder trial being solved, and here you are letting Hayes take credit in the spotlight!"

Reed chuckled. "Being in front of the cameras isn't my thing, Vic."

I leaned over to whisper, "But what about—you know—? The death-curse money? Kirk put a spell on a rock. Do you think he's the GK?"

"After seeing Wagner's apartment, I don't think he's big on organizing or planning. It doesn't fit. But he could have been a tool wielded by someone smarter."

"The GK got Wagner to attack Patty? Knowing it would kill my mother because of the money curse?"

"Exactly."

Great. We still had a mysterious contract killer running around Grimsby, and they could kill at a distance.

"My boss is letting me stay so I can help my dad close Victor's case. But unless I find more evidence that the Ghost is in Grimsby, he'll recall me."

I hadn't figured on Reed not being here, helping me. My expression gave me away. "Don't look so deflated, Vic. Look how much you've gotten done. How you've succeeded beyond all odds."

The waitress came back with our ticket. I asked him, "Do you want any pie? I think I have room."

After all the sleep and food, I felt reborn. I was in the mood to get things done. To conquer the world. Or at least my little corner of it.

While Reed paid for the meal, I started reading phone texts from my sister. When he came back to the table, I told him, "Phillipa. She's with Liam and Nell, looking at a building to lease for the bakery. You want to go by?"

"Sounds good."

Grimsby wasn't a big town, and we quickly found the location. In moments, Reed pulled into another parking spot a couple of blocks over from where we had eaten.

"That wasn't far! We could have walked."

"You don't need to tire yourself out."

Reed pulled open the door for me, and having him behind me gave me a moment of nervousness, a reminder of my encounter with Kirk Wagner. I stepped through quickly.

Inside the vacant store were Phillipa, Liam, Nell, and Nell's mom, Lottie Hoffman, who seemed about to give her daughter some unwanted advice. Seeing us, Nell asked me, "What do you think?"

Sensing my opinion was about to arbitrate some argument, I hedged. "About what?"

"Taking this place. After all, you're the one paying for it."

Before I could frame an answer, Lottie gave her opinion. "I only think, dear, that you should wait until you hear from the insurance company and get their settlement. Take a few months off. You could help me at the salon."

Nell rolled her eyes. "Make appointments, sweep up hair, and check out clients? No, Mom. I'm not in high school anymore."

Liam was standing off to one side, his bare hand touching the brick wall, his eyes masked by sunglasses.

"What are the differences between this place and the old one?" I asked him.

Like I'd expected, he rattled off all the details.

"This one has lower rent by a hundred fifty dollars a month, with an increase of two hundred forty-three square feet. There's an outdoor patio at the back of the building, increasing the number of tables. It has a commercial kitchen area, but an expert should inspect the roof, electrical, and plumbing before signing a contract."

Phillipa, the agent, flipped open the portfolio she was holding. "They upgraded the electric and plumbing a year ago for a restaurant."

"Why isn't that restaurant still here?" I asked.

"It failed," said Lottie. "This location had two other failed businesses. It's cursed."

Being in Grimsby, I didn't know if Lottie meant an actual curse or just a metaphorical one. Regardless, I knew a lot about curses. I said blandly, "Since you asked, I'd say you need to get those experts first to confirm it's all okay so it can help get the bank loan approved."

Nell wasn't pleased to hear my words. She turned to my brother and asked him, "What does the building tell you? Would it like to be a bakery?"

Liam cocked his head, and after a moment, told her, "It's skeptical. It's been let down before, so you'll have to convince it you really mean to stay."

While Liam and Nell discussed the building and its need for love, Phillipa pulled me aside. "They've released her body."

"Ugh. Reed told me the coroner ruled Mother's death as natural. We all know it wasn't."

Phillipa shrugged, the long waterfall of her blond hair sliding over her shoulder. "Do you care who did it? I don't think I do. Neither does Liam."

"Not knowing could cause us a problem. Another problem like Kirk Wagner."

"It's over, Vic. Stop making it into more than it was. Wagner is going away for a long time, and the rest of the town won't do anything like he did. People think the book went up in smoke with the store fire. With Patty's killer found, Grimsby wants to move on."

I hadn't told her about Reed's Ghost Killer, but she knew about the money spell. I opened my mouth to remind her when she said in her Big Sister tone that brooked no argument, "You need to return to the city. Go back to your life and let us deal with ours."

I crossed my arms, growing angry. "You seem stuck on wanting me gone."

"It's best for everyone."

I narrowed my eyes suspiciously. I could feel Phillipa's bristly irritation and frustration.

"Vic, you act like you know people here, but you don't. Not really. You should go back to where you belong."

"Fine, I'll go, but first I'm visiting the funeral home. See Mother one last time before she's fried to a crisp."

"Why? You've said your goodbyes."

I gave my sister my best blank stare, causing her to frown at me. "You're not planning on something, are you, Vic?"

I said innocently, "I'm going back home. Isn't that what you want, Phillipa?"

Later, I told Reed I wanted to go home.

"Are you sure? I mean—"

"I want to be around my things. My place."

"Okay, Vic, whatever you need."

I asked him to take me by the crematorium so I could say goodbye to my mother before we left town.

"You want me to go inside with you?" he asked in the parking lot.

"No. There's something I need to do. Privately." So his feelings wouldn't be hurt, I patted his upper arm before leaving the car to go inside. That was too easy. Reed wasn't suspicious enough.

It only took a moment to cut off a swath of my mother's hair and to put it in my purse.

Chapter Thirty-Three

Reed insisted on driving me back to the city so I could sleep in the car if I wanted. Knowing what I was carrying in my bag, sleeping was the furthest thing from my mind. I felt bright, like a spark ready to start a blaze.

"How is your dad coping with knowing Victor's death wasn't a murder?"

"Better than I would have thought." Reed paused a moment, casting me a sideways look. "He's totally in your corner now."

Wow, that was a change.

"How does Deacon Hayes feel about it?"

Reed shrugged, his eyes on the road, his beautiful hands resting easily on the steering wheel. "It was my dad who was committed to the idea that your family were murderers. Hayes doesn't care. Besides, he has his hands full with Wagner. The Grimsby PD is as busy as a hit hornet's nest."

"Regardless of what Hayes thinks, we know that there is a connection between the deaths."

We talked about mundane things for the rest of the trip. When Reed dropped me off at my apartment, he wanted to come upstairs, but I told him I was heading to bed.

"Hey, you know, I never got your phone number."

He gave a half-smile again before giving it to me. I stepped out of the car and got my bag from the back.

"Thanks, Reed, for everything."

"Look, when will I see you again?"

"Soon, but I've got a few things to get done." I waved and started towards my apartment door, texting him a string of numbers.

He waved his phone at me, shouting through the open window of his car, "What's this mean?"

"Security," I called back. "Just in case."

Over the next week, I returned to my daily schedule. Through emails, I learned that Nell and Liam had gotten the building inspected. It had passed, and they would proceed with the lease. Liam sent me a long list of the equipment they would buy, as if I knew anything about commercial ovens and refrigerators.

Phillipa let me know she had met up with Betz at the house. Her crew had packed up all the valuable furniture, and it was now in the climate-controlled warehouse reserved for antiques. The collection would wait there for probate to finish.

Once Victor's case was closed, I would strip that room clean, too. I was also waiting for Kirk Wagner's case to be finished, and then I could do Mother's room. I would handle the sledgehammers myself this time.

I stopped by Hunter Garrick's law office to record a deposition about Victor's death. It was mostly a repetition of what I had already told them at the house.

When I was leaving, Hunter let me know he was going down to Grimsby to do another deposition with Greg Easton and my brother. It was obvious he was more interested in meeting up with Phillipa than in taking formal statements.

"What type of flowers does your sister like?" he asked, while I had one foot out the door.

"Probably expensive ones," I told him, before escaping.

I finished the paintings for the department well within the deadline, and the university picked them up. I delivered the private commission to its owners and collected the balance of my fee. Reed was off on some FBI assignment that had come up at the last minute. I missed him, but I had work to do.

With my calendar cleared, I was ready to implement my plan to expose the Ghost Killer.

On my worktable, I spread out a piece of clean, undyed muslin. On it, I uncoiled my mother's hair.

"Hello, Mother," I said.

It didn't reply—not yet. But I had plans for making that white hair talk.

Art is the most primal form of magic. We used shapes before words. In caves, we painted animals, detailing the world around us. Our handprints stained the walls of our temples. In our sacred places, we used art to bring the world of the gods closer to us.

Art is the bridge that connects us to the uncanny.

You learn plenty of skills by taking art classes: how to stretch a canvas; making paint; and the different brushes and their uses.

I always had materials to make a new canvas. After I had stretched and primed it, I set it on my easel to dry.

Next, I rummaged through my supplies and found four new brushes. They were still in their wrappings. Each brush had a wood handle with a metal piece that held the bristles, shaped and crimped onto the wood.

With small, delicate pliers, I worked open the metal heel and tugged out the bristles, then cleaned out each ferrule.

I would make four brushes from Mother's hair. A Filbert

would be the largest. Its curved, bristled end would do well for applying a lot of paint and blending colors.

The Bright brush would have a flat cut across the bristles. It made short, controlled strokes. And the final two would be my thinnest brushes, with long bellies whose tapered ends would make them excellent tools for detailed work and long strokes.

You can't rush making a magical ritual tool to reveal a murderer. First, the hair had to be cleaned and prepared. While I waited for it to dry, I cut off some of my own hair and made a prototype. I found that, all in all, it didn't yield a durable brush that accepted paint well.

Oh well; I didn't plan on using these for long. They had only one task.

"Tell me your murderer," I whispered, bundling my mother's hair together.

"Who killed you?" I asked, sanding the wood handles before staining them with drops of my blood.

I glued the bristles into the ferrule and delicately snipped the end hairs to shape the brush tips.

"Reveal your killer."

Surrounded by the tools of my trade, I thought of my mother and her talent. I was about to ask her to reveal the biggest secret of all.

I was less concerned about whether my idea would work, and more that it would work too well. Calling one's dead mother back to life probably wasn't a great idea, especially if it was my mother.

However, it was the only way I could think of to discover her murderer. I'd use magic to fight magic. It would be a balancing act. I wanted my mother to control only the brush; possession wasn't my plan.

As an empath, you must know how to clear your mind, or you don't survive. I took several deep, meditative breaths, calming myself. For the artist, drawing and painting are trance-like activities. Creating art leaves room in the spirit for little else.

You empty yourself to fill it.

I laid out my colors on the palette and picked up a brush. Facing the canvas, I began my chant.

You who guard the gate between life and death,
You who close the door,
Whose voice is silent,
And whose eyes are darkness;
Open the door.
Permit the shade of Rachel Rowan
To return to this time and place,
To complete this single task.
This one task and only this task.
I offer these tools, which I have prepared,
Born of her flesh and mine.
(I spat on the brushes, mixing my saliva into the hair)
As conduit and vessel
To reveal her truth
As she has revealed the truths of others.
By my power,
Which is a blessed curse,
And her power,
Which is a cursed blessing,
I ask this.
Open the door.
Open the door.
Open the door.

It was as if the world was holding its breath. There was a moment, a suspension, before the brush in my hand quivered. My hand moved to dip it into the pool of paint.

My descent into madness began.

Hello, Mother.

My mother sat on her couch in a familiar pose, chin slightly elevated, a half-smile on her lips. The familiar scent of her perfume started me shaking.

"Here I am, darling daughter." Her half-smile deepened, as did the contempt.

"Finish the job and leave," I commanded.

"The job? Do you think I'm a servant to be ordered about? Have you ever thought I may not be able to answer? If I even wanted to?" She gave a slight tsk-tsk. "Not a very well-conceived plan, my dear. Magic doesn't take straight paths, Victoria. You should know that. There are limits. Laws that govern even the Uncanny."

It wasn't like my mother to admit she wasn't all-powerful. I felt a moment of indecision. "If you can't answer, return to whatever hell you came from."

She was dead, and there was no need to be polite.

"I'm in no rush to leave. Maybe I like it here, inside your head. I could guide your life and keep you from making those stupid mistakes you always do."

She looked down at her manicured nails, her thick black eyelashes hiding eyes that looked like mine. Her hair, the same as from my childhood: a soft dark brown with streaks of red highlights. My color. Her mouth was mine, but the arrogance was only hers.

"Sticking around won't be an option," I said curtly.

"Oh, Vic." She shook her head, her mouth giving a small smirk. "Darling, I'm way above your class. You can't make someone like me do anything."

I clenched my teeth. I needed her help. Her cooperation. Then I could get rid of her. My mother continued to lecture me. She was still the same, rejoicing in being an authority on everyone and everything.

"Always emotional, lacking ruthlessness to make your talent

useful. Crying over that stupid brother of yours, mooning after that boy in school. Your talent still needs your mother to shape it, train it."

"I'm not a bonsai tree, Mother!" I snapped.

She gave a laugh that pricked the hairs on my neck.

"Gardens need care and attention. Pruning at the right time. You needed training to prevent you from growing wild."

"You tortured us!"

Not responding to my accusation, she continued.

"I saw you empathize with people. Wasting yourself on useless, weak friendships. Like that little friend you brought to the house back in first grade. What was her name again?"

"Ashley Taylor," I whispered.

How my mother had convinced Ashley's mother to let her daughter have a sleepover at our house was a riddle. But my mother could charm those who didn't know her well.

I remembered that evening. She'd let us play dress-up with her make-up and clothes. She'd dabbed perfume on our wrists, and I had hated the smell ever since.

My mother tenderly brushed Ashley's long blond hair while she whispered into her ear all the ugliness she knew about the girl's parents. I felt as my friend's bright joy turned to shame, fright, and finally, terror.

My mother, the witch from a fairytale with no happy ending.

"That poor kid transferred schools, she was so scared!"

"You let her lead instead of being her master. And your soppy devotion to your brother? Sentimental mush that made you soft."

She stood up, growing taller than I remembered her ever being in real life.

"Now you summon me because of a misplaced affection for that inferior Easton boy. Put yourself in danger because of silly sentiment. Necromancy is a dangerous spell, Victoria. How will you hold me?"

Maybe it was the mention of Reed, but I regained control of

myself at last. My voice was flat and cold. "You will do what I ask, Rachel Rowan, and then go. My art is more powerful than your hate."

"You must feed me power so I can paint. If you wish to help Reed, let me inside."

"You will paint what you know. Then you will go."

"I will," she said, giving another secretive smile.

I opened the door and let her in.

Chapter Thirty-Four

One day I will need you.
That day is today.
Come to me.

The girl sitting outside the door of the principal's office was small and thin for a teenager. Her dark brown hair, almost black, with red highlights, obscured much of her face. Only sometimes did it reveal old eyes and a mouth that rarely smiled.

A boy about the same age walked down the short hall. He put his backpack on the floor and sat down in the chair beside her. Lost in her thoughts, Vic didn't notice him for a moment. But as the minutes passed, and he said nothing to her, she gave him a sideways look.

He was a lanky young man, finding it difficult to get comfortable on the hardest chairs you could find at Grimsby High School. Vic recognized him: Reed Easton. Star athlete on the swim team. The boy noticed by all the girls, especially when he was standing on a starting block at a swim meet.

Normally, she never gave him a second look, but being this

physically close to him finally made her aware of his strangeness. There was no emotional radiation from him. He was cool as a mountain-fed stream on a hot summer's day.

Instinctively, her talent reached for him, taking a long, soothing drink. Vic's emotions calmed, becoming settled.

The door opened and revealed the secretary, Mrs McGillicuddy, a woman as round as an orange. Her bifocals hung on a chain around her neck, resting on a fussy blouse patterned with riotous flowers. She gave them both an impatient glare.

Mrs. McGillicuddy was not happy. Mickey-G lived her life slightly irritated, but there was an extra layer of it today. She was disappointed. Vic knew she would never produce that concern, so it must have been because of Reed, son of the police chief. Mr. Goody-Two-Shoes. He who never put a foot wrong must have tripped.

"Reed. Mr. Grant will see you now. You," she pointed a finger at Vic, "can wait."

Reed stood up and gathered his bag before entering the dragon's lair. Closing the door after him, Mrs. McGillicuddy showed Vic a stern, foreboding countenance.

Vic gave her a grin, widening her eyes into a maniacal stare. She felt the secretary's stone-heavy dislike crack with a line of fear. Mickey-G pivoted on her high heel and stiff-walked back down to where her desk was located.

Another boy approached Mickey-G's desk, and she pointed with her pencil to where Vic sat.

"Take a seat," she ordered him.

The other student had a cocky walk, but Vic knew it was a pretense. Scott was in her history class, and she found him repellent both inside and out.

"Hey, weirdo. Reed inside with Coach?"

When she didn't answer, he gave her a knock on the back of her head. She jumped up, fists clenched, ready to fight. The principal's door opened.

"Scott Ballard," barked Mr. Grant, the Grimsby high school principal. Grant was an ex-football player who returned to his hometown in glory. He wasn't a small guy. "About time you showed up. I'm told you have some information about this unfortunate event."

"Yeah," said Scott, in a more subdued tone than he had taken with Vic.

Mr. Grant waved Scott into his office. Vic could see Reed standing inside. He had an expression like he was facing a firing squad. Before the door could close, Vic stepped forward and raised her hand.

"Do you have something to contribute, Ms. Rowan?" asked Mr. Grant.

"Yes."

He waved her in, and Vic took a position between Reed and Scott to watch them both. Reed was almost as tall as the principal; his face was flushed red, either in embarrassment or anger. Vic didn't know which, and she was enjoying the novelty of ignorance.

Scott emanated his usual icky, superior asshole vibe: cheap drugstore cologne applied too heavily mixed with a bottom-of-the-clothes-hamper smell.

On Mr. Grant's desk was a baggie filled with something. Uh-oh. This was more serious than Vic had expected.

"Mr. Easton has denied knowing how this," Mr. Grant pointed to the baggie, "got into his locker. But it seems his teammate has an idea about that."

With Scott being exposed as a tattle-tale, Reed's face went from red to white. Perhaps sensing the turn in his mood, Scott said quickly, "That's Reed's stash. He brought it to school yesterday. I saw him put it in his locker."

Mr. Grant gave a heavy sigh, crossing his massive arms. To Reed, he said, "You've disappointed me, son."

Both were on the swim team, and Reed had broken a state record last month earning admiring glances from girls sitting on the bleachers. All the students knew Scott Ballard resented Reed Easton. Scott's emotions were rank with jealousy.

The problem with being an empath was you knew too much about people. Well, Vic knew a lot about Scott Ballard and didn't like any of it. She licked her lips, about to speak. Seeing it, Mr. Grant asked, "What about you, Rowan? What do you know about these drugs?"

Vic pushed at the principal's emotions. It was so easy to increase his doubt in the direction she wanted. Coach didn't want to believe Reed was a rotten apple.

"I sit behind Scott in my history class. Yesterday, when he opened his backpack to get his textbook out, I saw that. I remember seeing it had a tear in the closure. I thought the stuff might fall out."

"Are you implying this contraband is Scott Ballard's? If so, how did it get into Reed's locker?"

Vic shrugged. "I don't know. But their lockers are right by each other. I passed them on the way to my art class and saw them there."

Mr. Grant picked up the bag and inspected it. Just as Vic had described, there was a slight tear at the top of the plastic bag's closure.

"She's lying!" cried Scott, panicked. He came closer to Vic, giving her a shove with his shoulder.

"Sit down, Ballard, and shut your trap. What do you have to say to this, Easton? You've been quiet."

"I know nothing about what she's saying, sir."

Mr. Grant transferred his gaze back to Vic. He remained skeptical. "You have a reputation for lying."

Vic knew she was incapable of looking innocent, so settled for a bored expression. "Why would I make up a story? I'm not friends with either of these guys."

"Did you see Ballard pass anything to Easton?"

Vic shrugged, pushing hard on Scott's flammable emotions. She would get him into trouble. "Maybe Scott's a dealer?"

Vic hadn't allowed for the intensity of a teenager's emotions; leaning on Scott's worked a bit too well. He lunged forward to tackle Vic. As she went down, her cheek hit the corner of Mr. Grant's desk.

Mr. Grant wrestled Scott off Vic, and Reed stretched out a hand to help her get back on her feet. Holding Scott in a bear hug, Mr. Grant ordered, "Escort Rowan to the school nurse, Easton, while I deal with this."

Reed quickly grabbed some tissues from a box on Mr. Grant's desk and hustled Vic out of the office. He handed the tissues to Vic, who pressed them against her bleeding nose. As he guided her down the hall, he said, "You're going to have a black eye."

"Won't be my first."

"That weed was mine."

"I know. But it was fun to see Scott take the fall."

"You're a strange girl, Vic Rowan."

"Not the first time I've heard that."

He knocked on the nurse's door.

"I owe you."

Vic moved the tissue sideways to look at him.

"You'll pay me back. You're that type. Sickeningly loyal."

One day I will need you.
That day is today.
Come to me.

Chapter Thirty-Five

"Vic. Vic!"

Reed was calling my name. It took a moment before I could unglue my eyes and respond. "Whud—?"

"Easy. Don't get up yet."

I was lying on my stomach. Slowly, I rolled over to stare up into Reed's face. He was kneeling beside me, bending over me, one hand on my neck, the other taking my pulse.

"Talk to me, Vic. Do you know where you are? The date?"

This scenario seemed painfully familiar.

"You c-c-came." Was that stammering, tiny little voice mine?

"You think you can sit up?"

With his hand under my back, I could, but my arms were floppy. Looking down at them, I thought it was blood until I realized it was only paint that stained my hands.

"I was painting," I explained stupidly. I blinked, trying to bring my vision back into focus. Reed's face kept getting blurry.

He looked over my head before returning his attention to my face. "What's the last thing you remember?"

I swallowed and found my voice.

"Making a spell to raise my dead mother so she could tell me who killed her."

As usual, Reed took my statement calmly. For me, everything felt very disjointed and floaty.

"Can you get to your feet if I help?"

I moved my legs, trying to force them under me, but they were wet noodles. With Reed's hands under my armpits, he brought me up. I staggered, and his grip changed to my waist to prevent me from falling.

"You're pretty strong," I mumbled as he dragged me out of my painting studio and into my living room. There, he sat me down in a chair. In a moment, he brought me a glass of water. My hands were shaking so badly that he held it against my mouth while I drank.

"Should I call an ambulance?"

That woke me up. Not again. "No. I'll be okay. Give me a moment."

"You don't look okay," Reed said in an unusual tone of voice.

I rubbed my eyes. The paint on my forearms was dry and crusty. How long had I been lying on the floor? "What day is it?"

At his answer, I gasped. I dreamed and painted for two days.

"Your sister got worried when you didn't return her calls. She knew I was back in the city and asked me to come by. But you knew this was going to happen. That's why you texted me your door code."

I ran the back of my hand against my mouth and tasted crusty paint. I spat it out. "No. Not exactly. You were my backup plan."

Reed's expression made me shrink back into the softness of the club chair. Seeing my fear, he closed his eyes and forced his features into a friendlier cast. His voice gentle with the patience you give children who have misbehaved, he asked, "When did you eat last?"

He made me an omelet. After I wolfed it down, he made me a second one. My hands stopped shaking.

He insisted I take a shower.

"Do I smell?" I pulled my T-shirt collar out and tried to sniff myself. Yeah, I did. Nice of him to let me eat first.

"Take a shower. But leave the bathroom door open so if you fall, I can help you."

I would have protested, but I feared a spanking if I did.

I made it to the bathroom on my own; seeing myself in the mirror, I understood Reed's concern. Paint was in my hair, on my face, all over my arms. I looked like a madwoman.

I leaned closer, bracing my hands on the sink so I could stare into my eyes. They were bloodshot, with deep shadows under them. Was it only me I saw reflected?

"Are you in there?" I whispered. Nothing answered me. Surely she couldn't be here any longer.

It took time to remove the coats of paint from my hair and skin. Stepping out of the shower, I rubbed in moisturizer, reclaiming my body with each stroke. The wound on my side was looking better all the time.

Wrapped in a towel, I peeked out of the bathroom door and found a stack of clothes right outside. Reed had picked some soft pajamas—my penguin ones. I grabbed them and shut the door again.

When I finally emerged, Reed told me in a stern voice, "Go to bed, Vic. You look like utter crap."

I bowed my head and shuffled off to my bedroom. There I collapsed onto the mattress, not bothering to get under the covers. I wondered briefly who was snoring before my mind drifted away.

When I woke up again, my mind was more alert. I was on my side, and Reed was lying on the bed, watching me. This close, I could see that his eyes had hints of brown-green in the blue.

Seeing me awake, he asked quietly, "What are you thinking about?"

"How did you know to come here?"

"You needed me, so I came." I blinked and opened my mouth to say something about the magic of love, but Reed's next words stopped me. "And your sister called me, wondering why you weren't returning her calls."

My hand came up to give him a playful punch on his arm, but he grabbed it mid-strike. My fingers loosened and became entwined with his, falling to land on the bed together.

"I'm glad you came."

He gave a slow smile. "This place is a fortress, so your text with the door code was helpful. Otherwise, I'd probably have needed a SWAT team to get inside."

"Could you do that? Call a SWAT team, and they'd show up?"

"You seem to find yourself in situations that need an extract team." Reed's face became serious as he asked, frustrated, "Why do you keep doing this?"

"What?" I asked defensively.

"Trying to destroy yourself."

"I'm not—" But the tears beading in my eyes contradicted my words. He'd struck upon something deep inside me. A truth about my quest for self-destruction I would never have shared with anyone, least of all myself.

"It's okay," he said, pulling me close so his shoulder cradled my forehead. "I didn't mean to upset you."

"Kirk Wagner wasn't my fault!" I cried, shaking.

"No, he wasn't. That was mine. I shouldn't have left you alone."

"Apology accepted."

Without missing a beat, Reed continued to push me to self-enlightenment. "But this time, it was your fault. And you take risks I wish you wouldn't. Like breaking into Patty's house."

He stroked my hair, moving strands away from my forehead. "I waited across the street to see if you'd try breaking in like you said. When Hayes showed up, I thought I'd better head him off. When your head popped up in the window, I practically had a heart attack."

His hand was on my lower back now. My penguin top had hitched up in my sleep, and I could feel the warm, rough skin of his palm and fingers against my back. I snuggled closer, draping my hand over his hip. Why was he wearing jeans in bed?

"But what was this? This thing—whatever you did?"

"Magic."

Reed said nothing, so I rushed to explain. "I used magic to make my mother paint who murdered her. I wanted to help you catch the Ghost Killer. She's so good at revealing secrets, and—"

"You shouldn't have risked yourself. I'd rather have you than any Ghost Killer, Vic." I looked up, tilting my head back. His thumb smeared the tears sideways across my cheek. When he kissed me, we both tasted salt. "You've always been enough for me," he whispered.

This time I kissed him. Both of his arms came around me, and he rolled, so I was on top.

"I want you. Is that okay?"

I knew what he meant. Kirk Wagner. I shoved that asshole out of my mind and gave Reed a deeper kiss.

"This is us. Now. This moment. Just be careful of the nose."

He laughed. I almost slipped off him as his ribs shook. He caught me in time.

"I'll always take care of you, Vic."

We fell asleep together and I found it strange to wake up with someone else in my bed. Feeling his body beside mine, his breathing, and the warmth from living. Thought about Reed. How he shook out everything I didn't need and put me back together again.

The rhythm of his breathing changed, signaling he was awake. I rolled over and asked, "Still here?"

"Yep."

Making my face fierce, I said, "I could throw you out of here."

"You could," he agreed with a small smile. "But I'm determined to earn my keep. Make myself indispensable to you, Vic Rowan."

After a few kisses to disarm me, Reed caressed my hair and added, "I want to talk to you about something."

"What is it? Is it bad? What did I do wrong?"

He placed a forefinger over my lips. "Stop. Will you listen to me? I want you to stop destroying yourself."

"I—don't."

He tapped my lips with his finger.

"Yes, you do. Rachel was a cruel, selfish woman who was your mother by an accident of birth. You aren't her. You will never be her. So stop thinking you have to fall on a sword to atone for things that were out of your control."

I lay still in his arms. Frozen.

"People care about you, Vic. You are loved."

Looking at his face squeezed my heart. I didn't want to talk about choices and guilt. Especially knowing what was in my art studio.

"I need to get back to Grimsby to meet up with the DA."

"I could take you back in my car."

"Okay."

I rolled over, grabbed my discarded T-shirt from the floor, and wriggled it over my head.

"Your side is looking good."

My head was through my T-shirt, and I looked down to where he lay in my bed—not wearing anything now, let alone jeans. "It'll leave a scar."

"Tigers don't let their scars bother them."

I headed to the bathroom, where I locked the door. I needed time to think. Alone.

Standing in the shower, washing my hair, I thought about it

last night. I didn't feel real, as if I had slipped into someone else's body. I probed every corner, trying to find why I felt new, changed.

In the mirror, steam was fading away, revealing my face in pieces. I was smiling. Grinning.

Oh. It was happiness. That was what it was.

Chapter Thirty-Six

When I exited the bathroom, I found Reed gone from the bedroom. I dressed quickly, picking a clean, long-sleeved T-shirt and jeans from my closet. I dumped out my bag and repacked it. I found Reed in the living room. He gave me a grin, putting away his phone.

"Ready to go?"

"Not yet. I need to see that painting."

I hesitated only for a moment before entering my studio. The place was a bit of a mess, but less than I had expected. Mostly the floor would need to be cleaned of paint and spilled water. I stepped over to my easel, careful to avoid the brushes discarded on the floor.

"Recognize her?" I asked Reed.

"No."

The woman in the portrait looked about my age—thirty-odd. She had sandy-brown, straight hair that fell to her shoulders. Her heart-shaped face and a symmetry to her features that I would have loved to draw.

Her mouth smiled, but she had haunted eyes.

Looking over my shoulder, Reed mused, "She looks nice. Not how I imagined the Ghost Killer to look at all."

"Well, Mother says this is who we're looking for." I snapped a photo of the canvas with my cell phone. "Let's go before I miss that appointment."

We went down the stairs, but before I could open the outer door, Reed stepped closer, preventing me from reaching for the doorknob. Suddenly afraid, I stepped back quickly, a reflexive reaction courtesy of Kirk Wagner.

Reed asked, "May I?"

"What?" I said nervously, licking my lips, my eyes wide.

"Kiss you?"

I relaxed. Imagine Reed remembering that Rowans didn't invite casual touch. I stepped closer to him, tilting my chin up.

"Why don't you see if you can take one?"

His eyes were solemn.

"I'll take as many as I please once I know you want them."

We stayed there for some time, letting Reed know exactly what I wanted and in what quantity.

We reached Grimsby with little time to spare. Reed went around the square twice and still couldn't find a parking spot. Outside the courthouse were Liam and Phillipa. Seeing us, my sister waved us down.

"Look, I'll just get out here." Before I could jump out, Reed said, "I'm heading over to the Grimsby PD. I've got some questions for Hayes about Patty's case. Something I wanted to clear up with him."

I frowned as I unbuckled my seat belt. "What do you mean? I thought we knew who killed Patty? We need to find the GK."

"Paperwork always has mistakes, inconsistencies, Vic. It's a formality. Dotting the i's."

Phillipa shouted again that I needed to hurry.

"Okay. I'll come over to the station when I get done here."

I was half out of the seat when he grabbed my forearm, stopping me. "You'll be okay in there without me?"

I gave him a quick kiss to reassure him. "It's nothing. Hunter already recorded our depositions, so Liam and I are here to answer a few questions. Sign some papers."

Reed still looked indecisive. "Maybe I should find a parking spot and talk to Hayes later?"

"I can do this, Reed." I added, without irony, "Besides, your dad will be there so I've got an Easton man to protect me."

I leaned over and gave him a deeper kiss to prove my statement. Someone behind us honked their horn—whether as a comment on us being parked in the road or at the quality of my kiss was unknown. I waved to the SUV behind us and blew another kiss to Reed before running up the sidewalk to meet Phillipa.

As we entered the courthouse, my sister asked with amusement, "Something you want to tell me?"

"Have you and Hunter started picking out china patterns yet?" I countered.

After passing through the metal detector, we headed up the stairs to meet Liam. My brother knew where to go and brought us to a room that held Greg Easton and Jack Ingram, Phillipa's first husband. Both men stood as we entered.

We took seats, and after Phillipa had briefly chatted with her ex about his twins, we got started. The questions were more involved than I had expected, but at least we weren't being interrogated by a hostile police chief such as Deacon Hayes.

Ingram wanted to know why I hadn't offered information about Victor's death sooner. He even seemed to want to make it some Rowan plot.

"Convenient that you waited until your mother died to bring this information forward."

"Convenient?" I gave an exasperated snort. "It would have been convenient never to mention this at all."

I would have been more aggravated if I didn't feel that a lot of Ingram's bark was for show. He was curious, but I didn't pick up any outright hostility. His attitude towards Phillipa was mostly regret, and irritation for feeling it. For Liam, he had nothing but contempt.

"Anyone who went against her, Rachel Rowan punished. I don't think it's surprising I waited until she died to tell you about Victor."

The room became silent. I mean, what could they say to the truth? Greg Easton cleared his throat.

"The important thing to remember is that Victor Rowan killed himself. A woman who couldn't deal with the shame—or maybe the reality of it—covered it up."

"The cover-up allowed Rachel to collect a three-hundred-thou-sand dollar life insurance policy. That's fraud," said Jack sternly.

Phillipa spoke up. "We've contacted the life insurance company and are negotiating a settlement."

"I'm sure you'll sweet-talk them around, Phillipa," said Jack sarcastically. Phillipa was hurt by his comment, and I decided I had enough of him.

"It was our mother who lied. Are you going to charge a dead woman?"

Jack didn't enjoy being directly challenged by a woman. He turned to Reed's dad and asked, "Why are you here, Mr. Easton, and not Chief Hayes?"

"Since I was the one involved in the case at the time, he sent me over. I know far more about the matter than he does. And he's busy wrapping up that Kirk Wagner mess."

Jack shuffled through paperwork, pretending to read it to save face. Meanwhile, I sat there and thought about Reed. Looking up, Jack snapped at me, "What are you smiling about, Victoria? You find your father's death funny?"

I snapped back. "I was thinking of something else. Are you the smile police?"

Before things could deteriorate further, Phillipa took it all in hand.

"Jack, we're just on edge because of everything that's happened since Mother died. Her shop burning down. Vic being attacked." She gave some sniffles, her big eyes becoming wet. "I'm so scared."

Jack patted her hand.

"Don't worry, Pip. We'll get this wrapped up today."

Seeing my sister soothe Jack's hurt pride made me quietly furious. It must have been hell living with a guy whose ego was that delicate. Phillipa had probably bent herself into pretzels to be what he wanted. I regretted that Hunter Garrick couldn't be here today, but I satisfied myself with fantasies about how I would introduce the two men.

Jack turned back to his paperwork.

"I've reviewed your depositions, the autopsy report, the statement from the doctor treating Victor for depression, and the recommendations from the police department. I'm declaring the case closed. Your additional evidence supports that Victor Rowan shot himself. But if you can't settle with the insurance company, I might reopen the case as fraud."

At the door, Greg Easton stopped Jack to talk.

"I'm glad that's done," said Phillipa, giving an enormous sigh. Her eyes were clear of tears, her nose wasn't pink, and she had an honest smile. What a faker.

A thought struck me.

"You know everyone in Grimsby, don't you?"

My sister laughed. "You're right! I guess I do. Especially if they own a piece of prime property, I want to broker for them."

I pulled out my phone and accessed my camera files. I flipped it so my sister could see the one I took that morning of the painting.

"Oh." She took the phone from my hand and turned up the

brightness level. As she enlarged the photo, I asked, "So you know her?"

"Of course I do. That's Stephanie."

"Where does she live?"

Phillipa handed the phone back to me.

"In the cemetery. Stephanie Hayes died last winter in a car accident."

Chapter Thirty-Seven

I didn't know what to think, but emotionally I was having a five-alarm fire. I demanded quickly, "Hayes? Was she related to Deacon?"

"His wife," said Phillipa. "Is that important?"

Frightened, I babbled, "I need to get to Reed."

Shoving past Jack and Easton, I barely heard Phillipa's hasty apology to them as she followed me out of the room. I dialed Reed and cursed as the phone went to voicemail. I practically flew down the stairs, sending a clerk and her papers flying.

"What's wrong, Vic?" cried Phillipa as she ran after me. Outside, I stopped and grabbed her arm.

"Tell me everything you know about Stephanie Hayes. Now."

By the time Liam had caught up, we were all standing on the corner of the town square. I texted Reed's phone: *911. Call me NOW*.

"Not much. She was a city girl. Came to Grimsby to be the manager of the Regency hotel—that place you stayed at with Reed."

I was jogging towards the police station a few blocks away,

barking questions at my sister. "How long was she married to Hayes? What was their marriage like?"

"I don't know. Maybe ten years? I didn't see them much as a couple. They weren't part of my circle."

I called Reed again. When I got his voicemail for the third time, I shouted into my phone, panicked. "Answer your phone, you dumbass! You're in danger! Don't go anywhere alone with Hayes. Call me. Now!"

My sister asked, "Who's in danger? What's going on?"

By this time, my frantic walk-jog had brought me to the police station. I ran to the front desk and found a woman wearing a police uniform sitting at the desk.

"Where's Reed Easton? I was to meet him and Chief Hayes here."

"They aren't here. You can sit over there in the waiting room until they get back."

I paced, thinking. The front automatic door swished open. For a moment I thought it was Reed—but no, it was Greg Easton. He must have followed us from the courthouse.

"Greg, I think Reed's in trouble."

"Why?"

"Reed told me he was meeting Deacon Hayes here to discuss something about Patty Maxwell's death. But he isn't here, and neither is Hayes. Hayes is mixed up in Patty's death somehow. I know it. Because of his wife."

To give him credit, Greg took my disjointed words seriously.

"You think Reed discovered something? Something that would put my son in danger from Deacon?"

"Yes. Maybe. I don't know, but I think Stephanie Hayes was being blackmailed by my mother."

Liam, who was standing behind me, confirmed it. "Yes. She was in the book. Something to do with porn."

Liam—! I could almost choke my brother.

Easton tried calling his son, and when no one picked up, he asked me, "What exactly did Reed tell you?"

I frowned hard, trying to think. "Reed was going to discuss something he found in Patty's paperwork with Hayes. He wanted it explained."

"Are you sure that's what Reed said?"

"Are you calling me a liar?"

"No." Easton was patient, controlled, with his emotions firmly locked down. He was a man who had dealt with many emergencies over his career, unlike me. "I'm trying to find out why my son would be in danger from Deacon Hayes. Where is Reed now?"

"I don't know. That woman said he and Deacon weren't here." I pointed to the receptionist. Easton called over to her. "Do you know where Deacon and Reed are?"

"You just missed them," she told the former police chief. "They went out for coffee."

"Would you get Deacon on the radio? That would be a big help, Joy." She gave him a nod.

"Don't worry, Vic, I'm sure he's fine," said Phillipa beside me. Liam said nothing, but his face was not giving me a reassuring lie. I wanted to scream.

Joy reported, "The chief's not responding."

I begged her, "Do you know where they went for coffee?"

Before she could answer, Easton replied, "Everyone here goes to Busy Beans. They give twenty-five percent off to officers."

Joy added helpfully, "It's right down the street."

Why hadn't anyone told me that to begin with?

They were not inside Busy Beans. I shoved past the people standing in line, waiting to order their iced coffees and cappuccinos.

To the complaints at my presumption, Easton told them,

"Police business." No one asked him for a badge. They all knew him, or maybe his demeanor and haircut screamed 'cop'.

The guy at the register was the same employee I had seen weeks back when I visited the place with Crackers, the Grimsby librarian. He wore a light tan polo shirt emblazoned with a smiling coffee bean, part of the Busy Beans logo.

I asked quickly, "Have you been here for the last hour?"

My simple question touched a nerve. He rolled his eyes and said sourly, "I've been working my ass off since eight this morning. I'm the only one here, since Darla and Nathan didn't bother to come in for their shifts."

"Did you wait on Deacon Hayes? The police chief? He might have been in here about thirty minutes ago? With a tall, good-looking man with dark hair."

"Yeah, I got the chief his coffee. And his usual discount, even though he was ordering two coffees, which isn't policy. Didn't see the other guy."

My voice shook. "Did the chief say where he was going? Give any hint at all?"

The guy shrugged, his gaze going over my shoulder to the restless customers beyond. His attention was straying. I pushed on his emotions, but the flash of bills from Easton's wallet encouraged him just fine.

"He asked where Darla was. Everyone likes her, but I'm sure it has nothing to do with those tight T-shirts she wears. I told him she called in sick, but that I know for a fact she went to the lake. Her dad owns a boat, and she likes to water ski. Me? I'm stupid, *Mr. Responsible*. I come in and do my shift. But do *I* get a raise?"

"The lake? That's all you talked about?" I demanded.

"Yeah, he said going to the lake today sounded like a good idea. Then looked out the window to where his car was parked outside and gave a weird laugh. Got up all in my face and started telling me to hurry or else. But it wasn't my fault that the machine was throwing fits. Maybe next time he shouldn't order a fancy coffee to milk his discount."

Phillipa came to my side and applied her charm. "Oh dear, was he rude?"

The barista leaned over the counter, coming closer to my sister. "Bit my head off. But the guy's on drugs. Isn't that like a cop? 'Do as I say, but not as I do?'"

"Oh my, drugs? How do you know?" Phillipa's blond hair fell forward, the ends brushing her breasts.

The barista pointed to a counter that ran against the wall.

"There's a mirror there to prevent people from bumping into each other when they round the corner from the bathroom. His hands were shaking so bad, he could barely get the pill bottle lid off before dumping it into his coffee."

That's all the info he had. We moved away from the counter and huddled together.

"So you think, the lake?" I asked them.

Easton said, "Deacon has a cabin up there. A good spot for fishing. He once told me jokingly that it would be a good place to dump a body, because the inlet up there has a lot of submerged trees and the divers won't go down."

Easton and I exchanged looks as heavy as lead.

Liam came back, clasping an empty medicine bottle in his hands. "I found it buried in the trash. It's a prescription drug for anti-anxiety. The bottle has Stephanie Hayes name on it."

"Do you have a car?" I asked Greg Easton.

Greg Easton's vehicle was the truck I'd seen Reed drive a few times. Before he could protest, I grabbed the keys out of his hands and jumped into the driver's bench seat. I used a hand crank to roll his window down. *Primitive.*

I told Phillipa, "Send a map link to Deacon's cabin to my phone."

Easton still had one leg out of the passenger door when I started reversing out of the parking slot. I heard the squeal of brakes and the honking of a car horn behind us. *Screw them.*

Beside me, Easton pulled the seatbelt strap over his chest and locked it down. Good idea. I strapped myself in too, still holding the enormous steering wheel with one hand. The damn thing drifted to the right, hard. I felt like I was driving a school bus.

"You really believe that Deacon would harm Reed?" Easton asked.

"Yes." Oh, good, this old thing had a V8 engine. I pressed the pedal to the floorboards, and it roared up the hill. Cars scattered like chickens.

I continued sharing my thoughts with Reed's father.

"I didn't get the impression Reed suspected Hayes. But for some reason, Deacon must have panicked. Maybe Reed asked the right question at the wrong time."

My phone dinged. I pulled it from my pocket and tossed it to Easton, giving him my password. "Give me directions."

"The place is up on the north side. I think I've been there for a cookout and fishing. When I was still working as chief."

There was a nice paved road circling the lake. I grabbed my phone, gave a quick look at the map, and pitched it back to Easton. "That's a long drive."

"We could take an old logging track that would cut off about fifteen minutes."

I didn't ask if he thought his truck could do it. It would do it if I had to carry it.

"How do we get there?"

As we bounced and the truck tires dug through ruts and hills, I wondered if Deacon had taken Reed somewhere else. No. The cabin felt right. Hayes wasn't a creative thinker; he'd go to ground somewhere familiar, but also quiet. A private place. Where he could sink a body.

"Tell me about Deacon Hayes. What type of man is he?"

Greg Easton's hand stretched out to the dash to steady himself as we hit another pothole. I'd probably need to buy him some new shock absorbers when this was all done. Maybe a transmission. I'd buy him a brand new spanking fancy truck if we found Reed alive.

"Good cop. Works hard."

"Good cop?" I snorted. "When I was there with Liam, I saw a lot of plaques on the wall. Trophies. It seemed to me he was a show-off and a phony. Reed said he closed the case on my mother's death to keep his perfect record."

"Deacon thinks a lot about his image. How people in the community think about him. You could call him a proud man I suppose."

"What about his wife? Stephanie Hayes. What was she like?"

"It's hard being a cop's wife, with the hours, and living with the idea your husband could get shot." He stopped.

I needed someone to talk to me, to hold back the darkness. I prompted him, "Go on. What else?"

"I always thought Stephanie was a nice gal. Always supportive of Deacon. Waited on him hand and foot. Worshiped him. But I never understood how they got together. She was a looker."

We had arrived at a T-branch. Easton directed me to go right.

"How much longer before we get there?" I asked, stopping myself from wailing the words.

"Maybe another ten minutes. We weren't that far behind them. If they're at the cabin, we'll know soon."

Now that we were back on asphalt, I would shave those ten minutes to five.

Chapter Thirty-Eight

Easton was the first to sight the cabin. Parked down a picturesque drive was Deacon's black SUV with the Grimsby PD logo on the door.

The tires spun out on the gravel entering the drive, spinning me so we almost hit a tree. Slamming on the brakes, I put the truck into park at the same time. I was out the door as Greg shouted a warning to me. "He'll have a gun!"

Deacon's SUV was empty. On the cab's floor was a spilled cup of coffee, and in the brown puddle was a tiny silver key. I picked it up and pocketed it while I ran to the cabin. The screen door squeaked, but I found the cabin door locked. There were cobwebs in the corners; they hadn't come through this way.

I jumped down from the porch and ran to the back, which had a screened-in four-season room. It looked as unused as the front. *Was my guess wrong?* Frantically, I turned and saw a slope down to the water—an inlet that was a feeder to the lake. Framed like a postcard, there was a stone path winding between the trees that ended at a boat dock.

On the planks of the dock, Deacon Hayes was trying to subdue a struggling Reed.

I shouted. I was an avenging angel, a Valkyrie. Nothing would stop me.

Hayes looked up the hill to see me charging down to them. Seeing me, Reed tried to escape Hayes, but cuffed he was easy to throw off balance and Hayes shoved him in the back. Reed fell to one knee on the dock planks.

Greg was right. Hayes had a gun. It was a wonder he hadn't already shot Reed. We must have been hot on their trail. Or maybe he didn't want his car to get messy with blood and brain matter. Easier to drown Reed in the lake and leave no bullet hole.

I stopped right before the boards of the boat dock. I'd kill him. Mind-wipe him like I had Kirk Wagner if I had to. Seeking to capture his emotions was like grabbing a fish. I tried to make his emotions grow hotter so they would be easier to hold.

I shouted, "Your wife's secret? Everyone in town knew it!"

"Shut your lying mouth, bitch."

The gun swiveled from Reed to me. I didn't care. No one was going to hurt Reed.

"Don't do it, Vic." His voice was hoarse and foggy.

I mocked Hayes, drawing upon the scornful power of my mother's voice.

"People laughed behind your back about Stephanie. Did you think your fellow cops didn't know she did porn? How naïve you are, Deacon. They all knew. Did you kill Stephanie, Deacon? Kill her because she wasn't perfect?"

Deacon's eyes were mad, black holes in a red-blotchy face.

"My wife died in a car accident."

"Did she?"

Before I could get a deep hook into his emotions and pry out his confession, he pulled the trigger. I jerked, expecting to be hit, but he had aimed it to go wide. It was a warning for the man behind me. Reed's dad had arrived.

"Get back, Easton, or I'll shoot this Rowan bitch." He told me, "Come over here. Into the canoe."

The first rule of staying alive: don't go with the guy holding a gun. Seeing my hesitation, he pointed the weapon at Reed's head. "Or would you rather I kill your boyfriend?"

"Don't, Vic!" shouted Reed, trying to rise, but he was unsteady, and Hayes knocked him back down again.

In the distance, I heard sirens. Greg Easton pleaded with Hayes. "I called an ambulance! Please, Deacon, I can't lose my boy. You know he's all I got!"

Deacon demanded I come closer, and looking at Reed, I did.

"Get in and grab a paddle, or Reed gets a bullet. Want to see him go splat like your old man?"

As I stepped into the canoe, my sneakers slipped on the wet wooden planks of the deck, causing me to fall. As the canoe rocked under me, my fear leveled up. With his gun still trained on me, and despite his weight, Hayes got into the thing with more grace.

"Paddle."

"Which way?"

"We'll go across. There's a holiday cabin where I can get what I need to escape."

Behind Deacon's shoulder, I saw Greg Easton rush to Reed. I hoped they found the handcuff key that I had dropped right under Reed's nose.

The paddle slapped the water. I was pretty ineffectual at it, but I didn't think Deacon would put down the gun to help me out. Irritated, he barked at me, "Are you stalling for time?"

"No!" The stress of the situation made me answer truthfully. "I just suck at this."

I tried again, and this time, got the paddle working. I eyed the gun, wondering how much I could push Deacon for answers. At least it would get my mind off wondering how deep the water under me was.

"You didn't kill your wife?"

"No," Hayes said curtly. His eyes were moving back and forth from the Eastons shouting at us on the boat dock to the other shoreline as if he could hurry me up with his gaze.

"How did she die?"

"We fought over money. She wouldn't tell me where she was spending it. When I accused her of having a lover, she left in that little hatchback of hers. The damn thing was nothing but a soda can on wheels. She hit some black ice and slid it into a tree."

"I'm sorry."

"No, you're not," sneered Deacon. "You're a stone-cold bitch like your mother." When I didn't respond, he continued in a voice soaked with hatred. "Patty came around a month after Steph's funeral, demanding that I pay to keep my reputation. That's when I found out Steph was paying blackmail to Rachel."

I nodded. "About the porn."

"She didn't do any porn!" He shouted angrily. Barely regaining control, he said in a furious undertone, "When my wife was in college, her scholarship money ran out. Steph did some glamor videos. Lingerie stuff. Your mother made it out to be a bigger thing than it was. Steph was only a model."

My back started hurting, and the old wound on my side wasn't feeling so good either. I slowed down, and Deacon waved the barrel of his weapon at me. I dug deeper into the water with the paddle.

"When Rachel ended up in the hospital, I figured it was over. Instead, Patty showed up."

Patty definitely wasn't the sharpest tool in the shed, threatening the police chief of Grimsby. We were now in the middle of the inlet. The murky water gave the illusion that it wasn't deep, but I knew better. The canoe moved in an unsettling, rocking way.

"That's when I started planning my revenge."

"The money curse."

My comment made him laugh.

"It was so easy. When I was there to deal with the alarm system,

I got into your mother's room. Who would suspect a police chief? I lucked out that Kirk Wagner was there for me to blame later."

"Wagner didn't kill Patty, did he?"

"I enjoyed every moment of throttling that bitch. Seeing the life fade out of her eyes."

The look Hayes gave me said he would soon enjoy doing the same to me. He had no plans to let me go. Behind him, someone from the ambulance was now on the dock. Reed had his hands free and was pointing in my direction, saying something to his companions I couldn't hear.

I couldn't hold on to Deacon Hayes or influence his emotions. I had been trying for the last ten minutes. He had strange protections I couldn't break. Stubborn man. Of course, he wouldn't make this easy. Well, I wouldn't make it easy for him either.

I asked, curious. "I've always hated this lake. People always said there were caves under the water that trapped people. Is that true?"

"In places. When they put the dam in, the trees on the shoreline died under the water. Now their branches can hold swimmers under."

Getting up, I threw the paddle away as far as I could. It made a sound on the water surface like a beaver's tail slapping a warning.

"What are you doing!?" Hayes cried.

I ignored him.

Standing with feet wide, I rocked the canoe. It took more effort than I'd expected, probably because Hayes was still sitting on his fat ass. I needed him standing, needed his greater weight to disturb the balance.

"Stop that!" he commanded. His hands went to the side of the canoe as he tried to slow the rocking.

"Steph always thought you were a fat toad of a man."

Blinded with rage, Hayes forgot his gun. He lunged at me as the canoe capsized.

I heard a shot. Water rushed into my gaping mouth as the branches of the dead trees dragged me under.

Chapter Thirty-Nine

The girl was six when her mother learned she had a talent.

"Stop that and get in here for dinner," Rachel Rowan said to her middle child, sitting in the garden's dirt. The girl looked up, tears on her pale face, and gave a crying hiccup.

"It stopped talking to me."

Rachel's eyes narrowed. She saw the dead bird in Vic's hands and had a sudden suspicion. "The bird? What did it tell you?"

"It won't wake up! Fix it, Mommy."

Rachel grabbed the girl by the wrist, and the dead robin dropped to the ground. Vic wailed, leaving her friend. At the back door of the house, Rachel shoved the child against the door.

Her mother crouched down to look into Vic's eyes, probing them for information. For secrets.

"Tell me what I'm thinking, Victoria. What I'm feeling."

"I don't—don't know," stammered the child.

"Try again."

Vic closed her eyes. When they opened again, she shrank back, fear in her eyes.

"Very good," said her mother. "You might be useful after all."

. . .

Thrashing, my arms tried to climb up on a ladder that didn't exist. I broke the water's surface, panicked. Choking. Struggling, I went down again.

When Vic was nine, she didn't tell her mother where Liam was hiding. It wasn't until the next day that she learned never to go against her mother's commands.

Rachel Rowan announced to the family, "Vic will help me fix dinner."

Vic was wary of her mother's attention, but being invited to help with dinner was an exciting idea.

"You sit here." Rachel Rowan brought a stool to the counter, and Vic climbed up on it. From a box, Rachel pulled out a live lobster and set him in the sink.

"Isn't he funny-looking? You can pet him."

Vic reached a tentative hand to touch the back of the creature, connecting with it. Bonding with it. Loving it.

"He's a girl," she said, proud to show off what she knew. She enjoyed being smart and the praise of her teachers at school.

"Oh, is that so? We'll have to call her Mrs. Lobster. What does she think of that?"

Vic told Rachel more about the lobster as her mother moved around the kitchen. How it loved the water, how it waved its claws, and how funny its eyes looked.

"Why is that band around her claws? She doesn't like that."

"We wouldn't want it to snip off your nose, silly." Her mother made a grab for Vic's face, making the girl giggle. As Rachel set a large pot on the stove, she told her daughter, "Mrs. Lobster will love to swim in here then." She gave a laugh. An honest one.

"Mrs. Lobster isn't as smart as Ashley's new kitten."

"Who's Ashley?"

"A friend I met at school. She's new to town. Ashley's awfully pretty. She has a cool lunchbox, and we both like to draw."

Vic told her mother about Ashley until Rachel interrupted her.

"Time for our lobster to go back to the water."

Vic clapped as her mother dropped the lobster into the boiling water. Suddenly, the child's face went white, her mouth opening to scream. Before she could make a sound, Rachel placed her chilly hand over her daughter's mouth.

She whispered into Vic's ear, "When I ask where your brother is, you tell me. Or next time, we play a game with Ashley's kitten."

I gasped, sucking in air. My hand struck something. The paddle! I grabbed at it, but my hand slid off.

The child was now a teen who slouched through the house, not as easy to control.. Her sister, Pip, had escaped. Rachel Rowan wasn't omnipotent; she had a chink in her armor.

Rachel felt Vic slipping away. She needed to gain back control. Bring her back to heel. Discover her secrets.

Holding up a sketch pad, Rachel entered the dining room where Vic was bent over homework.

"Who's this boy?"

Vic sprang up, crying, "Give that back! It's private."

"Nothing is to remain private to me, Victoria. Sit down and control yourself."

Rachel flipped through the pages of her daughter's sketchbook. "Very nice. You're improving. Maybe someday you'll be able to achieve something with it." She threw the pad down on the table. "I'll ask one last time: who's this boy?"

Vic gave her mother a scornful look. She was no longer innocent. "He's no one. Someone at school who I thought would be interesting to draw."

Rachel gave that cruel, superior smile. Her chin tilted upward. "You know I see your lies."

"You didn't know Pip was going to run away to get married," snapped Vic, earning herself an open-handed slap across her cheek.

"When we play games, Victoria, I always win. Do you want to lose again?"

Vic looked sullenly down at her papers. It was algebra, and the numbers were now floating off the page.

"He's Reed Easton."

"The son of the police chief?"

Vic said nothing.

"Forget this boy. I have plans for you, and they don't include the son of a small-town police chief. Phillipa disappointed me, but you will not."

"Pip loves Jack! Something *you'll* never understand."

"Does she? The girl jumped at the first opportunity—the first good-looking male that crossed her path. But she'll regret her choice."

Hands on the table, Rachel bent forward, bringing their faces closer together. "Sometimes I see the future, Victoria. And I give that loving relationship ten years at most. Jack Ingram is a weak, foolish man."

Horrified at the idea of her mother having this new skill, Vic asked, "You know the future?"

Rachel gently brushed a strand of hair away from her daughter's face.

"Would you like to know how you die?"

"Stop!"

But even covering her ears, Vic could hear her mother's husky chuckle.

"In the dark, Victoria. In the dark. And all alone."

. . .

In the dark, all alone, I was dying.

I always knew you were weak. Worthless.

Shut up, I feebly told the voice in my head. Couldn't I die in peace?

One day you will need me.

And I shall come.

A second voice, young and strong, pulled at me, trying to awaken me to action.

I can't, I screamed back. *It's too hard.*

Worthless, said my mother.

A fresh voice became louder, drowning out the old.

Look up, look up to the light.

I opened my eyes to see the sparkle of the surface above my head. Dumbly, I reached up, trying to touch it, but it was too far. I couldn't do it.

Someone grabbed me and pulled; I broke the water, choking, trying to gulp air at the same time I heaved.

"Hold steady. I've got you."

Droplets of lake water beaded Reed's eyelashes, and his hair was plastered flat to his head. With a stroke of his free arm, he drew us both closer to the overturned canoe.

"Hold on here."

My tired arms were blue-tinted. They flopped over the bottom of the overturned boat and would have slid off, but Reed held them there. He was breathing hard, and his face was like milk, his lips white-pink.

"They'll be here in a moment. Hang on, Vic."

I laid my cheek against the cold aluminum. It was hard to breathe, so I only mouthed the words thank you with numb lips.

He squeezed me weakly with the arm holding me up.

"Don't pass out, Vic. I don't have the strength in me to do this again." I heard a motor noise, getting louder. "Dad and the ambulance crew got a boat from the cabin next door. They'll be here any second."

I mouthed, Don't leave me.

He gave me his lopsided grin. "You're a slippery fish, Vic, but I caught you in the end. I don't have any plans on throwing you back."

Romantically, we got to share the ambulance ride back to Grimsby. Wearing an oxygen mask on my face, I felt more aware and ready to hear what had happened between Reed and Deacon.

Reed's vitals were being monitored, as he told me.

"It was Patty's cross. The crime scene photos showed the cross on the ground beside her, the chain broken. But I found the same gold cross with rubies on the list of things at Kirk Wagner's apartment. As one of the sick trophies he took from his victims."

I tried to remove the oxygen mask to speak, but the paramedic shook his head, putting it back in place.

"Don't talk, Vic. Let me. It's helping me shake off the dope Hayes gave me."

Thankfully, Reed had stopped drinking the coffee when he'd started feeling sleepy, but it had dulled his responses, and when they'd got to the cabin, Deacon had handcuffed him.

"I thought someone had mixed up the evidence between the cases. Labeled it wrong. Hayes wanted to talk it over, away from the police station so none of his staff would hear themselves being accused."

The ambulance hit a rut, and it threw me sideways against Reed. It was cramped quarters with both of us and the paramedic trying to monitor our read-outs while eavesdropping on Reed's story.

Reed's arm came around my waist to steady me against the jolts. "You promised me you'd take care of yourself. Stop sacrificing yourself."

"Sorry about that," I rasped from under my mask. While the oxygen helped, my lungs hurt with every breath. As did my side, where Kirk Wagner had stabbed me.

"Where's Deacon?"

"Dead, I imagine. He sank like a stone. I didn't swim out there to save him."

"But did you beat the fifty-yard freestyle record of 20.01 minutes?"

Reed chuckled, squeezing my hand gently.

"How you remember that from high school, I can't imagine."

"You made an impression at the time. Especially in a swimsuit."

My head nodded, my eyes getting sleepy. I forced myself to stay awake by asking Reed, "What type of fish do you think I'd be?"

"Hm?" Reed started to fade, his eyes drooping. He was probably being hit with a post-adrenaline drug crash.

I prompted him. "Probably something pretty, like an angelfish?"

"Rainbow trout," suggested Reed.

"What?" I sputtered.

"It's a beautiful fish!" Reed said defensively.

I didn't know what was worse—almost drowning, or having to listen to Reed and the paramedic discuss fly-fishing for the rest of the trip.

Chapter Forty

Saving my life won Reed the right to come with us to disperse my mother's ashes.

We found a maze of overpasses and interchanges which, according to folklore, should confuse any spirit trying to find its way back home. It wasn't easy to find a place to pull off the highway safely. The traffic coming out of the city was heavy, and it seemed semi-trucks didn't believe in speed limits.

From the shoulder, we exited the car and walked down a slope to a small creek under the bridge. The rattling of passing cars and trucks gave me a headache. Or maybe it was the box of ashes that Liam carried, or the bundle of paintbrushes I held.

"We have to cross the water three times," I explained to Reed.

He didn't ask questions. Probably he would later; he had grown curious about all things Rowan.

Thankfully, some rocks and a fallen tree trunk helped me and Phillipa scrabble over the creek. Liam had to be different. He shed his socks and shoes and waded through.

"Looks like a good idea," said Reed. He removed his own and followed Liam.

Three times we went back and forth. Done with crossing,

Liam set down the box of cremated remains on the grass. He brought out a camp shovel and started digging a hole. There was a brief argument over how deep it should be, but soon we poured in our mother's remains. My brother quickly covered her up before any of her ashes could blow out.

"I'll take the box."

The packing box was cardboard and would do nicely. I unwrapped the brushes and set them inside it, then pulled some things out of my pockets: cotton wadding dipped in wax and a box of matches.

The paintbrushes caught fire quickly; the wax helped them become little torches. Under my breath, barely audible, I chanted:

The need is passed,
The question answered.
The task is done and won.
Reclaim and return,
To the dark embrace,
The shade of Rachel Rowan.

"I need to wait until the fire finishes," I told them.

"We'll meet you at the car," said Phillipa, giving me a meaningful look. When Liam didn't move, Pip put her hand on his shoulder and shoved him in front of her. They crossed water three times before washing their hands. Grabbing his shoes and socks, Liam and Phillipa walked up the hill, their mood lighter.

They were halfway up the hill, out of earshot, when Reed spoke.

"So, Fish, it's over."

I froze until realizing he was talking about the case.

"I'm not sure how I feel about Wagner taking the rap for what Hayes did," I said, watching the fire. The wooden handles were becoming charred and the hair, gone in flames.

"If Wagner ever regains his mind, I'll make sure he isn't

charged. But your mother's death isn't officially a murder, and if we reveal Deacon as the Ghost Killer, we'd have to expose her blackmail scheme. That would hurt a lot of people."

Reed was learning. He hadn't used my mother's name.

"Yeah, I get that." The fumes were smelly, but the wind changed direction and the smoke blew away from us.

"We'll go through the book together, and anyone who did something criminal that deserves to be investigated, I'll pass it to my dad."

"Mr. Easton?" I said, surprised.

"He's going to be the interim police chief until the city manager hires a new one. It's temporary, but gives Dad a chance to mend some fences. Make things right."

"Well, when he thought he had a clear shot, he tried to bring Hayes down."

"And missed," said Reed sourly. His dad had found his son's weapon in the back of Deacon's SUV and had brought it down to the lake. Reed had been too woozy to try a shot.

"Unlike your dad, you know how to swim, and that was more important."

The fire licked away at the cardboard box. It wouldn't spread; the grass was still wet from yesterday's downpour.

Reed interrupted my thoughts.

"What's your next move?"

I snorted. "I'm not living in Grimsby."

"You're selling the house?"

"I've got an idea on how to get rid of it, but I have to wait until the estate is out of probate. Our lawyer says that may take a year."

The fire was sputtering. I found an old fallen tree branch and smashed the coals with satisfied vengeance, then I cupped my hands into the running water and spilled it all over the coals. Reed helped.

With the fire done, he put on his socks and shoes, and we

headed back up the hill together. The traffic noises grew louder with each step.

"What about you? Back to the secret-agent work, I suppose."

"I'm not a secret agent, Vic, I'm FBI."

"Secret agent sounds cooler."

We were almost at the top, and Reed's hand slipped down my arm to cradle my wrist. I turned to face him.

"Why don't you come back with me to Chicago?" he said. "For a visit."

"Hm. Why should I?"

"They have an amazing art museum there."

"Oh, so I'd be there looking at art, would I?"

"Among other things."

I made Reed sweat it out for a few moments before I leaned over and kissed him.

"Okay. But I've got some things here I need to get done before I can come."

"More important than this?" His hand waved behind him, down the hill to where my mother's ashes were.

"Yes. Because I'm planning for the living."

The Grimsby public library was a red brick building built in the 1920s by Carnegie. It was a noble building, proudly sitting next to a town park with a statue of one of my father's great-great-grand-fathers.

Entering the front door should have brought back a wave of memories, but the interior had changed so much. I stopped at the front desk and asked where I could find Mrs. Crackenberry.

After my discussion with Crackers, Phillipa did some investigative work with her contacts. Pip discovered Crackers had officially retired, but was working a few hours at the library to earn extra money. Still, she was barely scraping by. My mother's blackmail demands hadn't helped.

I found her re-stacking books in the children's section. She was sitting on one of the round black step stools.

"You look very well, Vic. Radiant, in fact."

I gave her a grin. "Thank you. I was wondering if you'd be free to have some lunch with me? There's an idea I want to talk with you about."

"Now you've intrigued me."

Crackers' volunteer work at the library let her make her own hours so she could leave with me. I asked where she would like to go. When she hesitated, I reassured her it would be my treat. "Pick a place you don't get to go to very often. I got a bonus from a restoration project. I'm ready to spend some of it."

She picked the steakhouse where Liam had said my mother had humiliated Patty so long ago.

"They have very good steaks," Crackers confided to me as we entered the door. Over our New York strips, I told her my idea.

"I don't want the house. Phillipa has her own condo, and Liam's moved in with his girlfriend. So the question is what to do with it."

"Being a historical home, I'm sure it would sell."

I cocked my head. "Would it?" Before she could answer that, I went on, "We three are forming a nonprofit. A foundation. To pay back the Grimsby community."

Crackers gave a husky little chuckle. "You mean pay back all of your mother's victims?"

I gave her a brief grin. "Some of them. A few are going to be investigated for serious crimes—but my lips are sealed. That's now Chief Easton's business."

As Crackers got her coffee refilled by the server, I asked for the dessert menu. Then I cocked my head and asked, "I was wondering if you care about ghosts?"

Crackers' eyebrows rose in astonishment. "Ghosts? I don't give them a thought. They don't exist."

"Good. That will make things easier. I want to offer you a position to head up a literacy program with offices at Victor's house. You'd live there rent-free, plus have a salary. I've already checked the neighborhood zoning. It's in a mixed-use area, and some houses are now law and accounting offices."

Her mouth parted in surprise as her eyes widened, showing their faded blue. "My dear, you don't have to do this," she protested. "It was your mother—"

I ignored her. I was going to get what I wanted.

"I talked to the library board of directors. They told me that improving literacy and reading was one of their most pressing concerns."

"My dear," repeated Crackers, flabbergasted.

"Let's consider this a down payment." I slid over a check for the amount of what Rachel had bled Crackers over the years.

Crackers' hand trembled as she took the envelope. She didn't open it before sliding it into her purse.

The server returned with two dessert menus. I asked, "Which one do you want? To celebrate your new job?"

It took some convincing, but I got Liam to come back to the city and meet Betz Zachary at the Hennessey auction house. Not that Liam doubted his skill—he just couldn't believe that anyone other than Mother would pay for it.

We were in a conference room on the 20th floor with a beautiful view of the city. I was staring down at the traffic, thinking of Reed, when Betz entered. With her were two men carrying jewelry boxes. They laid out the black boxes in a row on the table, spaced out like place settings. One man handed Betz a clipboard before leaving.

"Vic's told me of your extraordinary talent, Liam. I have to say I'm skeptical, but I told her I'd give you a chance to see what you can do with it."

Betz thought nothing would happen. I almost laughed.

The first box she opened revealed a necklace of diamonds, each stone as large as my thumb, on black velvet.

Liam was wearing the clothes Nell had bought for him: a nice navy turtleneck and khaki pants. He rolled his chair over to the box. Taking off his gloves and sunglasses, he carefully laid them aside. His bare fingers gently touched the necklace.

It didn't take long.

"He bought it with Gold Rush money, around 1850, as a wedding gift. The first woman refused his proposal; the second accepted." Liam turned the clasp over in his fingers. "They replaced this at a later date. The weight of the necklace caused the clasp to weaken and break. I'm surprised the family is selling it; the necklace has a deep sense of family pride."

I hid a smirk behind my fingers, feeling the cold shock of surprise from Betz. She shot me a wide-eyed look, which made my smirk widen to a grin. She told Liam, "The family isn't selling it. It's here for an appraisal."

The next item was a man's gold ring with an emerald.

"The owner was a military man, a soldier." Liam frowned, concentrating, as he rolled the ring around with his fingers. "It feels like he was French, but I think he was actually an Englishman who had been in France a long time. I get images of the ring knowing about swords, horses, and cannons. I'm thinking late 1700s or early 1800s."

"What about the inscription inside? *Je pense toujours à toi*?" Betz asked. I translated it in my head: *I always think of you.*

Liam shrugged. "I don't read French. But the engraving says his lover had that done before she gave him the ring. They never married. He went back home without her."

We went through each box. I knew Betz had probably laid some traps, but I was confident. I had faith in my brother.

The first trap was a ring of three bands of gold, in rose, yellow, and white. Small diamonds studded the white band.

"They made it as a fake—a copy of something better. About forty years old. Made in South America."

Betz reluctantly told us, "It's a facsimile of a Cartier Trinity ring."

Some of Liam's answers surprised us, such as a Victorian ruby ring framed with smaller diamonds.

"The diamonds aren't the originals—the owner removed the better stones to pay off gambling debts. Cards. She loved playing cards. She replaced the ones she sold with smaller, flawed ones, so her husband wouldn't notice."

By the time Liam had gone through ten boxes, Betz called a truce.

"He's amazing, Vic, but how would I use this? Liam's information isn't something that I can explain. I mean, I know you and didn't believe it until I saw him do it."

Betz spoke directly to me—Liam had left the room to go to the bathroom.

"I'd use his talents as a springboard, Betz. For example, he told me the artist of one painting I was restoring was a woman. I started researching that idea and discovered it was similar in style to Judith Leyster. She's a 1700s Dutch painter. With Liam's tip, I contacted a few museums in the Netherlands, and they tied it to one of her sketches. My client is ecstatic, as you can imagine."

I could see the wheels turning in my friend's eyes.

Liam's financial future was settled.

It was two months later when my sister and I were at Nell's bakery enjoying her success. I looked around, taking in the crowd. It was the lunch hour, and the vibe was good.

"Nell's new place is busy," I said.

"Liam designed her website and set up the social media for her to get the word out. She's always had a loyal customer base."

"I don't see her?"

"She's taking a decorating course on wedding cakes." Pip suddenly became nervous, toying with her napkin. "I wanted to talk with you about Hunter, since you know him. He wants to introduce me to some people. About a project I'm working on."

"What project? What people?"

"It's a block improvement, changing the warehouse area to a mixed living-business use, but the project needs investors. The grant we got won't cover everything we want to do. And we need businesses to commit to renting the converted space."

"Are you talking about the brick-making plant? Hasn't that fallen down yet?"

Phillipa smiled. "Not yet, Vic."

"So, what people is Hunter introducing you to?"

"Lots. There's a chef that wants to start a farm-to-table cooking school that would also have a restaurant, and I got a call from a non-profit looking for warehouse space to convert for an interactive children's museum. It's part of a state initiative to support small-town development. I'm meeting them next week."

"Sounds great, but I sense there's a problem."

Phillipa blinked rapidly, her eyes growing misty. She said in a quiet, small voice, "I think Hunter is doing this because of my talent. I'm influencing him to help me. He's not doing it because he really believes in me."

"Hunter isn't a charity, Phillipa. He's far too hard-hearted for that nonsense. He's ruthless—or haven't you noticed? If he's telling people about you, it's because he believes in you. In you, Phillipa."

"No one has believed in me before." She gave a helpless shrug. "Jack, Alec... I'm a disaster."

"You married Jack to escape Mother. Don't blame yourself for that decision. And maybe it would have even worked out if he hadn't proved to be such an arrogant prick."

"And Alec?" She was sniffling now.

"Pity. You always want to make people happy, please them. That's how Mother kept you under her thumb. The problem is that once you're done fixing, you grow bored. No one can survive on a continuous meal of baked potatoes."

Phillipa laughed, choking on her iced tea. She put the glass down and patted her lips with a napkin.

I told her, "Hunter Garrick is no bland potato."

That made her smile. "No, he isn't. But I may not be up for rich food."

"The trick to that is to eat a little bit every day. Before you know it, your palate adapts."

"That sounds like the reverse of dieting."

"Dieting is overrated."

For once, my big sister asked me for reassurance.

"Everything is going to be alright, isn't it?"

"Life has its difficulties. Challenges. Problems. But love makes it easier to deal with it."

I stood up and grabbed my jacket, and we walked out to be greeted by a beautiful fall day. By my side, Phillipa asked, "Are you talking about Nell and Liam, or you and Reed?"

"Weren't we discussing you and Hunter?"

"Vic!"

"Love is magic. And magic comes in threes, Pip. I don't make the rules."

Epilogue

EIGHT MONTHS LATER

I was sitting at a table in front of a judge. To my left was Phillipa, and on my right was Rebecca Massey, our attorney. On the other side of her sat Liam.

It was now the end of winter, so he had an excuse for wearing a trench coat and heavy gloves indoors. His sunglasses were in his coat pocket. Counseling was helping, and Liam now only wore those when he was outside.

We were in Grimsby to close the probate for my mother's estate. Massey had informed us how lucky we were to get it done so quickly. Usually it took a year or more, but it seemed that Grimsby wanted to be done with Rachel Rowan as much as her children did.

The judge, a woman with iron-gray hair, read off a bunch of legal stuff that I barely understood. We took our cues from Massey and were obedient little puppets in the courtroom.

When the judge asked if there was anyone here to contest the probate, the room remained silent. No ghosts, alive or dead, appeared.

"We can go now," Ms. Massey told us. "They'll need the room for the next case."

Finished, we all breathed a sigh of relief. In a hurry to escape, Liam knocked a folder off the desk. The papers fluttered out, scattering on the floor. He bent and picked them up while Phillipa tried to cover Liam's clumsiness with small talk.

"So it's all done? We can do what we want with the house, and the bank accounts?"

"Yes. You can distribute the estate according to your mother's will."

Liam handed the folder back to Ms. Massey. She tucked it into her soft-sided briefcase before shaking hands with us all.

Clasping her hand, I said with heartfelt honesty, "Thank you. We appreciate all you've done to get this settled."

"No problem," she replied with a thin smile. "Your mother was a client. She paid me for what I did."

We were in the hallway now, Phillipa's and Ms. Massey's heels clicking on the stone tile. As she pushed the elevator button, she told us, "They approved the final paperwork for your non-profit. I've sent the details to Phillipa."

"That's great news!" The elevator doors opened, and I snapped my fingers. "Sorry, Ms. Massey, but we have to meet up with the DA. Still wrapping up some things. Another time maybe."

After the elevator door closed on Ms. Massey, we three Rowans rushed toward the stairs.

Phillipa asked me, "How long before the spell works? When the money death curse activates?"

"Probably when she touches it. Regardless, I don't want to be anywhere near her. I'm not looking for one of us to be accused of another murder."

Phillipa persisted with her questions. "Do you think it will work?"

"I think the curse on the money we found in Mother's things should work again."

"Really?" Phillipa insisted.

Liam shrugged. "I guess we'll see."

On the steps of the courthouse, Phillipa asked me, "Are you sure?"

"That she's the Ghost Killer? Of course she is," I said scornfully. "You didn't think Deacon Hayes had the smarts for that type of operation, did you?"

"But how can you be certain?"

I tapped my temple. "Brainpower."

Liam, who was more detail-oriented, explained.

"Deacon killed Patty, but his cousin, Rebecca did the death spell. Vic was suspicious about her—Deacon had a natural protection in the same way Rebecca Massey did, which shielded them from her knowing their deeper emotions. After Deacon's death, Vic brought me to her office. While they talked about the nonprofit, I sorted through the pens on her desk. I found a black ballpoint that knew all about the Ghost Killer contracts."

"But why not tell Reed? Let him deal with it?"

I told her impatiently, "The case would fall apart in court. Call Liam as a witness because a pen told him Rebecca was a contract killer? Or that she put a curse on a piece of money? Think, Phillipa."

Finally, the car I had been looking for pulled into a parking spot. My breath quickened.

"Reed!" I shouted, waving.

He started walking down the sidewalk to me. I ran. Ran towards my light.

Acknowledgments

A Spell of Rowans is a deeply personal book. I know firsthand how harmful and long lasting childhood trauma and abuse can be for adults who still find themselves struggling.

I appreciate the alpha readers who read the project in its infancy: Bronwyn Kotze, Jenn Halverson, Merricat Alexander, and Giselle Jeffries Schneider. Beta Readers caught my mistakes, typos, and duplicates, as well as providing valuable insight are: Amirah, Diana (Artemis) Page, Laurie, Linda Lou Oliphant, Jada C., Abi, Asha, Eileen Townsend, Cirila Lilly Marie Phillips, and Elizabeth Close all have my sincere thanks.

My editor Emma O'Connell gave many helpful suggestions on the developmental edit, and brought it home on the copy edit.

Thank you, team.

BYRD NASH

Find Byrd at her website, Goodreads, Bookbub, or join the private Facebook Fan group for giveaways and discussion.

If you enjoy Byrd's books,
visit her website at ByrdNash.com
and join her newsletter for insider news
and 10% off future purchases.

www.ingramcontent.com/pod-product-compliance
Lightning Source LLC
Chambersburg PA
CBHW071727190726
48292CB00003B/639